DEATH OF AN IRISHMAN

"Morning." Jack looked from Charlene to her room and the partially open door. "Silva's still sleeping?"

"Out like a light, lazy cat. What's on the news?"

Jack glanced at her with a hesitant expression that put her on guard. "Connor Gallagher died last night in the hospital."

"Oh no!" She sighed, immediately thinking of her new friend from the AOH. "I'll reach out to Shannon Best and send a card or something. Did they say what happened to him?"

"Police haven't given an official statement yet." Jack shrugged. "No surprise there. What do you think?"

Charlene dredged up the memory of Connor on his back, arms to his sides, unconscious but breathing. "I didn't see any injuries on him . . . a stroke or a heart attack because of being attacked? He'd been drinking, so a part of me wondered if he'd just passed out cold when the guy pushed him. Maybe he hit the tables?"

"Could be a head injury of some kind." Jack laced his fingers over his bent knee. "Sam will know what happened."

"You're right." Charlene snugged the afghan close around her lap. "But there is no guarantee that he'll tell me. He'll be by later."

Jack gave a slow nod and sent her a smile. "My money is on you to get him to tell you what he can . . ."

Books by Traci Wilton

MRS. MORRIS AND THE GHOST

MRS. MORRIS AND THE WITCH

MRS. MORRIS AND THE GHOST OF
CHRISTMAS PAST

MRS. MORRIS AND THE SORCERESS

MRS. MORRIS AND THE VAMPIRE

MRS. MORRIS AND THE POT OF GOLD

Published by Kensington Publishing Corporation

Mrs. Morris
and the
Pot of Gold

TRACI WILTON

Kensington Publishing Corp.
www.kensingtonbooks.com

I would like to dedicate this book to our readers and fans who have supported us for the past few years and helped make this series a success. We love you all.

Also I wish to thank my friends, my family, and all those who have suffered neglect for all the hours Traci and I have put in to bring you the best enjoyable books that we possibly could.

Love always to my grandchildren—Caelan, Blake, Bryn, Andrea, Cameron, and Bryceton. You are the best!
—Patrice

This book is for all the readers out there who love Salem as much as we do. Patrice and I keep you all in mind when we craft our tales, wanting to create the perfect escape. To my family, always, and to Christopher, with love.
—Traci

ACKNOWLEDGMENTS

We would like to thank our editor, John Scognamiglio; our agent, Evan Marshall; and the team of folks who make each book and story possible. From edits to cover design and everything in between, we are so grateful to be living our dream.

Our families are so important to us, and we know that without their support and love this journey would not have been as sweet.

CHAPTER 1

Charlene Morris checked the time on her cell phone, encased in emerald to celebrate Saint Patrick's Day, and called, "Ten minutes!" up the grand staircase of her bed-and-breakfast from her foyer.

"Charlene." Six-year-old Mason Fishburne tugged at her green skirt. "Will there be real lepercons at the party?"

Charlene cupped her chin and peered down at her hopeful young guest. Salem's Irish community hosted an annual corned beef and cabbage dinner. She'd gotten lucky with tickets and a private table to the sold-out event. Each stub included green beer or green lemonade, all-you-can-eat corned beef and cabbage, and live music by an authentic Irish band. Surely there would be a leprechaun!

"Could be." She glanced over Mason's curly brown

hair to smile at his dad, Ken Fishburne. "We can hunt for one *and* his pot of gold."

Ken gave her a thumbs-up and continued his search through Mason's jacket for his son's mittens. Deana Fishburne upended the contents of her purse to the table by the front door.

"What do lepre—lep—what do they look like?" Mason, dressed in a green sweatshirt with a shamrock on the front, shuffled his feet nervously.

"Oh, leprechauns are tiny people, about your size," Charlene said. "I hear that if you catch one, you can make them share their stash of gold at the end of the rainbow."

"They've got scraggly orange beards!" Minnie, her housekeeper, chased Silva, the cat, across the foyer between them. "And a green top hat." She swiped for Silva's tail but missed.

Charlene noticed a small stick stuck in the cat's green collar. "Here, kitty, kitty."

Silva darted past them and up the stairs, watching them all with golden eyes from the second-floor gallery, tail swishing in satisfaction at having evaded capture.

"I'll get the twig later," Minnie said to Charlene. "After I rescue the bread from the oven." She hurried to the kitchen, where a yeasty smell emanated.

"I sure hope we see one." Mason stood next to his dad—at six, the boy barely reached Ken's knee. "And catch him."

"Got 'em!" Deana held up two black mittens from the pile and dumped the rest of the assorted junk back in her purse. "A pot of gold would be awesome. I'll help you look."

Ken dropped a casual arm around his wife's shoulders. "We could trade in the Buick for a Cadillac Escalade with

TVs in the back and Bose surround sound. Big enough amp to knock our neighbors off their feet."

Deana bumped her hip to his. "There is nothing wrong with our car." She grinned at their only child. "What would you buy, hon, if you had a pot of gold?"

"I dunno." Mason looked at his sneakers and up at them. "Could we trade it for a brother?"

Charlene witnessed the quick flash of hurt in Deana's eyes and the way Ken pulled her close to kiss the top of her head. She commiserated with them, as their grief was very familiar.

With her husband gone too soon, and at the ripe old age of forty-three, Charlene's chances were over. She'd resigned herself to this hard fact and now enjoyed the sound of laughter that her guests and their children brought to Charlene's.

"Where's the rest of the gang?" Charlene eyed the stairs as a door slammed on the second floor. That had to be either the Brookses or the Prescotts, but she'd put her money on the fortysomething couple who had an air of snobbery about them: Dell and Harmony Brooks.

The Prescotts were from the English countryside, the Cotswolds. Refined and retired, in their seventies, they were not the door-slamming type. The Leonards had checked out of a suite this morning. Her other guests were two brothers in their mid-twenties, Marc and John Ward from Rhode Island. The Fishburnes were in the largest suite, since they were staying a little over a week.

"I'm hungry," Mason said, patting his tummy.

"I reminded everyone at breakfast that we'd meet at four sharp." It was now 3:59. Charlene's reservation was at four-thirty, but she wanted to leave early in case there was a problem with the rental van or parking. She'd learned in the last year and a half to allow wiggle room with a large group.

"We're ready." Ken wrapped a green scarf around his neck and tucked it under his navy jacket. Deana and Mason both wore black puffer jackets and jeans, though they'd accessorized with green *Kiss Me, I'm Irish* buttons.

"Silva is so cool." Mason waved at the cat, who was licking her paws on the edge of the gallery. "Wish I had a cat like her." The boy gave his father an entreating glance.

Ken ruffled Mason's curly hair. "What happened to getting a dog?"

"If I make friends with the leprechaun and he gives us some of the gold, can I have both?" Mason clasped his hands adoringly.

Laughing, Charlene turned as Harmony and Dell descended the stairs. Each had styled brown hair and pleasant features. "Right on time," Harmony said, chin hefted for an argument. Shamrocks dangled from her ears as she and her husband swept past in matching leather jackets to wait by the front door.

Ken raised a brow but said nothing. Deana's pretty face turned pink. Charlene took it in stride, as the variety of personalities in the world was endless. Some perhaps were a *tiny* bit nicer than others. She kept her smile in place.

It widened as Jasper and Lila Prescott reached the stairs. Lila's hair was silver and styled in a bob, and Jasper's was more of an iron-gray. Lila's dark tweed trench coat had been paired with a cashmere scarf.

"We hope we didn't keep ye, luvs," Lila said in her

lyrical British voice. Arm in arm, she and Jasper reached the foyer. "I couldn't find a touch of green. What was I thinking? Traveling in *March*."

Jasper rubbed his hands together and waggled his brow at his wife of fifty years. "I think she's askin' to be pinched."

"Oh no! You gotta have green on or a lepercon can pinch you. You can borrow my glasses, Mrs. Prescott," Mason said, holding out the flashy green frames in his hand.

"Thank ye, lad. You're saving me from a sore derriere." Lila held the frames to her chest as a shield against her chuckling husband.

"What's that?" Mason asked. "De . . ."

"Why don't we get into the van?" Charlene suggested, hoping the activity would save the Fishburnes an explanation on the French word for *butt*.

Just then the Ward brothers raced down the stairs as if it was the last leg of a triathlon. Since they'd checked in on Friday night, she'd noticed that everything was a competition between them.

"Sorry to be late!" Marc grinned at them all in a way that made it easy to forgive his trespasses. Charlene knew the brothers had stayed out last night, but the dark-haired, brown-eyed pair appeared none the worse for wear.

John elbowed his brother. "I was pounding on your door while you were taking your shower. Sober now, huh?"

"I wasn't drunk!" Marc denied.

Still heckling each other, they followed the Fishburne family out the door and into the sleek black rental van.

Last to leave, Charlene grabbed her camel-colored

wool coat. She had green leggings on under a mid-length, slightly flared green skirt. She added a green felt hat just for extra fun.

A shiver of cold air at the front door threshold stopped her mid-step. No draft—it was her closest friend in Salem, her resident ghost, Jack.

Jack didn't appear all the way as he warned, "Chasing after a pot o' gold combined with too much green beer can be a deadly combination. Be careful driving home."

Her lips twitched and she gave a slight nod just in case anybody was watching. She could never answer Jack unless they were alone. She was pretty sure all her guests were in the van and Minnie in the kitchen, which left Silva on the stairs. The cat meowed under Jack's scrutiny. The two were old friends. Silva could see Jack, but not touch him, and he loved to tease her.

She fluttered her fingers and shut the door, walking down the porch stairs to where the shiny black van waited, her guests already inside. A year and a half ago, she'd bought this mansion at a steal with plans to create an elegant bed-and-breakfast . . . she had no idea that it was haunted by the previous owner, Dr. Jack Strathmore, tied to the property because he'd been murdered.

So much had changed in such a short amount of time. Like, she now believed in ghosts.

Charlene started the van. She hoped to buy her own if business remained steady, but for now, it suited her to rent on the occasion she needed something large.

"Everybody buckled in?" she called.

They chorused *yes* and she left her property, driving the main road that led to downtown Salem. Charlene pointed out the famous Hawthorne Hotel, telling them about the episode of *Bewitched* that had been filmed there. Next was the Waterfront Hotel by the harbor. She slowed as they passed the House of the Seven Gables, the Peabody Essex Museum, and the two touristy witch attractions, skipping the scary stories of ghosts often seen in the Old Burying Point cemetery. She wanted Mason to sleep tonight.

Charlene turned on Boston Street and followed her GPS to the two-story building with a parking lot to the side. It was almost full, but her reservation included a parking space as well as their own table. It didn't hurt to pay a little extra to make her guests feel special.

"This is my first time here at the AOH for their famous Saint Paddy's Day party," she told Deana once they'd all disembarked. She locked the van with the fob and stepped toward the line of about twenty people handing over their tickets to get inside. Music leaked from the partially open windows downstairs.

"What does AOH stand for?" Ken asked.

"The Ancient Order of Hibernians—Irish folk," Charlene answered. She'd practiced saying the long name in case someone asked. "They've been in Salem for over a hundred years."

"I love the history of Salem," Deana said, eyes bright.

Charlene turned to her guests as they moved forward in line. "My friend Kass Fortune says this event is known for the great music and you can't beat the price for dinner and drinks."

Deana clasped Mason's mittened hand. At half-past four, the sun was hidden behind clouds and fog. Off-key singers danced their way down Boston Street, arms over shoulders. Charlene had never heard "Danny Boy" so, well . . . forlorn.

"Kind of tame after last night," John said to Ken, who

had stepped protectively between his family and the singers. "The pubs were packed."

"Lots of chicks ready to *parteee*," Marc said. "Not like the girls at home." The brothers were in IT of some sort from Michigan and had picked Salem randomly off a map to visit. Charlene shook her head and smiled at the Prescotts. The Brookses were on their phones and not engaging with the other guests or each other.

Luckily, the line moved fast, and Charlene ushered her group to check in. "Private table for Charlene?"

"Dinner's upstairs, but the bar and games are on the first floor here," a man with a thick brogue said, winking at Mason.

"Is there a lepercon?" Mason dared to ask.

"Leprechaun," Ken corrected automatically.

"Oh, aye," the man said. "If you're good, you can get a picture with him—he's got a giant pot of gold."

"Yes!" Mason pulled his mother forward. "I'll try and make him my friend."

Charlene shepherded her crew inside, then up the narrow flight of stairs to the second floor, looking for a single table that read *Charlene's*.

There wasn't one.

Embarrassed and disappointed, she scanned the large room packed with an outlandish crowd of people. They were smacking each other on the back, speaking in raised voices, and seemed half-tanked already.

She had to do something quick, as her gang was standing around with perplexed expressions. Marc and John rolled their eyes and whispered to each other. Most likely making plans to escape.

Tables were jammed together and stuffed in every corner, and her single had become three separate tables. Complaining was not going to make the situation any better, so it was time for plan B.

"Hey, guys. This isn't quite what I expected, but we're here, so let's make the most of it." Charlene set them up in groups and got everyone settled. She would have sat with the Fishburnes, but their table was an oval for three tucked against the wall. The Brookses and Prescotts sat together, which left her and the Wards at a table for five.

Even though her name was on the cardboard name-plate, a very attractive red-haired woman and a younger man with a similar shade of hair occupied two of the five seats. "I'm sorry, but this table was reserved," Charlene said in a strained voice.

The woman, dressed head-to-toe in green, rose and fluttered her hands. "I'm the one who's sorry. We're short of tables and I spent half the day scrambling to fit every-one we'd sold tickets to." Her blue eyes batted back tears. "I had to bring in card tables from home." She pressed her fingers to her chest and held Charlene's gaze. "Would it be all right if my son and I joined you? We won't dis-turb you—it's just that . . . well, I work for the AOH. I plan the party every year! This has never happened to me before."

"Mom!" The young man cut her off with good-natured exasperation. "You're babbling." He held out his hand to shake. "I'm Aiden Best, and my mother is Shannon. We hope you don't mind our intrusion?"

Charlene gestured to the Ward brothers. They shrugged, leaving the decision up to her. She smiled at Aiden, then Shannon, aware of how uncomfortable this was for the woman. "Pleased to meet you. I'm Charlene Morris. This is Marc and John Ward. Guests at my bed-and-breakfast."

"Oh!" Shannon said. "I just love bed-and-breakfasts.

They're so quaint and charming compared to a large hotel chain."

Charlene sat and scooted her chair close to the table. "I think so too."

The Ward brothers said hello and Marc added, "Charlene's is practically a mansion. Her happy hours are the best."

Aiden tugged the top button of his forest-green oxford. "Maybe I should rent a room, huh, Mom?"

His mother gave him a disapproving purse of her lips, which he completely brushed off.

Feeling a little discord between them, Charlene changed the subject. "You work here at the AOH, Shannon?"

"I own an accounting business and they're one of my clients." Shannon sipped from her glass of lemonade. Aiden drank green beer.

Charlene looked to see how her guests were doing. The Fishburnes were laughing over something. Such a sweet family! The Brookses had put their phones away to converse with the Prescotts . . . progress. Their coats were on a long rack in the rear of the room. She preferred to keep hers over her chair.

With a sense of relief, she returned her attention to Shannon. "Accounting—that's my least favorite part," Charlene admitted. "My degree is in marketing."

Aiden stood and spoke to the Ward brothers. "How about a shot of whiskey and a game of pool downstairs? I'll buy the first round."

The guys grinned and scrambled to their feet. Before Charlene could give Marc and John a reminder, Shannon said, "You lads can drink your weight in green beer at no extra charge—for anything else, it's a cash bar."

The three made their way toward the staircase, anxious

to get away from the older people, Charlene imagined. Beer, games, and single ladies were a greater temptation. She'd been so intent on getting upstairs that she hadn't even peeked at the main floor.

Shannon patted Charlene's hand. "You're sure it's okay that we share a table with you? I doubt we'll see much of my son. Aiden's home on a small break from medical school and is only here for the band."

Aiden was a smooth, well-spoken young man. Being a doctor might suit him.

"It's absolutely fine." Charlene meant it. "I just need to check on my guests occasionally to make sure they're having a good time." She waved toward the Fishburne table, where Mason was drumming his heels on the chair leg. "I promised my youngest guest I'd help him look for a leprechaun."

Shannon laughed, her cheeks rosy. "Take him downstairs, opposite the pool table. We've got a photo booth set up with Gil dressed to the nines. The boy's family will want pictures, trust me."

"Gil?"

"He's been our lucky leprechaun for thirty years. I hesitate to tell you that he's close to my age, but you'll never guess because he's hidden under layers of makeup."

Her brow rose, intrigued.

Shannon nodded. "Wait till you see him. He's a favorite attraction and much nicer than he looks."

Charlene was starting to like this woman. "I feel like I'm deserting you if I take Mason downstairs."

"Go! I've lived in Salem all my life. I know most of the people here. I'll get us drinks while you take pictures with the leprechaun."

"You don't have to do that!"

"It's no problem." Shannon scrunched her nose. "I did mess up your reservation."

"Well, thank you. I'm driving, so something without alcohol." Charlene didn't really want the green dye either, but figured she'd go along with it in the Saint Paddy's Day spirit.

"I'm a tea drinker myself. Should I get you one too?"

"That would be great." Charlene leaned close to Shannon, who smelled like rose water. "But I have to confess that my drink of choice would be wine. Flint's Vineyard supplies my house wines at the B and B."

Shannon's giggle should have been strange from a woman ten years older than herself, but she liked it just the same. Charlene had a hunch that they could be good friends. "I have a martini every night."

"Cheers to that! Guess it's leprechaun time." Charlene left the table, accidentally bumping into a few people as she struggled to reach the Fishburnes. "I'm so sorry that we aren't all together," she said when she arrived at the oval table.

Ken and Deana put her at ease. "It's all right," Deana said after Charlene explained the mix-up. "It's very festive! Shamrocks everywhere." She lifted her glass of green beer and Ken did too. Mason raised his glass of green lemonade.

"So, Mason," Charlene said, her hand on the boy's shoulder. "I heard there's a real leprechaun downstairs. Should we go find him?"

His eyes widened with excitement. "Yes!"

"Ken, Deana, want to come along?"

"Wouldn't miss it!" his mother said.

"Dad. We need to Google how to catch a lepercon!"

Mason used his legs to push his metal folding chair backward.

Deana smacked her palm to her forehead. "Now why didn't I think of that?"

"Magical creatures probably aren't on Google," Ken said, thinking quick on his feet. As an elementary school teacher, he was no doubt used to it. "Let's go!"

Charlene led the way to the staircase, leaving behind the room decorated with green shamrocks, gold streamers, and the tantalizing smell of savory corned beef. Shannon waved to her from the refreshment table.

If upstairs had been festive, downstairs was like landing in a bad eighties movie. Neon orange, bright green, and fluorescent yellow flashed from a disco ball in the center of the ceiling. Bagpipes blared from a small corner stage near the bar. There was a pool table and dartboards. A lot of the kids were pretending to be Irish dancers with crossed arms and fancy footwork.

But Mason didn't care about that as he tugged her forward and pointed. "Look, Charlene! It's the leprechaun!"

Charlene's eyes adjusted to the lights and she blinked again. Sure enough, there was a black pot the height of a dining table, filled with gold coins. On top of the coins was a hunched figure in green and black.

The leprechaun was terrifying with wrinkled skin, a long orange beard, and a green hat with a gold buckle. Minnie had been right, but she hadn't mentioned a thing about being scary. She shivered, even knowing that it was a costume.

Black fingernails attached to a gnarled hand lifted the coins and let them fall through his fingers back to the pile. The jingle sounded less authentic than gold, but it was still an impressive sight.

"Want your picture, Mason?" Charlene swallowed her distaste and stepped forward.

Mason hesitated. "Is he gonna eat us?"

"Leprechauns don't eat people. He's just protecting his gold." Charlene winked at Deana and Ken. "Right?"

"Right." Deana grinned. "My birthday is March seventeenth, so I definitely want a photo. Charlene, can you get us all?"

The leprechaun saw them coming and revealed rotted teeth. Fake, but well done. As if sensing Mason's fear, he tossed the boy a chocolate coin.

It was all smiles after that.

Charlene captured photos of the Fishburne family with Gil the Leprechaun, sure to be lifelong memories.

CHAPTER 2

Mason gave up trying to make the leprechaun his friend in exchange for a pocketful of gold chocolates. His disappointment that the gold wasn't real didn't keep the boy down. Charlene was impressed by his resilience.

John, Marc, and Aiden wandered over to Charlene and the Fishburnes. Aiden raised his hand to the leprechaun. "Hey, Gil. How's it going, man? You need a beer or anything?"

The leprechaun pointed to the full stein beside him. "I'm good, thanks."

Aiden gestured for them all to come closer. "All right, everybody. Gather together so I can get a picture of you all with our 'leprechaun' and his pot of gold."

Mason high-fived his dad and the Wards bumped each other's shoulder. Charlene handed Aiden her phone. Despite the rocky beginning, everybody was having a good time. She'd put the photo on her website to entice new guests. "Thank you!"

After the pictures were taken, Charlene glanced at her phone screen and realized it was after five. She nudged Aiden. "Should we eat?"

Aiden nodded, clapped his hands, and raised his voice. "Let's get some chow. Once the corned beef is gone, there's no more till next year."

That got everyone's attention and the group weaved their way through the dancers. They reached the staircase and climbed up to the second floor, two by two.

"It smells so good," Charlene told Aiden next to her. She couldn't pinpoint the exact scent. Cumin or coriander?

"The secret is in the pickling spice." He grinned with pride. "Mom's been planning this event since last Saint Patrick's Day. She loves it." He patted his chest. "Most people can claim a wee bit of Irish in their DNA, but our family can trace its roots directly to Dublin."

Overhearing their conversation, Deana asked, "How long have you been in Salem?"

"The O'Briens have been here more than a hundred years. My uncle still lives in the family home."

"That's quite something these days." Ken acknowledged Aiden's remark as they all reached the second floor. "Most families drift apart once they're adults and have children of their own."

Aiden shrugged, a smile flickering around his mouth that didn't reach his bright blue eyes. "That's what I hear." He flung his arm to the left. "Food line is this way. Drinks on the right."

They all split off and Charlene followed John and

Marc to the buffet line while the Fishburnes took Mason to wash the chocolate from his hands. He held tight to the crumpled gold foil wrapper.

Charlene filled a plate of tender corned beef, red potatoes, and buttery cabbage and returned to her seat next to Shannon. On the way, she passed the Brookses and Prestons, who were eating and laughing like old friends.

Her heart warmed. If they hadn't been forced together, the two couples might not have found this common ground.

"Here you are, Charlene. Hot black tea with lemon and a packet of honey, if you have a sweet tooth?" Shannon nudged a white cup with a matching saucer toward her.

"Thank you." She sat next to Shannon, who was halfway through her meal. Aiden broke open a round roll and spread mustard on it before adding a slice of meat.

Charlene took a bite of her corned beef. "Delicious." She speared some of the cabbage and devoured it. "Guess I was really hungry!"

"Our mom never made corned beef and cabbage like this," Marc said. "Too bad!"

"Are you boys Irish?" Shannon asked.

"Isn't everybody this week?" John countered with a laugh. "Our roots are American mutt."

"So probably you are then," Aiden said, lifting his glass of beer to them. "Welcome to the family."

Charlene chuckled and sipped her hot tea.

"Is there anythin' left for a hungry Gallagher?"

Charlene turned toward a gruff-voiced man swaying at the top of the stairs. Red hair, blue eyes. Ruddy cheeks in otherwise pale skin and freckles. She'd guess about fifty. He had broad shoulders and his green sweater was askew over dark denim jeans.

"Cousin Connor?" Aiden rose in a hurry and brought him to his own chair, setting him down. Connor shoved the plate before him away and Aiden said, "I'll get you something else."

Shannon flushed with embarrassment and wouldn't quite look at Charlene. "Connor. What are you doing here? This is by ticket only."

"Since when does a Gallagher need a damn ticket for Sunday dinner? Gil didn't want me to come up, but that didn't stop me neither." He shook his fist—there was heavy makeup on his knuckles. "Punched the squirt and here I am. What are you going to do about it, cuz?"

"Connor Gallagher!" Shannon leaned back with a red face—anger, this time. She got to her feet. "If you all will excuse me?"

Charlene hunched over the table to keep her chair out of the way as Shannon marched to Aiden and whispered in his ear. Aiden hovered near Connor.

Shannon swept away from their group with her head high, but her shoulders shook. Aiden left and quickly brought Connor a steaming plate of brisket. He took his mother's seat. "Eat up, Connor. I'll drive you . . . where are you staying?"

"I'm not goin' anywhere, boyo. Not till I'm good and ready. Where's your uncle? We gotta talk."

"Home." Aiden put his elbow on the table. "Where else? He never leaves."

The Wards stood to make a hasty retreat. "Thanks, Charlene." John put his napkin on his dinner plate, ignoring the intruder. "Heading downstairs for the music."

Aiden's jaw clenched, but he remained in his chair across from Connor. He swiped at a chunk of potato on his elbow. "See you guys later if you wanna stop by the pub."

"Maybe," Marc said, not making any promises. "Coming, Charlene?"

"I'll get the others . . . go on ahead."

Charlene felt sorry for the O'Briens and their black sheep, knowing all too well that every family had one. Even hers—Uncle Mark had eaten all of Aunt Susan's rum cake and fallen asleep under the dining table more than once. It was almost a Christmas tradition.

The upstairs closed at eight when the food was gone so that the AOH club members could clean up. She glimpsed Shannon in the kitchen, organizing.

Charlene brought her brood downstairs. They clustered around some high-top tables slightly away from the music, but not so far that they all weren't tapping their feet or dancing in place.

The Brookses snapped pictures around the pot of gold, taking turns wearing Gil's green hat. He must have left early because Charlene didn't see him after Connor punched him to get upstairs.

Mason was in heaven with all the chocolate coins he could eat. He had a paper cup filled with his riches for later. Jasper and Lila tapped spoons in time to the bagpipes and taught Ken how to play. The Ward brothers didn't stop dancing. The lads knew how to have fun.

When the lights began to flash, signaling the good times were over at nine, Charlene gathered her flushed guests. She didn't see Shannon to tell her goodbye, or Connor. The band packed up its instruments to play another gig down the block and continue the party. Charlene's group went outside to the sidewalk.

Laughter echoed into the night as revelers traveled by foot en masse from one pub to another. No police officers in sight, but she knew they were out there safely guarding the partiers and controlling the crowd.

John danced up to her. "See you later, Charlene! We're going to hang out a little." He had his arm around a pretty girl.

Marc had two—a young lady on either side. "Thanks! Don't wait up." And off they went.

"I remember the days when you and I would dance all night," Jasper said to Lila.

"We certainly had our fun. And still do." Lila gave him a warm glance.

How lovely, Charlene thought as she led them to the gleaming black van in the parking lot. There was only one other car—a white sedan. The Camry had an AOH sticker on the window. Could it be Shannon's?

Everyone who was going home with her had boarded, so Charlene climbed into the driver's seat. "Ready? I'll put on Irish music if the majority is still in the mood."

"How about 'Danny Boy'? Or anything of Dean Martin!" Lila and Jasper were in the seats directly behind Charlene. "Oh, pigeon crap! I'm sorry, Charlene."

"What's wrong?" She swiveled to Lila.

"I've left my coat upstairs."

"Tweed, cashmere scarf?"

"That's it. I should go . . ." Lila started to rise.

"Stay here," Charlene instructed. "I'll get it! It'll just take a sec."

Charlene left the van running and went to the front door. The handle didn't turn. Locked. Dang it. She went around the side of the building and saw another entrance leading to the second floor.

That's where Lila's coat should be, anyway. She hurried up the stairs. It was chilly tonight, especially without the crowd around, dancing and having fun.

She knocked loudly.

She hoped the solid wood door would be unlocked or that someone would hear her knock and let her in.

Nothing. She tried the door handle.

Twisting the brass knob, she let out a sigh of relief when it gave. "Hello?" she called, opening the door slowly to see inside.

The only light came from the kitchen area and spilled to the room. It was eerie and she stayed in place to get her bearings. The tables were pushed to the side and chairs stacked high.

". . . give me my share, Finn!" A square-shouldered man in a hoodie pushed another figure back. The man stumbled but stayed upright. "Who's there?" Suddenly, even the kitchen light went out, leaving them all in the dark.

"Hello?" Charlene said.

No answer. All she heard was the sound of someone dragging in labored breaths. Charlene's heart thudded. She hadn't brought anything with her. Not her phone, not her purse, not her keys for a weapon . . . she'd just meant to get Lila's coat and leave.

She heard a *thwack* in the dark, then a crash as the man fell to the ground. The figure in the hoodie pushed past Charlene, causing her to land hard against the railing, cracking the wood.

"Hey," Charlene called to the retreating figure. Something bulged in the man's back pocket. He almost lost it but caught it in time before he disappeared.

Charlene rubbed her shoulder and reached inside the door, her fingers searching for a light switch.

Finding it, she flicked it on and hurried toward the figure sprawled on his back. She knew him. The red hair. Freckles. Green sweater and dark jeans. The smell of booze. "Connor?"

He groaned. She couldn't see any blood, no life-threatening injuries, and when she lifted his eyelids, his orbs were a haze of red streaks. Only a feeble pulse at his wrist.

She whirled as footsteps pounded up the stairs. Had the stranger come back?

"Charlene?" Ken Fishburne looked shocked as he took in the scene. "Are you all right? We saw someone run by and then you didn't come down . . ."

"I'm fine," she said in relief. "Can you call 911? I left my phone in the car." And Sam would give her hell for that.

"Yeah." Using his cell phone, he gave the operator the address of the AOH. "Yes, on Boston Street. What is the state of the emergency?" Ken asked Charlene.

"A man's been injured, but he's alive," Charlene said, and Ken repeated it to the phone dispatcher.

She scanned Connor for any wounds but didn't see anything. He still had some theater makeup on his knuckle from where he'd brawled with Gil. Had that been who she'd seen run out? The frightening leprechaun out of costume?

Connor gave another moan and Charlene reached for his hand to comfort him. Inside his palm was a gold coin . . . the chocolate melted. Another gold disc peeped from his front denim pocket, the color bright against black fabric.

He brought his other hand to his temple, an expression of pain crossing his face. Had he hit his head on a table when he'd fallen?

"Help is coming," she assured him.

Ken waited on the small square landing of the outdoor staircase. Deana had come to see what had happened.

"Ambulance is on its way, hon," he shouted down. "Why don't you go stay in the car with the others? Lock the doors."

"Okay," Deana agreed. "Uh, Charlene's phone is ringing. Should we answer it?"

Charlene shook her head. She knew it would be the handsome, dashing Detective Sam. "I'll get it later."

She would have some explaining to do, but not now. This mess was not her fault. Not this time. She hadn't raced into danger; she'd gone to pick up a jacket and scarf. An innocent bystander who happened to be in the wrong place at the wrong time.

There had been no reason to be suspicious of anything. Nothing had seemed wrong until it had been.

Bright lights filtered through the door, and seconds later the paramedics burst into the room; one with gray hair, the other with acne. They strapped the unconscious man on the stretcher to cart him carefully down the stairs.

"His name is Connor Gallagher." Charlene followed the medics across the floor. "His cousin Shannon Best was in charge of the party here tonight."

"I know Connor," the older medic said. "Surprised to see him here, though. He made a big deal about leaving Salem and never coming back."

Charlene recalled the surprise and anger on Shannon's face when she'd seen him enter. The rest of the evening had passed in a blur of music, bagpipes, and dancing.

"When was that?"

"Five years ago?" The older medic took a careful step backward on the stairs. "Had a farewell party for him right here."

Charlene rubbed her arms against a chill. She trailed the men out, but at the last minute grabbed Lila's coat and cashmere scarf. They were hanging on a metal rod with wheels, the only one dangling between empty hangers.

She descended the staircase and reached the sidewalk. To her dismay, Officer Jimenez arrived in her patrol car to take Ken's statement. The two women didn't see eye to eye and never would. "Why am I not surprised to see you here?"

Did her lip just curl?

Charlene didn't react, though she was tempted to be snarky too. "My guests and I attended the Saint Paddy's dinner tonight. I'd like to get them home."

Officer Jimenez jotted down Ken's name and number. "What happened?"

"Lila forgot her coat inside, so Charlene ran up to get it," Ken replied, oblivious to the tension between Charlene and the officer. "From our spot in the van, we saw someone fleeing the building. I just had a bad feeling, you know?"

"And then?" the officer prodded.

"I decided to check on Charlene and found her helping that man, Connor, who wasn't moving. She'd forgotten her cell phone, so I called the ambulance."

"Can you describe the person?" Jimenez asked Ken.

"Not really. I just saw a man in a hurry to get away. Besides, it was dark." He shrugged, concern on his face.

"No discernable features? Skin color? Hair?"

Ken stuck his hand in his pocket. "He was wearing a bulky jacket with a hood, and I only saw the back."

Officer Jimenez turned to Charlene, her stylus pen poised over her tablet. "What did you see?"

"A guy in a black hoodie running down the stairs. He took me by surprise." Charlene stepped toward Ken. "I wasn't expecting to see anybody . . . I mean, maybe Shannon. It definitely was not her."

"Come on, Mrs. Morris. You can do better than that." When Charlene didn't answer, Jimenez sharpened her tone. "Was he short or tall? Fat or thin? You're used to this drill. Shannon who?"

"Shannon Best. She's the event coordinator here. She's also Connor Gallagher's cousin." Charlene inhaled slow and steady. "I don't recall more than that."

Ken clued into their animosity as Jimenez focused on her guest with stony gray eyes. "When are you leaving town?"

"Not until Friday."

"Good. I'll be in touch with more questions." Jimenez got into her patrol car and shut the door, lights flashing as she typed on her computer.

"She's tough as nails," Ken said to Charlene.

"You should try being on her bad side," she joked.

Charlene opened the van and ushered Ken in before her. He took his seat next to his wife, while Charlene presented the coat and scarf to Lila.

The guests applauded and cheered.

"What on earth is going on, luv?" Lila asked, leaning forward. "Your phone won't stop ringing."

Charlene turned around to calm her guests, glancing at the missed calls from Sam. He'd texted for her to call him, right away. The man could wait until she returned the guests to her bed-and-breakfast.

"Who here would like a glass of cheer when we get home? I'll give you all the details of our unpleasant experience at the same time, all right?"

Charlene kept her silence as she blared Irish music and everyone sang along.

Once home, Charlene and her guests went to their rooms to shed their outer clothing, then returned for conversation and a drink that was not green beer. Having a few minutes alone she returned Sam's texts, reassuring him she was fine.

I was never in danger . . . not even looking for it.

That's a first.

I promised to try!

Please don't talk to your guests about what happened tonight. Coming by tomorrow morning around ten. Let Minnie know? She's the only one who likes me.

Spoils you, you mean. And Avery is very fond of you.

She finished the message with a winking emoji.

After a quick, two-minute shower she changed into a pair of jeans and a camel-colored turtleneck, clipping her still-damp hair high on her head.

"Jack?" she whispered. The television was on low, but Jack wasn't around. He liked to hear about her day or evening out, as she was his link to the world. He claimed to be lonely when she was away.

Well, she couldn't worry about it now—her guests were her priority. As she turned to leave, she was attacked with tiny claws at her ankles. "There you are, kitty cat." She cradled Silva and kissed her on the furry head.

"Where is our friend, Jack? Did you scare him away?" Silva licked Charlene's hand with her rough tongue. "I'm sorry I can't stay, but you can keep the bed warm for me."

Charlene scratched Silva behind her ears, then placed her on the bed and darted out the door, closing it firmly behind her. She went straight for the living room and the new bar Parker had designed for her across from the fireplace.

Glasses hung from a small cabinet above. The maple countertop and base cabinet held a variety of liquor, wine, and tumblers. An ice machine was built in underneath, and two high-backed upholstered swivel barstools added more seating. She checked the wine supply and placed a bottle of red and a white on the corner of the countertop.

The fire was lit and one velvet wingback chair next to the fireplace was occupied. Jack stood up slowly, his eyes on hers. Her heartbeat kicked up a notch and knowing they only had a few minutes of privacy, she hurried to his side. "I wondered where you were. You lit the fire! How nice."

"I knew you'd be home soon." He had on a dark green velvet jacket over black slacks, and his ebony hair was swept back. His gorgeous blue eyes filled with warmth. "How did it go?"

"The food was excellent, and everyone had a good time. Until . . ."

"Oh, no. Until what?"

"If you make yourself comfortable and out of sight, I'll tell you about it later."

"Out of sight is never a problem with me."

Charlene laughed in surprise when Jack blew her a kiss and disappeared—she knew he hadn't gone far.

CHAPTER 3

Hearing footsteps, Charlene turned toward the double doors that she rarely closed. "You're the first to arrive," she told Jasper and Lila. They hadn't changed their clothes. "Take one of the sofas and I'll get you a drink. What would you like? We have practically everything."

"We'd both enjoy a sherry if you have a bottle in this very attractive bar." Jasper took his wife's hand and they stood next to the fireplace before the crackling flames.

"I'm sure we do." She smiled at the compliment. Finding the sherry and proper glasses, she poured the sweet wine. "This was my treat to myself after my first anniversary in this house. Now I don't know how I did without it."

As she carried the drinks on a small silver tray to the couple, they lifted their glasses and clinked before sipping. "It's a beautiful place you have, Charlene. You must be very proud of it."

"I am." She swallowed a sudden lump, seeing this sweet couple still in love after a lifetime together. She'd thought that she'd have Jared by her side forever too, but fate had intervened.

"What brought you here?" Lila asked softly. She sat on the sofa and patted the seat next to her.

Remaining upright, Charlene answered quickly . . . the pain less after so many times of retelling. "My husband was killed in a car accident, and the memories were too much. I had to get away from Chicago."

"I'm sorry," Jasper said, sharing a look with his wife. He joined Lila on the sofa.

"It's not easy and I'll always miss him. I love running the B and B." She headed for the bar and poured herself a small glass of merlot from Flint's Vineyard. "It makes me happy."

The entire room made her happy, from the flowered yellow-and-rose print sofas, the four-by-four square mahogany coffee table, and the exquisite matching chairs in laminated rosewood and yellow brocade grouped around the ornate fireplace.

Perhaps it looked like something straight out of *Downton Abbey*, but now, eighteen months later, she wouldn't change a thing.

The other guests arrived in varying stages of casual— Ken and Deana, with a tired Mason, were in sweatpants. Dell and Harmony had matching designer loungewear. She got them all something to drink, with a glass of milk for Mason, and everyone found a seat near the fire. Charlene stood, her back to the flames.

The chatter among the guests turned to questions about what happened when Charlene had gone back for Lila's coat.

"Can you tell us now?" Harmony asked. She and Dell had chosen the brocaded armchairs while the Fishburnes sat cross-legged on the floor. Mason sprawled against Deana. His face had been scrubbed clean of chocolate.

"I wish I could, but Detective Sam Holden will be by in the morning, and he's asked me not to talk about it."

Jack appeared with an elaborate eye roll.

Charlene sipped her merlot and glanced at Ken. His cheeks flushed as he said, "I won't say another word."

Lila clasped Jasper's hand. "How frightening! I'm sorry to have put you in a dangerous situation, Charlene."

She gave the couple a consoling smile. "It wasn't your fault. What happened was out of our control."

"Is the man dead?" Dell demanded. "Are we in danger?"

"No! And no. Now, how about a game of trivia?" Charlene did her best to steer the conversation away from Connor Gallagher, but she could tell that her guests were going to burst unless they talked amongst themselves.

"Ken told us that it was the drunk guy that got into a fight with the leprechaun," Harmony said.

Ken bowed his head. "Sorry, Charlene."

Deana smoothed Mason's hair, winding a brown curl over her finger while he finished his milk, eyes half-closed. "I remember thinking he'd embarrassed the red-haired lady."

Shannon. Charlene nodded but then caught herself. "We can do a puzzle or a game of UNO to unwind."

Dell ignored that suggestion. "The guy was that woman's cousin, right?"

Charlene hurried to the bar and added another half-inch to her glass. Jack laughed. "Want me to turn out the lights?" he asked. "You can claim power failure and send them all to bed."

It was tempting, but she sipped her merlot and shook her head.

"You mean the guy with the red hair that didn't have a ticket, and sat at your table?" Jasper asked with concern. "Bonkers. What was his agenda?" He made a *tsk* noise. "Whatever it was, it backfired."

"Can't feel sorry for him," Dell muttered. "Guy like that deserves his fate."

Jasper sipped his sherry and set the glass down. "Easy to condemn his actions, but I'm sure a few of us have skeletons in our closets."

Lila patted his hand. "Not mine, my dear. But definitely yours."

Her jest brought laughter and reduced the tension.

"Well, that calls for another drink." Dell stood up and reached for his wife's empty glass. "You ready for another gin and tonic, hon?"

"Sure . . . but make it small. We still have a few things to see in the morning, and we need to get something for our dog sitter. What time is checkout, Charlene?"

"Noon. If you need a little later, just let me know."

Harmony scooted to the edge of the armchair. "I know you can't talk about it, but what happens next?"

"Detective Holden will be here in the morning, but since none of you were there, he might only need a statement from me. Perhaps Ken. The police will find out who is responsible for the attack."

"You said that with a straight face," Jack said from his position by the fireplace. Charlene didn't answer but waited a little longer for her guests to say good night and leave for their rooms.

She brought the used glasses to the kitchen and washed them. Jack made the curtains at the kitchen window sway.

"Come downstairs, Charlene. I opened your favorite wine." He used his most persuasive voice, doubled with the look he gave her that she couldn't refuse.

If he wasn't a ghost, she'd have melted on the spot. But common sense dictated she would not melt, now or ever. Friends forever, that's what they were. On earth and in heaven.

"Just for a bit."

She followed him down to the wine cellar, closing the door behind them. No one could hear them surrounded by stone walls and it was their safe place.

He poured her a half-glass of the best French wine she'd ever tasted. It was a rare treat.

She took an appreciative sip, watching him over the rim of the glass. "What do you want, Jack?"

"Me?" His eyes blinked innocently. "I want to know about your day, and to heck with Sam's directive. I'm different."

"Above the rules." Charlene sipped again.

"Rules, *shmules*." He rested his forearm on the custom table. "What happened tonight?"

She smiled even though she felt a pang of hurt for this sweetheart of a man who was trapped between worlds. He'd given up salvation once to stay with her and now had to wait until the next time a knock came from heaven's door. If it ever would.

"All right, I'll tell you." There was a cushioned bench next to the door that she'd recently put in. Jack took the far end, not wanting to give her a further chill. She kept a warm fleece blanket on the bench and wrapped it around her shoulders.

Once she was comfortable, she related the story of finding Connor upstairs, having been attacked by a stranger in a hoodie. But Jack wanted more.

"Tell me about the party," he said. "What was it like?"

"It was nice—but also very crowded. Shannon Best is the one who arranged the event. Guess she does it every year. Green, gold, and shamrocks covered every surface." She put more emphasis on her tone, knowing Jack wanted to see it through her eyes. "We were on the second floor, elbow to elbow, practically. There wasn't room for one more chair."

"How was your table? Did everyone fit?"

She shook her head. "No. Charlene's didn't get private seating like I'd ordered. We were broken into three groups, all at separate tables. Guess who I was put with?" She made a face.

"From that clue, I can only imagine it was with the kids' table in the back of the kitchen."

"Not quite kids, but yes, the Ward brothers and I shared a table with Shannon Best and her son, Aiden. We probably won't see the boys until morning." She worried about them in a strange town.

"Relax." His soothing voice was a reminder that she wasn't responsible for them while they made a brief appearance in her life. "This weekend is a getaway. A chance to do the things they don't do at home." He waited for her to sip her wine. "They're single. Have steady jobs, but still live at home with their parents. Sometimes we don't get what we want."

Charlene adjusted the blanket and glanced at Jack. "We both understand that more than anyone—having been robbed of happy lives. Yours was cut short and mine was ripped in half."

"True. But look at us here together. Though not the regular kind of life, it's still a good one." He held her gaze with compassion. "Mine is better with you in it. You're shivering." He stood up to put a few feet between them. "Sam and I just want you to be safe. Even though I don't like him, I understand that."

"I wasn't in any danger tonight. I barely saw what happened to Connor. He's alive and in the hospital as we speak."

He chuckled. "Alive and not dead. A much better ending than some of the other drama around you. Do you think you have a guardian angel—Jared, perhaps?"

Her heart leaped as she considered the idea. "I wish, I really do." She bent her head and released a sigh. "I don't feel him. If he was around, he'd stop me from running even accidentally into danger." She bristled against the warning she knew Sam would give her. "Am I a fool?"

"Hardly. You're a very strong, hardheaded woman who fights for what she believes in. Justice shall prevail!" His chin tilted to the ceiling.

She laughed at his theatrics. "You're right. I'm no victim and never will be." Charlene stood and raised her fist like a gladiator, the blanket slipping to the bench.

"Look at all that you've accomplished in less than two years. Everything you've done to make Charlene's a success." He waved the blanket like a cape behind her. "You are amazing, and the world . . ."

"Don't you dare say the world is my oyster, or I'll have to clobber you."

He snickered. "You'd have to catch me first." Like a beam of light, he blinded her and when she opened her eyes again, Jack was gone and she was alone in the wine cellar. And much warmer.

"Jack, come back." She waited, knowing he might not return, but hoping he would.

He didn't.

"Night, Jack." She climbed the stairs, cradling her glass in her hand. At the sink, she sipped and savored her wine.

Like life, it was too special to waste.

Charlene woke up feeling refreshed and eager to start her day. She took a shower, washed her hair, then dressed in her favorite jeans and a long-sleeved Tommy Hilfiger tee.

The scent of fried bacon, fresh coffee, and savory croissants made her mouth water as she stepped into the kitchen from her suite, passing Minnie in the hall to the dining room. "Good morning, everyone," she called out cheerily as she entered.

The Fishburnes were enjoying their breakfast, but they looked up with a smile when they saw her. The Prescotts weren't down yet, neither were the Wards. The Brookses were also absent.

"This is delicious, Charlene," Deana said. "The brochure stated full breakfast on weekends only, but it hasn't been that way. Every morning we have something substantial. It's a great surprise."

Charlene pinched a slice of bacon from the center of the table. "Minnie can't help herself. This is her idea of a 'light breakfast.'" She used her fingers for quotation marks.

"Well, we certainly appreciate it." Ken buttered a croissant. "It helps with the budget."

"Where's Silva?" Mason asked. The little boy didn't appear the worse for wear after his night of chocolate coins.

"I don't know." Charlene wondered the same thing. She hadn't seen the cat when she'd gone to bed, and Silva hadn't been with her this morning. "I'm going to grab a coffee and have a peek. Sometimes she stays outside at night, but not when it's cold."

"Can I come too?" Mason blinked big brown eyes at her.

"If it's okay with your parents, then yes, I could use a helpful person like you."

"Huntin's a lot of work so we should have another crawsant. I'll need the enagy."

She smiled at his mispronounced words and patted Mason's shoulder. "You stay here and have as many as your little tummy demands. I'll be back."

Charlene hurried into the kitchen for her mug of java. "Minnie, you're wowing the guests again. Are you sure it's not too much work?"

"I'm fine, dear. If there are leftovers, I take a little home for Will."

"I'm sure he appreciates that." She grabbed her favorite mug, added cream, and filled it to the top with dark roast, then chose a green pear from the fruit bowl that looked ripe and sweet. "Have you seen Silva today?"

"No. I haven't." Minnie covered a loaf of bread with plastic wrap. "She didn't come around for breakfast and I know she loves bacon. Don't think I've seen her since yesterday. I finally got that twig out of her collar, but she didn't like it. Maybe she's pouting?"

Charlene frowned. "Can't imagine that she'd hold a grudge. She's got the run of the house."

Minnie patted the loaf. "Little Queen of Sheba."

"Who is?" Lila asked as she and Jasper entered the

kitchen. The couple was dressed for the day in matching tweed. Very English countryside.

"Silva, our cat." Charlene shrugged. "I'm worried. It's not like her to miss a meal or not climb into my bed at night."

"Another crime to solve," a deep voice rumbled from behind her. "I knocked but nobody answered. The door was unlocked, so I let myself in."

"You're early," Charlene griped, cutting a slice of the pear. "You said ten-ish."

"I'm Detective Sam Holden." He offered his hand to Jasper and then to Lila.

Jasper gave a firm shake. "Jasper Prescott and this is my lovely wife, Lila."

"Are you here to question us?" Lila's charming English accent brightened as she eyed Sam.

"Not unless you want me to." Sam wore a devilish grin on his handsome face, then pulled on his thick mustache. He had that whole young Sam Elliott thing going on, and Charlene wasn't even sure he knew it.

"Would you like some coffee, Detective?" Minnie blushed to the roots of her gray hair. "I made fresh croissants." She shoved her hands in the pocket of her apron.

Jasper and Lila exchanged an amused smile.

Charlene shook her head and focused on her delicious pear.

"The ones with bacon and cheese?" He sniffed. "Chocolate with almonds?" Minnie had poured him some coffee and he took a sip.

"Some imagination you've got!" Dear Minnie, who was more a friend than a housekeeper, put her hands on her plump hips and gave him a saucy look. "Mozzarella, basil, tomatoes, and a light touch of hollandaise sauce."

"I'll have one of those too." Jasper wetted his lips. "How 'bout you, my love?"

"I'd choose the bacon and cheese, if it's not putting you out." Lila studied Minnie to be sure.

"Not at all." Minnie shooed them down the hall. "Go join the Fishburnes in the dining room and I'll bring it to you, along with fresh coffee."

"Thank you." Lila gave Sam a quick wink as she passed by him.

Sam was a large man, six-foot-six, with wide shoulders like a linebacker, yet he was lean muscle through and through. His presence took up the entire kitchen.

He plunked himself on the stool next to Charlene, who tried to ignore him but couldn't. Her pulse skipped.

"So, Silva's gone missing," he said, taking another drink of coffee. "Need help?"

She darted a glance his way and swallowed over the lump in her throat. He'd offered her more than friendship when she'd first moved to Salem, but she'd declined. And kept declining. Until Jack was free of the property, she couldn't share her life with anyone else.

"Nope. Mason has offered to search for Silva with me."

"Then I'll quickly take your statement, and Mr. Fishburne's, then be on my way."

Minnie slid a plate in front of him with her new creation, plus the chocolate croissant, another favorite. "I'll take care of the guests while you two talk."

Charlene hadn't had the chance to tell Minnie about what had happened yesterday—she'd do it later. She gave Sam her full attention. "How is Connor Gallagher this morning?"

"Unconscious," Sam said bluntly. "I'll feel better when he wakes up and tells me who did this. Until then, I'm doing the standard background stuff. Connor Gallagher is the black sheep of a respected Salem family. He isn't well-liked by them or his peers."

"I saw that for myself at the dinner yesterday. I was seated with Shannon Best and her son, Aiden. He's bright and going to med school."

Sam bit into his croissant, but she could tell he was listening.

Charlene kept talking. "She works for AOH and it was glaringly obvious that Connor's presence disturbed both of them." She sipped her now-cool coffee. "Connor was drunk and obnoxious. Fighting with the leprechaun, who is a mainstay. It was humiliating for her."

"Bad blood between them. Is it a motive for an attack?" He took another bite, then wiped his mouth. "What did you see upstairs?"

"I told Officer Jimenez already."

"Tell me again." Sam swallowed coffee and she pulled her gaze from his throat.

"A man in a hoodie." She shook her head. "I didn't see many details."

"What did you hear?"

Charlene thought back. "The person said, 'Finn, give me my share' or something like that. It wasn't clear. And of course, that wasn't Finn but Connor."

"That wasn't in Jimenez's notes."

"She didn't ask what I'd heard. She asked what the guy looked like." Charlene raised her brow.

He didn't push. "What about the dinner? I've never been. Heard the brisket is amazing."

"The food's great, but the real party is downstairs after the meal. Dancing and having fun."

"Tell me about the leprechaun and the brawl. I noticed

abrasions on Connor's knuckles and wondered about that."

"I didn't see it happen. I guess Gil, the man dressed as the leprechaun, tried to stop Connor from coming upstairs, but Connor wasn't listening. They fought."

"Tell me more." Behind the mustache, she could see the hint of a smile.

"About the leprechaun? Well, he scared poor Mason, who's six, and he gave me the creeps too." She helped herself to a quarter of Sam's chocolate croissant. "He wears a lot of makeup, which is what I saw on Connor's hand. I didn't see Gil after the altercation."

"Gil's last name?"

"I don't know."

"Okay. I'd like to talk with Ken Fishburne."

"He's in the dining room. I'll introduce you."

"I read the statements from Jimenez. She seems to think you were holding back." Sam finished his croissants and brought the plate to the sink.

That woman! "I wasn't. Just leave them." Charlene ushered him toward the dining room. Minnie stacked empty plates and joked with the guests.

Sam introduced himself to Deana and Ken. Charlene caught Mason's eye. "Ready to find Silva?"

"Let's go!"

Charlene grinned at his enthusiasm. For a half hour, they searched every corner of the downstairs, starting with her room—even under the bed and out on the back porch. They called for Silva in the living room, lifting sofa cushions, and looking behind the bar. The guests' rooms were off-limits, of course. They were on the third floor in the vacant single room about to give up when Silva jumped from behind a drape and lunged at them.

Mason shrieked.

Silva's little paws were brown and gold. Charlene lifted another curtain and discovered a stack of gold chocolate wrappers.

"Oh no!" Mason cried. "Silva ate my stash."

"You were hiding gold coins?" Charlene asked, remembering the paper cup he'd brought with him last night. Silva must have found it. Wasn't chocolate bad for cats?

"It's treasure," he insisted, eyes welling.

"We'll get you more, hon." Charlene pulled her phone from her pocket and dialed Dr. Hendez, Silva's veterinarian. Life with cats and kids was never dull. As if her hands weren't already full with a handsome ghost.

CHAPTER 4

The Brookses returned at eleven from their tour and last-minute shopping, then dashed off to pack. Minnie would ready the blue suite for their next visitors. Sheffer LaCroix was due by two this afternoon.

Silva sat on her lap in the kitchen so that Charlene could monitor the cat's behavior. Chocolate could be lethal, but Silva acted fine. Dr. Hendez said the chocolate might have already been regurgitated. Ew.

Charlene made good use of the next hour by sprucing up her website on her laptop until the clumping sound of suitcases bouncing down the staircase interrupted her focus. She cringed at the golden oak taking a beating, but hopefully the runners on each step would keep it safe.

She put Silva down and entered the foyer. Harmony dragged a lighter bag behind her while Dell struggled with two larger wheeled suitcases.

"Do you need any help?" Charlene hoped they'd say yes so she could save her floor

"No. We're almost there," Dell panted. "Just a few more steps."

She breathed a sigh of relief once the bags were stacked next to the door. "Do you have time for a light lunch?"

"No. But thanks for the offer, you've been so kind." Harmony gave her a warm smile—so different than her original cool attitude.

Dell nodded. "We've already called for a cab."

They were traveling from Boston to Maryland and should be home for dinner.

Charlene realized she'd misjudged them, finding their aloofness cold rather than self-sufficient. They were pleasant and didn't require coddling. It was a reminder to her to keep an open mind.

The cab arrived and Charlene helped them to the car.

"We enjoyed our stay very much," Harmony said. "Your home is gorgeous and you're such a gracious host."

"Thank you! How kind for you to say." She touched Harmony's arm with affection. "I imagine you're missing your pup."

Dell smiled and put a hand on his wife's back. "He's our baby. A Labradoodle. Good-natured, doesn't bark, or shed. Bailey is sweet as can be."

"We have a dog sitter he adores," Harmony told her, "but Bailey will jump for joy when he sees us."

"That's the best thing about a loving pet." She had Silva and understood. The driver put the suitcases in the trunk and closed the lid. "Have a safe flight. If you have a moment when you get home, I'd be thrilled if you could leave a review on Tripadvisor."

"Of course." Harmony smiled. "And we'll tell all our friends."

In a good mood, Charlene sent Minnie home at lunch for some extra time off for herself. Avery would come right after school, since she'd missed work Sunday to study for a test. The teenager lived in a subsidized home for teens and worked between twenty and thirty hours a week at the bed-and-breakfast. Over the past year, she and Minnie had become very attached to the girl.

Avery was months away from graduation, then it was college at Salem State if one of her other choices didn't come through.

Charlene returned to her suite. She hadn't seen Jack since the cellar last night. She doubted she'd ever get used to the way he floated in and out. She didn't know where he went or whether he'd come back.

"Hey!" Seated at the computer in jeans and a navy sweater, he welcomed her with a relaxed smile. "You caught me playing a solo game of chess."

"You must be winning, right?"

He laughed and his turquoise eyes lit up. "There is that. But the competition is pretty poor."

"Nonsense. You just have to outwit yourself." She plopped down on the love seat and he shifted the entire chair to face her.

"How did the meeting with Sam go?"

She shrugged. "I told him what I knew, which was basically nothing. Then Mason and I searched the house for Silva. She'd been missing all morning."

The cat was curled up on Jack's armchair, snoring. "Where was she?"

"She's fine now, but she ate Mason's chocolate coins."

Concerned, Jack appeared at the cat's side in a blink, looking her over as she slept. "Chocolate can be deadly to animals. Did you call the vet?"

"I did. I think she's all right." Charlene tucked herself into a corner of the love seat. "Carry on! I want to watch you beat yourself."

"Ha, ha, ha." He reappeared before the desk. "How about you play a game with me? Although I am very clever, maybe too clever for you."

She threw a pillow at Jack, but it went right through his essence and hit the open laptop screen, then dropped to the floor. Embarrassed, she jumped up and retrieved the pillow. "Sorry."

"If you're afraid to lose . . ." He tugged a lock of her hair.

They smiled, enjoying the easy banter and friendship they'd formed. A knock sounded and she checked the time on her phone. Not quite two.

"It's probably our new guest. Avery won't be here until two-thirty." Charlene arrived at the front door just as she heard a second knock. With a flourish, she opened it wide and her mouth dropped. He was either George Clooney's doppelgänger or Charlene's reputation had reached LA.

The striking face, strong jaw, dark brown eyes, and a touch of silver glinting in his well-cut, dark brown hair all screamed GEORGE.

She clamped her hands together and squeaked, "You, you're not—"

"George Clooney?" He gave a mouthwatering smile. "I get that all the time, but unfortunately, no. Sheffer LaCroix. I have a reservation?"

"Come on in." She felt flustered and foolish as she saw his luggage on the porch behind him. Nice, but not George Clooney nice. "You have just the two bags?"

He drew himself up and smoothed his jacket in a reserved manner. He'd paid ahead for a full week. "Yes."

Sheffer walked past her and stood in her foyer. He admired her staircase and the galleries above. Silva stared down at him from between two posts. "Nice place you've got here."

"Thank you."

Sheffer turned to her with a slight furrow between his perfect brows.

She'd been eyeing him with appreciation as he had summed up her house. This man would rock a tuxedo. Dressed to impress, Sheffer wore a dark gray suit, a crisp white shirt, and polished shoes that gleamed. He carried an attaché and a rolling bag that would easily fit an overhead bin. He probably flew first class.

Gathering her wits, which had fallen by the wayside, she asked if he'd need help with his suitcases to the second floor.

"That would be nice."

She snapped out of it as she realized she had to help him—it was her job—and retrieved his luggage from the porch. "You'll have time to unpack before happy hour around four, depending on the guests' tours."

Jack shimmered behind her in a gust of cold. "You sounded out of breath and nervous. Decided I better check out our new guest for myself." He surveyed Sheffer with a critical eye. "Good-looking, but pompous. He's trying too hard."

Was he? She agreed that Sheffer was a tad overdressed

for the short flight from New York. He could easily be a male model or a Hollywood stand-in.

"Happy hour?" Sheffer showed off perfect white veneers. "I could use a drink after my flight. Short, but bumpy." He checked his black watch. "Perfect." His smile just missed the mark of genuine.

Charlene cleared her throat, gesturing to the stairs as she picked up his suitcase. It was heavy but she gritted her teeth to hide her surprise. Sheffer started to say something, but then bit his lip and lifted the other as if it were full of cotton balls. "Your suite is on the second floor, to the right."

Jack followed them up the steps. "We'll see about this one, Charlene."

She blew a strand of long hair off her face as she struggled up the next step. Jack had a teensy jealous streak that sometimes clouded his vision.

"Ask him why he's here," Jack said.

"What brings you to Salem? You reserved for a week, correct?"

Sheffer peered over his shoulder at Charlene, the attaché handle in two fingers. "I've always wanted to visit, and your place has good reviews."

She'd worked hard to earn those reviews and they were paying off. "Good to hear!" Charlene adjusted her grip. "We don't do much for Saint Patrick's Day, but my cook is making a special dinner Wednesday night. Most guests like to sample Salem's superb dining establishments, so this is just a fun get-together." Her arm muscles burned. "You're welcome to join us for corned beef and cabbage."

"I'm French, not Irish," he said with a grin. "Not even a little bit . . . but I'm willing to try some corned beef."

It was beginning to feel like a dinner party.

Sheffer reached the landing, then allowed her to lead. She went to the right and the first door down the hall.

"Here you are." Charlene opened it and moved aside. The linens had all been changed and Minnie had put a welcome basket with a bottle of wine, nuts, and crackers on the end table.

Sheffer entered and turned around with a nod of appreciation. "Love it when the online pictures match the room and aren't outdated by twenty years."

Charlene laughed. "I've been here for less than two." She stepped back after putting his suitcase of bowling balls next to the bed. "I'll let you get settled."

She shut the door and had a spring in her step as she walked down the hall. Jack blustered at her side.

What did Sheffer have in that suitcase? Her mind went to an array of things a single man might want in Salem and blushed.

"I don't like that smile you're wearing," Jack said. With a snap of cold, her roommate disappeared in a huff.

Charlene dreamed of oncoming trains and perilous tracks. With a start, she realized the sound was Silva, purring at her side. She chuckled and blinked herself awake, stretching carefully so as not to disturb the large Persian. The cat was better than an electric blanket against chilly spring nights.

The television in her suite was on, which meant that Jack was awake and had gotten over his snit about Sheffer, her handsome houseguest. George Clooney wasn't her thing, anyway. She'd always preferred Sam Elliott.

She brushed her teeth and slipped into her robe over

flannel pajamas, then opened her door. Jack materialized when he saw her, sprawled comfortably in his favorite armchair. His baby blues twinkled in welcome.

Charlene chose the left corner of the love seat and wrapped an afghan around her lap. Jack's essence emanated a chill that she didn't mind because it meant he was nearby. "Morning," she said softly.

Minnie could be heard in the kitchen, making coffee and setting out pastries for the guests. Tuesdays were light breakfast days.

"Morning." Jack looked from Charlene to her room and the partially open door. "Silva's still sleeping?"

She didn't bring up the Sheffer incident and neither did Jack. "Out like a light, lazy cat. What's on the news?"

Jack glanced at her with a hesitant expression that put her on guard. "Connor Gallagher died last night in the hospital."

"Oh no!" She sighed, immediately thinking of her new friend from the AOH. "I'll reach out to Shannon Best and send a card or something. Did they say what happened to him?"

"Police haven't given an official statement yet." Jack shrugged. "No surprise there. What do you think?"

Charlene dredged up the memory of Connor on his back, arms to his sides, unconscious but breathing. "I didn't see any injuries on him . . . a stroke or a heart attack because of being attacked? He'd been drinking, so a part of me wondered if he'd just passed out cold when the guy pushed him. Maybe he hit the tables?"

"Could be a head injury of some kind." Jack laced his fingers over his bent knee. "Sam will know what happened."

"You're right." Charlene snugged the afghan close

around her lap. "But there is no guarantee that he'll tell me. He'll be by later."

Jack gave a slow nod and sent her a smile. "My money is on you to get him to tell you what he can." He rubbed his hands soundlessly together. "What do we have on the bed-and-breakfast agenda today?"

"Well, we have an almost full house." She grinned, happiest as hostess of Charlene's. "Just a suite and one single room to let. We have preparations for our Saint Paddy's Day dinner tomorrow." Charlene tipped her chin toward the television and the newscaster complaining about the dreary weather. "That's such sad news about Connor. I honestly didn't think he was on death's door. Poor Shannon!"

"There are a lot of mixed emotions when a family member you don't like dies suddenly," Jack said. "You're affected and you just met them. How can I help?"

"I witnessed Connor's attack. It's personal." Charlene plucked at a strand of yarn on her afghan. "Want to find Shannon's contact information online, while I have breakfast with our guests?"

He was up in a flash of chill air and at her laptop, opening it without visible hands. "You got it. What was her last name?"

Truth was, she and Jack made a great team. Too bad that he had to be understandably behind the scenes.

"Best. Shannon. She owns an accounting business. Has a son, Aiden. Smart kid—going to medical school to be a doctor. When I say *kid*, I mean twenty-one or twenty-two." Charlene chuckled. When she'd been that age, she'd considered herself a grown woman. Little did she know!

"Medical school. Being a doctor is a very fulfilling career," Jack reminisced.

Charlene reached toward him but stopped short of patting his body that was now in full color as he strengthened his image for her. "I know you miss it, Jack."

His gaze showed his appreciation for her understanding. They were working on a way for him to fill the void of helping others that he felt. "I'll get started."

Charlene also got up. "Here's to another day! Oh—Avery isn't going to be here this afternoon since she's got a test. I don't want you looking for her and worrying when she doesn't show."

Jack watched over them all, in his way. "She's doing well on those aptitude tests. I've seen her study."

They shared a smile. "Avery was a little down yesterday because of being on the wait list for full tuition to Boston Academy. It broke my heart to see her so upset."

Harvard and Smith were out of the question, but that wasn't the college Avery wanted anyway. Boston Academy had great accreditation and offered both associate and bachelor degrees. The local community college in Salem had offered full-paid tuition, and that was a good backup if Avery didn't find something else.

"You've helped her send out a lot of applications, Charlene. She's got good personal recommendations and terrific grades. Something will turn up," Jack said with confidence. "Now go get dressed, or else your guests will see that you wear kitty cat flannel pajamas to bed."

She laughed and turned to her room. Thanks to the weather lady, Charlene knew it was going to be a cool forty-seven degrees and gray skies. No rain. She chose an espresso-colored turtleneck with a button-up cardigan over jeans. When she returned to the living room ten minutes later, Jack was typing away with his back to her as he sat at her desk.

"Any luck?"

"You can wait and get a full report after breakfast," Jack teased.

She chuckled and left her suite for the warm, blueberry-scented kitchen. Her housekeeper hummed along with a pop station on the radio. "Morning, Minnie."

"It's another gray day in Salem," Minnie crooned as she turned off the oven. Steaming blueberry muffins rested on the stovetop and Charlene's mouth watered. "Do you ever regret not moving to a tropical paradise to open your B and B?"

Charlene poured herself a cup of coffee over cream and leaned back against the kitchen counter as she breathed in the dark roast aroma, allowing it to enter through her system on multiple senses before she sipped. Delicious.

"Hmm. No regrets." That was the truth. The weather in Salem wasn't so different from her old hometown, yet the gray skies here didn't bother her as she was happy. "This was the best decision I've ever made." She'd made friends and a life that she wouldn't have if she'd stayed in Chicago with her grief.

"Glad to hear it!" Minnie put a blueberry muffin on a small plate for Charlene to nibble. "Here you are. I hear the Fishburnes upstairs, so they'll be down shortly, I'm sure. Not a peep from the Ward brothers, but the Prescotts have been down by half-past eight all week."

It was just now eight according to the digital clock on the stove. "Sheffer LaCroix checked in yesterday. He agreed to join us for corned beef and cabbage tomorrow night."

Minnie opened the refrigerator and pointed to a roast the size of a piglet. "I bought the largest brisket at the market."

"With you, Will, Avery, and now Sheffer, that makes ten." Charlene followed her bite of muffin with a sip of coffee. "We can comfortably seat twelve in the dining room, and what better time to have a party, than when the weather is gray?"

Minnie shut the fridge, cutting off the chill that reminded her of Jack's presence.

"Potatoes, cabbage." Her housekeeper ducked into the pantry and came out with a cylindrical container of dried oatmeal. "I think I'll make cookies later."

"The lacy ones with orange zest and pecans?" Those cookies were one of Charlene's favorites. "Perfect to dunk in hot chocolate on a dreary afternoon."

She heard the clatter of small feet and her heart warmed as Mason skidded around the bottom of the stairs.

"We're here, Charlene!"

Laughing, Charlene brought the platter of pastries Minnie had prepared and the carafe of coffee to the dining room and set it on the center of the table. "Hello, Mason. Deana. Ken."

The family gathered around one corner in good cheer. The Prescotts followed and even the Wards were up by eight-thirty. Sheffer dropped down long enough to get a coffee and a muffin. Stubble covered his cheeks and he'd thrown on a sweatshirt with sweatpants to get his breakfast and scurry back upstairs.

Charlene kept loose track of her guests, in the event they needed her, but didn't want to hover. Sheffer had joined the others yesterday for her happy hour and then had slipped out. She didn't know when he'd come back to the bed-and-breakfast.

Not a morning person, perhaps.

Once breakfast was over, Charlene wished her guests a fun day out to see the sights. "Office chores for me today," she said, escaping to her suite. Hopefully, there would be more news about Connor—like the cause of death.

Jack waited for her with a pleased expression.

Charlene perched on the armrest of the love seat, facing her handsome ghost. "What have you learned?"

"Shannon *O'Brien* Best. Not only does she own an accounting firm, she's been nominated for businesswoman of the year five times, and won it three. She's very attractive with those blue eyes and red hair. Irish to the last freckle."

She read the article over Jack's shoulder, then searched for her phone. "Have you seen . . ."

Jack floated the device from where she'd left it in her room to charge to her outstretched hand.

"Thank you." She squinted at the phone number Jack had found online, then dialed on the keypad, keeping the device on speaker.

"What are you going to say?" Jack gave her a slight smirk.

Charlene shrugged. "It's a sympathy call."

Jack's brow rose. "Uh-huh."

Before she could defend herself, a heavy voice said, "This is Shannon."

"Shannon—hello. This is Charlene Morris. We met Sunday at the AOH club?"

Sniff. "Oh, yes. I remember. Uh . . . this isn't a good time."

"That's why I'm calling. I saw on the news that your cousin passed away. Is there anything I can do for you or your family? I'd be happy to send over some food for you."

"Oh? Aren't you sweet?" Shannon dragged in an audible breath.

"Who is it, Mom?" a young man asked grouchily. Charlene imagined that Shannon too must be using her phone hands-free and that the male was Aiden.

"Charlene. The woman we met the night Connor . . . Connor . . ."

"It's okay, Mom." It sounded like he gave his mother a hug.

Shannon breathed in and out, then said, "It's just that we don't know what happened to him. The police are being coy. Asking all kinds of questions."

Charlene stilled and exchanged a look with Jack. "Did they mention to you that I found him and my guest, Ken, called 911?"

"You did?" Aiden's tone grew stronger as if he had stepped closer to the phone. "No. That didn't come up when the police were here this morning. Two cops showed up hassling us—well, me—as if I might know something about it. Did someone take Connor out? I bet—"

"Hush, son," Shannon said.

Charlene's antennae quivered. She closed her eyes. There was only one reason for the police to be that way.

Murder.

CHAPTER 5

Connor's death must be suspicious for the police to be tracking down Connor's last moves. Charlene swallowed hard, her fingers to her throat. Could the Bests be involved?

"Perhaps we should get together to discuss what happened." Charlene wanted to see their reactions in person and look for truth or lies.

"I say you tell us right now, lady," Aiden countered. "My mom's been through enough without you playing games."

Jack scowled. "What does he mean by that, that his mom's been through enough?"

It had to be the embarrassment of Connor barging into the dinner on Sunday, and then the police on her doorstep.

"What did you see, Charlene?" Shannon's voice quaked. "Was Connor already . . . dead?"

"No. Unconscious." Charlene went over going back in for the coat and finding the man threatening Connor. Sam hadn't told her that she couldn't share with the family. "I think I heard, *Finn, give me my share*."

Shannon gasped.

"He said, Finn?" Aiden questioned. "Are you sure?"

"Well, as much as I can be. It was dark and alarming . . ." Still, she was pretty sure those were the words just as she was sure this meant something to the Bests.

"Finn." Aiden's tone held a sneer. "My mom has a twin brother named Finn. He's a crazy old recluse."

"We don't talk about him," Shannon said abruptly. "Why would anybody call Connor, Finn? I mean, I guess they used to look alike when they were younger but . . . my brother isn't well. He's housebound."

"I'm surprised that the police didn't mention this to you. I was clear about the attacker threatening Finn by name." Clear to Sam, not Officer Jimenez. It was true she'd held back and now she felt bad.

"You told the cops?" The end of the sentence hitched upward as if Aiden wasn't sure this was a great idea.

Too late, kid. If he had a secret it was best to come clean now. "Detective Holden."

"I think we'd better meet, Charlene," Shannon said quietly. "To discuss this situation. As I said, my twin isn't well and the last thing he needs is the police badgering him about Connor."

Charlene raised a brow at Jack as he said, "Interesting reaction."

"Tell me where . . . lunch is usually open for me even

when I have guests." Shannon probably wanted to know exactly what Charlene had heard the night her cousin was attacked. If their roles were reversed, she'd want to know everything.

"I've got to call the family together. Give me until to-morrow—no, that's Saint Paddy's. I'm so busy already." She groaned. "Thursday? Maybe. I'll phone later."

"You got it."

"Charlene, I would appreciate it if you didn't tell any-body else about Connor's connection to Finn. They had a falling-out when Connor left five years ago, and they never made up. Connor was wrong. I'll explain later." Shannon hung up.

"Well, that's mysterious," Jack said dryly.

"I wonder if they're worried that her reclusive brother killed Connor?" Charlene set the phone on the desk. "They're concerned over something."

"What did you see that night?" Jack asked. "Could the figure have been an old man?"

Charlene tried to picture Shannon's brother. "Shannon and Finn are twins. Finn would be fifty-two. That's not old."

Jack hovered his fingers over the keyboard, then fo-cused his mind to put Connor Gallagher into the search bar, which brought up a news article in the Salem online paper.

"Connor was fifty," Jack read. "Says here that he is survived by his sister, Patricia Gallagher. Parents de-ceased, no wife, no children. Cousins . . . but not listed by name."

"Where has Connor been living since he left Salem, does the article say that?"

"No."

Her phone rang and she jumped, her stomach in her throat. "Oh!" She recognized the number. "Salem police department."

"Not Sam?" Jack clarified by peering down his elegant nose at her.

"No." She and Sam had devised a system so that they could be friends outside of the occasional mystery she found herself embroiled in. He didn't share details of cases, as he was concerned for her safety, which meant they were at odds.

So, if he was calling her on official business, he usually used her landline and his office phone—not their cell numbers.

"Hello?"

"Charlene Morris?" queried a deep female voice that brought apprehension along with recognition. Not Sam. She'd rather hear from Sam.

Her defenses rose and she rubbed the back of her neck. "This is Charlene."

"Officer Jimenez. We regret to inform you that Connor Gallagher has passed away. I need you to come to the station and describe the person you saw to our sketch artist. Your guest Ken Fishburne too. I have in my notes he's in town still."

"Oh!" Charlene hurried out to the lobby, but the Fishburnes were already gone. "The family just left for a day of tours."

"When can you be here?" Jimenez asked tightly.

"Within the hour."

Jimenez ended the call.

"She doesn't like you," Jack said with a barely straight face.

"Laugh all you want. You aren't the one who has to

beard the dragon in her den. She looks at me like she'd love to toss me in a cell and throw away the key."

Charlene rose and brushed her palms together.

"Tell Minnie where you're going, just in case we need to organize a jailbreak to get you out of the pokey." Jack's image shimmered with amusement.

"The pokey?"

Jack grinned. "I've been watching old detective movies. What can I say?"

She left her suite without saying goodbye, shutting the door on Jack's mirth. He did have a point, though.

Charlene found Minnie in the living room dusting the furniture. "Hey, Minnie. I'm headed to the police station to describe the man who attacked Connor Gallagher. He died, so it's now a murder."

Minnie waved the duster over the fragile porcelain lamp bases. "Poor man! Will you be meeting with Sam?"

"I don't think so."

Minnie winked. "If you happen to see him, maybe you should invite him to dinner tomorrow night."

It was on the tip of her tongue to say no . . . but then she shrugged. What better way to get information than directly from the source?

Charlene threw a lightweight green jacket in the back of her car, then drove her Pilot to the station as the sun broke through the gray clouds.

With luck on her side, she found parking on the street, a half-block from the station. A large flag fluttered outside the police headquarters. Wide stone stairs led inside the brick building to black double doors.

She knew the precinct all too well, but she kept the past behind her, glad she wasn't in handcuffs or being interrogated. Not this time. This morning, she was here of her own free will as a witness to describe what little she'd seen.

As she entered, Marsha, the older police officer who manned the desk, nodded at her. "Charlene Morris. The sketch artist is waiting for you in the fourth room down the hall, to the left."

"Thank you," she said brightly, even if her backbone was stiff as a board. This was a different room than the one she'd been interviewed in before.

Reaching the fourth door, she knocked and heard a firm, "Come in."

She entered a stark, unfriendly room. Black shades were half-drawn, which allowed some natural light against the shadows, but it wasn't enough. How could the man see to draw?

"I'm Officer Nathan Tate." The sketch artist shook her hand. He was thin with a pale face, small in stature, wearing a gray suit. Thinning brown hair and hazel eyes. Not a man who would stand out in a crowd, or for a witness to describe. He looked like a million other men on the street and had no distinguishing features.

"Charlene Morris." She shuffled her feet in place. "Can we turn on the light?"

He reached over her shoulder to flip the switch. Fluorescent bulbs flickered and settled, but one of the tubes was out. "That will have to do, I'm afraid. This is the only room available today."

It was on the tip of her tongue to offer to come back another day, but she smiled instead, determined to get this over with, for Shannon's sake. She blamed her nerves on previous experiences here at the station.

"You seem anxious."

"A little."

"I promise you this is painless and can be a big help in locating the person behind Connor Gallagher's attack at the AOH club."

"I know." She put one hand in her jeans pocket and adjusted her purse strap over her shoulder with the other. "I've done this before, but it was in a different room. Where is your uniform?"

"I'm from Boston, helping out while the other officer is on leave. Maternity."

Her shoulders lightened. All routine.

"Can I get you a coffee? Water?"

"Water would be great."

A long wooden table with eight chairs centered the room. Officer Tate's laptop and sketch pad were at one end, along with a cup of coffee. She chose the second chair from his.

The fluorescent lights above flickered like they were possessed, then stopped. Officer Tate got a bottle of water from the counter and passed it to her, then gestured toward the ceiling. "Horrible, I know, but this shouldn't take long."

"It's fine." She edged her chair backward, studying him as he studied her. Did he see her nerves?

"Are you comfortable?"

"Yes. I suppose." Charlene clasped her hands in her lap, eager to help, but fearing she wouldn't be able to give a description. "It's just that I never got a clear view."

"It's surprising how much our subconscious can pick up in a brief flash. You might not think you remember anything, but once we start talking, little things could occur to you that will assist with our sketch."

She shrugged apologetically. "Just don't expect any miracles. It was dark."

"Charlene . . . try to relax. We're just talking, that's all." Officer Tate took a sip from his probably cold coffee. "Now, can you tell me where you were the night of the attack? Let's just make conversation. I'm not going to sketch right now. I'm going to listen. Ask a few questions."

"Sure." Charlene fidgeted on the chair, her thoughts scattering as she tried to catch them like spilled grains of rice.

"If you want to close your eyes you can, but it's not necessary. Whatever helps shut out the chaos. When did this occur?"

She leaned back in her chair and closed her eyes, bringing the night into focus. "Sunday evening. I'd taken my guests—I run a bed-and-breakfast—to the Saint Patrick's Day party held by the Ancient Order of Hibernians, known as AOH."

"My wife is Irish, so I'm familiar. Go on."

"I'd reserved a table for our group of ten on the second floor, but when we got there it was so crowded that they had us at three separate tables. The woman who organizes the event shared the table I was at—she apologized profusely, but I understand that sometimes things happen out of our control."

"Who was that?"

"Shannon Best."

"You weren't angry?"

"No. It ended up being fun meeting new people . . . until her cousin Connor crashed the party uninvited. He's the one who died."

"How did Shannon handle that?"

"I thought she managed the situation gracefully. Connor was loud, obviously drunk, and had made a scene downstairs with the leprechaun, embarrassing both Shannon and Aiden, her adult son."

"Aiden Best."

"Yes." Charlene opened her eyes to see how Officer Tate was reacting.

He held his coffee cup and left his digital pen on the table. He must have one heck of a memory, she thought.

"What happened next?"

"My guests and I went downstairs to see the band and the leprechaun—my youngest guest is six and Mason wanted to see if we could make friends with him and get his gold."

Officer Tate chuckled. "I've heard that if you capture a leprechaun, they have to take you to their stash of gold at the end of the rainbow."

"Me too! Must be true." She laughed and relaxed a smidge. "The leprechaun was too scary for us to befriend. Oh . . . Gil and Connor got into a fistfight. Connor had stage makeup from the leprechaun on his knuckles when he came upstairs."

"I see. Do you mind if I jot a few things down?"

The tension in her spine had eased. "Not at all."

Officer Tate used his drawing pencil and paper, dashing a few lines. "Do you think there might have been someone else in the room who had a beef with this man? Besides the leprechaun. What was his name?"

"Gil. I don't know his last name."

Officer Tate nodded. "Did you see anyone else react when Connor charged into the room? Other than the two relatives? And Gil?"

She shook her head.

"Do you think his cousins might have a reason to harm Connor? As you said, he'd humiliated Shannon."

Aiden had seemed upset that the police had questioned them yesterday. Him, especially. Yet when they'd met, he'd seemed like a decent guy and hardly a killer. "I don't know any of them well enough to say one way or another."

"Okay. Back to later that evening when Connor was attacked. You saw Connor arguing with someone. Can you remember any details?"

She bit her lower lip. "Connor was being pushed and he stumbled."

"Did you know it was Connor right away?"

"No. I hardly recognized that this was the same place we'd eaten our meal, as the cleaning crew had already packed up the kitchen and stacked the chairs. Only the tables were left out."

"He was pushed . . ."

"Yes. It was all shadowy, but then even the kitchen light went out. Connor didn't speak. I heard a strange noise and then Connor fell to the ground."

Officer Tate continued sketching as she spoke. She couldn't see what he was drawing.

"Connor was on the ground, you say? Faceup or facedown?"

"Faceup. His arm was sprawled out." She demonstrated for the officer.

Officer Tate exchanged his drawing pencil for the digital pen and was marking things on his laptop screen. Again, she couldn't see.

"What did you hear? A scuffle? Voices? Words? Where were you? Take your time."

"I had just opened the door from the outside staircase to the second floor and it was dim. I heard footsteps shuffle. Saw two men. The attacker was in a hoodie, covering his face. He said, *Finn, give me what I'm owed.* No . . . was it, *Give me my share*? Yeah. *Give me my share*."

"You're sure the attacker said this and not Connor?"

She thought about where the figures were standing, and how Connor had been shoved back. "I'm sure. Besides, if Connor had said those words, that means the attacker would be Finn. But that doesn't make sense . . ."

"Why not?"

"Shannon said that her twin brother is a recluse. He's got issues that keep him bound to his house." Shannon had asked her not to talk about it, but this was the police and shouldn't count.

Officer Tate nodded as if this wasn't a revelation to him. Could be part of his job, though, to control his reactions. Charlene hoped this interview allowed them to cross Finn from the suspect list.

"What else do you remember about the attacker? When did you go inside the room?"

"I leaned against the door and it was unlocked so I opened it. I overheard the altercation, but it all happened so fast. I heard Connor fall and I was about to enter all the way when someone barreled into me. The wood railing cracked behind me and I was lucky it didn't break. I yelled at him but he didn't glance back. Flew down the stairs as fast as he could and almost dropped something."

"Was there enough light to see the nose or jaw? Any small detail to help flesh out this sketch?"

"No, and it was so brief. It was more important to see if Connor was all right." He'd been on his back between the tables, eerily pale in the shadows from the moon coming through the heavy panes of the window. She remembered the peep of gold in Connor's front pocket.

Gold made her think of Gil. Could the figure fleeing

the scene have been the leprechaun? As if Officer Tate had read her mind, he said, "What about the leprechaun? Maybe he wanted to finish the fight he'd been in with Connor earlier."

She held her water bottle tight. "I don't know. I didn't see his face. His body seemed bulky. He was wearing a dark hoodie and jeans. Boots."

"Taller than you, or shorter?"

Charlene, at five foot eight, was tall for a woman. "It's hard to say because he was hunched over, in a hurry."

"Skin color? Hispanic, Black, Caucasian?"

She dragged up a memory of the person's hands. "Light-skinned—or it seemed that way in the dark."

"Good. Slender? Broad shoulders?"

"Blocky body."

"Uh-huh. A hoodie, jeans. What about cologne? What did you smell in the room?"

"Spices from dinner." Charlene closed her eyes and concentrated. "Nothing like cologne or aftershave, but there was something—oh, cigarette smoke!" She widened her eyes as excitement filled her. "The real thing, not a vape cigarette." She recalled the object in the person's back pocket. "That must be what fell out of his pocket when he was running down the stairs. A package of smokes. I couldn't see clearly and assumed it was a hat."

"Taller than you?" Officer Tate tried again.

She thought hard, on the edge of her seat. "I'm not sure."

"Chin? Nose? Hair color?"

"It was all covered by the hoodie. Ken was sitting in my van waiting for me, and he saw the man dart around the corner. That's when he arrived and called 911, since I'd left my purse."

"Mr. Fishburne will be in tomorrow morning. What do you think?" Officer Tate showed her his laptop. Using digital magic, he'd created a hunched figure with square shoulders, features covered by a black hood.

"Wow." It wasn't quite what she'd seen, but it still gave her a chill. "A little stockier, but very close. I'm sorry I can't give you more."

"You did great." Officer Tate tapped his pen to the screen. "The cigarettes are a big clue, since smoking has fallen out of fashion in regular society."

Charlene uncapped her water and took a drink to ease her parched throat. "Nobody I know does."

Officer Tate typed into the keyboard. "I'll send this to the officer heading the case, Detective Holden. While there is no face on the drawing, we can say the person responsible for the attack was light-skinned, between five-six and five-ten at either extreme. Stocky. A smoker. This is helpful for the officers to track him down."

Her doubt must have shown, because the officer gave her a very genuine smile. "Trust the system. These days we have digital face-matching programs that work instantly if it matches a mug shot. We've whittled down those parameters." He stood and held out his hand. "Thanks for coming in."

Charlene picked up her purse, gave Officer Tate a quick handshake goodbye, and left the room feeling accomplished and much better than when she'd entered it.

She was striding down the hallway when she met Sam and she slowed until they were face-to-face.

He gave her a tentative smile. "You were in with Officer Tate? How'd that go?"

Sam knew darn well that she'd been called in to see

the sketch artist. Charlene decided not to make a big deal of the fact that he'd come to find her afterward.

"All right, I think. I doubted I'd have anything to offer, because it all happened so fast and it was so dark, but I smelled cigarette smoke on him."

Sam's brow rose. "Nathan—Officer Tate—is very good with witnesses. He's got a way of getting people talking."

"That's what he said—we're just talking. No pressure." Charlene laughed. "It worked."

"Did you see a face?" Sam gestured toward the closed interview room door. "Do we have a composite?"

"No facial features," Charlene said with a chuckle at his eagerness. "I saw a stocky body, light-skinned. Not taller than me by much, if at all, because they were hunched. Hoodie. No jewelry."

Sam sighed and rocked back on his heels. "It's a start. Thanks for coming in, Charlene. I know you have a full house."

"Yes, lucky for me." She held his gaze. "I saw the attack, Sam. I wish I remembered more."

His brown eyes warmed. "Look, it's almost noon. The least I can do is buy you lunch."

She pushed her hair off her face and tucked a lock behind her ear. "I remember the last time we had dinner . . ."

His smile flashed behind his luxurious mustache. "So do I. We were going to work on expanding our friendship and have dinner or lunch once a week, but we never seem to make it happen."

He'd been traveling for work outside of Salem and she'd been creating her bed-and-breakfast. "I know. Both of us are busy. Speaking of which, I should get back to my guests."

Disappointment shadowed his face.

She recalled Minnie's suggestion and acted on her impulse, "Sam, we're having a dinner party tomorrow night for Saint Patrick's Day. Will you join us?"

His smile returned and he nodded, tucking a thumb through his belt loop. "If I can get away, I'll be there. What time?"

"Seven. Cocktails at six."

"I'll do my best." His deep, rumbling voice washed over her senses and she shivered when he asked, "What can I bring?"

"Minnie's making the traditional corned beef and cabbage. You should see the size of the brisket she bought!" Her cheeks heated as she realized she was rambling. "We could probably feed two-dozen people."

"Are you telling me that *Minnie* invited me to dinner?" Sam's tone was full of mischief.

"Who else? She adores you."

Sam burst out laughing. "Maybe I should stay home, then."

"Suit yourself." She lifted her nose and gave him the side-eye. "I suppose you'd rather be glued to the TV watching March madness with your dog?"

"I'm a Notre Dame fan, but they fell short this year." He raised both shoulders and let them fall. "Trust me, I'd give up a night of basketball for Minnie's cooking any day. And Rover understands."

She laughed, missing this version of Sam. Fun and flirty without all of the rules. "We can send you home with a doggie bag."

He touched his fingers to his forehead in a salute. "See you tomorrow night, then."

Charlene left the station feeling a teensy bit brighter.

She trusted Sam to solve this case and then she could go back to doing what she did best: running Charlene's.

Arriving home an hour later, she climbed out of her car and lifted the rear hatch of her SUV to unload her purchases.

She'd stopped at Witches Bloom for a green, white, and gold centerpiece for the sideboard in the dining room that matched the gorgeous arrangement in the living room. At the party store, she'd snatched up two packages of *Luck of the Irish* cocktail napkins and a centerpiece with four glittering shamrocks in small vases. She'd bought pot of gold window silhouettes with LED lighting for the front windows. To add to the fun, she'd purchased green shamrock-shaped eyeglasses.

She rushed up the porch stairs and opened the door. "Minnie?"

Minnie hurried to the foyer, a scarf around her gray curls askew. "What is it, Charlene? Did you buy out the liquor store?"

"Very funny. No, but I picked up a few things for tomorrow night's dinner. Sam's coming! I don't think he wants to disappoint you."

Minnie blushed. "Charlene, as much as I love you, if you aren't going to grab that man, then I will. The hubby won't take to him too well, but he'll get used to it."

With a chuckle, Minnie followed Charlene to her car and grabbed the flower arrangement and two plastic shopping bags. Charlene brought in the rest.

Silva decided that was the best time to get their attention and wound her way between their legs. Somehow, they managed to get the flowers and shopping bags to the kitchen without serious injury. Charlene gave her demanding Persian a few of her favorite treats. "Sweet kitty."

"Ha!" Minnie returned to the stove, where she was creating a pot of Irish stew for tonight's dinner. "She's a rascal. Got out of her collar again."

"Again? I'll keep trying. There has to be one she can't remove." Charlene unloaded the bags from the party store.

Minnie washed her hands and dried them on her apron. "Want a taste of stew for lunch?" her housekeeper asked. "Or the minestrone I made earlier."

"The soup sounds great. The stew needs time to stew." She grinned.

They sat at the counter with their delicious soup and fresh-baked whole wheat bread. Minnie was worth her weight in gold and Charlene would take Minnie over a leprechaun any day.

CHAPTER 6

Charlene adored hosting a party.

As she surveyed the festive green tablecloth, her white dishes, and the shamrock centerpiece, she counted her blessings that she was able to earn her living doing what she loved.

Her guests were spread out, with the Fishburnes at one end and Charlene, Sam, Minnie, Will, and Avery at the other. The Wards were opposite Sheffer and the Prescotts. Everyone had been served and started to eat.

Mason was chatting nonstop about the scary *lepercon* with the bad teeth that he would have to trick out of gold.

"I think I saw that leprechaun guy walking out of the police station today," Ken said to the group. They were all interested in the Gallagher case because they'd been there.

Sam glanced at Charlene with a warning brow. She

shrugged. This was how conversation went—people shared the juicy bits. It wasn't her fault Connor was the topic of discussion.

"Why were you at the police station?" Jasper asked. He cut off a slice of brisket. "Minnie, this is so tender."

"And delicious!" Lila agreed, dabbing her mouth with a white cloth napkin.

"The police station?" John grinned. "What for, Ken? Fess up! Are you the killer?"

Marc elbowed his brother.

"Oof." John rubbed his side.

Luckily, Mason hadn't heard John and said, "My dad tol' the police what the bad guy looked like!" Mason turned to Ken. "Right, Dad?"

Ken took a drink of beer to wash down a bite of roasted potato. "Yes. That's right. I don't think I was much help." He asked Sam, "Do those sketches ever work? I didn't have a lot to add."

Sam edged his fork into the potato and cabbage. "You never know what will help in an investigation." He turned to Minnie. "This is great. I want your recipe."

Did Sam even know how to cook?

"Me too!" Deana chimed in. "This corned beef is a thousand times better than what we ate at the AOH. Sorry, Charlene! What's your secret, Minnie?"

Minnie smiled with pleasure. "Oh, just a few spices. Slow cooking, that's all."

Charlene bit her lip to keep from sharing that her talented housekeeper had watched the pot all day, adding a dash of this and dollop of that.

"Minnie, I've had what is supposed to be corned beef and cabbage before." Avery's nose scrunched and the diamond in her piercing twinkled. "Not like this."

"Will, you're a lucky man," Sam said, leaning across Charlene to Minnie's husband.

"I know it." Will patted his flat stomach. He was tall and slim, while Minnie was on the short and plump side. "Minnie reminds me of that when my memory lapses."

Everyone around the table laughed.

"Can you pass me the salad, Detective?" Sheffer spoke directly to Sam. Charlene noticed the dish of leafy greens was equally within Sheffer's reach as Sam's.

Her hunky detective didn't quite meet Sheffer's probing gaze. Had he already realized the man was full of himself? Sam passed the wooden bowl with wooden salad tongs down the side of the table. "Here you are."

"What," Sheffer said, adding salad to his plate, "was the leprechaun doing at the station, Ken? Had someone stolen his pot of gold?" He chuckled to himself.

Ken shrugged. "I'm not sure it was the same guy. Gil. That night he'd been in costume while he sat on his pot of gold . . . he had that orange beard."

"The lepr—lep . . . he had fake teeth!" Mason piped up from his seat between his parents.

"Leprechaun. Exactly." Ken cut a piece of meat and dipped it into a small dish of mustard. "That's why you have to brush your teeth, son. Anyway, today Gil had a messed-up eye like he'd been in a fight. A couple of days old. You know? Purple-blue and yellow rather than red."

Charlene straightened in her chair. She'd told Sam and Officer Tate about the confrontation between Gil and Connor. Was he at the station to confess?

She snuck a glance at Sam, who was studiously ignoring her to enjoy his meal.

"Gil glared at me when I started to talk to him this morning." Ken dismissed this with another shrug. "I doubt he remembered me from the other night. It was dark downstairs at the AOH."

Had Gil been the one to push by her? What if the person had seen Ken come to her rescue? Giving the details to the sketch artist had allowed her to reaffirm what she'd seen . . . "How tall is Gil?"

Ken tapped the table with his finger. "Shorter than me. I'm five-ten. Average."

Sam turned to Minnie with a desperate tone in his voice. "How are the grandkids?"

"Oh, they're wonderful." Minnie went on for a few minutes, bragging about her brood. Most of her family lived nearby. Being a local with history was a big deal here in Salem.

Charlene gave Sam points on steering the conversation away from an open case.

Or trying to.

Sheffer took a drink from his water glass. "Never had kids. Never wanted them. I know my shortcomings. I love my job more than any woman. Just like Sam."

Sam hid his annoyed expression by smoothing his mustache. Why was Sheffer trying to bait Sam? Some people had a wariness around police officers. Usually, people with things to hide.

"Salem is fortunate to have Detective Holden," she said, really not caring for Sheffer at all. He probably used his job as an excuse as to why he didn't have a woman in his life when he should look in the mirror behind his handsome façade.

"That's true!" Avery, Minnie, and Will agreed.

Sam finished his brisket. "Salem is home now after all these years. And I've got Rover, my Irish setter. Not quite a nomad, Sheffer."

The rebuke sounded personal.

"You have a dog?" Avery said, sitting back from the table after giving her empty plate a forlorn look.

"I do. Had her since a pup and she's eight now."

"What's Rover like, Charlene?" Avery put her elbow on the table by her plate and cupped her chin.

"I've never met her." Charlene and Sam's friendship hadn't progressed to her being at his house. "Seen cute pictures." She'd been careful to keep the line of friendship between them. It was easier to do when he traveled. He'd told her once that Rover stayed with a friend of his, male, at the department, which was like a second home for the dog.

Sam shifted and regained his composure, his eyes warm. "You come on over anytime and I'll introduce you. These days Rover likes her soft bed by the heater."

Nothing wrong with comfort, she thought. She'd kept a slice of brisket for Rover aside for Sam to take home since she'd promised a doggie bag.

"Can I come?" Avery asked.

"Sure!" Sam said.

Minnie gave Avery a little elbow to the side and a head shake. Avery blushed. Her housekeeper-friend wasn't subtle in her hints for Charlene to let Sam beyond the friendship bar.

Charlene stood before she gave away her attraction to the man. "Who's ready for dessert? Minnie made an Irish cream cake." She'd decorated it with gold chocolate coins and had some leftover jingle that Charlene wanted to give Mason.

"Let me help." Minnie got to her feet. There wasn't even a wilted piece of cabbage left of their feast.

"I'll get the dishes!" Avery said.

Within moments the trio, used to working as a team, had cleared the table, and cake was served on green paper plates with shamrocks printed all over them. Charlene was hesitant to bring up the leprechaun again at the table. It was obvious that Sam didn't want to talk about it, but she wanted answers.

Had the police connected Gil to Connor's attacker? Why had they questioned Aiden? Had they talked to Finn?

Mason was creating a tower with his gold pieces. A gold coin dropped off the table to the floor, where Silva, who'd been watching from the doorway, pounced and batted it around.

Mason squealed and chased the cat, who was reluctant to give up her treasure. Avery helped and scooped Silva in her lap to pet her before setting her back on the floor.

"Silva wants to be rich too!" Mason declared.

"She likes the shiny wrapper—but, remember, chocolate can be very bad for cats." Charlene explained to the rest of the table, "Silva found Mason's treasure before. I called Dr. Hendez, who assured me that cats are smarter than dogs—no offense, Sam—and usually won't eat it, though the wrapper is fair game."

Sam scraped his fork along the dessert plate to get the last of the delicious cream frosting. "None taken. Silva is a superior feline in any event."

"What's that mean?" Mason asked. He stacked what was left of his gold pieces.

"Silva's the best," Avery said. "I agree." She and Sam high-fived.

Lila leaned across the table to address the others. "Chocolate and gold. No wonder that leprechaun was guarding the pot so fiercely." She lifted her wrist to show her gold bangles. "Two of my favorite things!"

The folks around the table chuckled.

"You are a good sight lovelier, *dahling*." Jasper kissed his wife's hand.

"Charmer." Lila winked.

Sheffer, on Lila's other side, admired the bangles. "Eighteen karat?"

"Are you a jeweler?" Lila asked, discreetly placing her arm in her lap.

Charlene perked up. She was curious as to what Mr. LaCroix did for a living. He hadn't said and had danced around direct questions.

"No, no. My mother was also fond of gold jewelry, that's all." Sheffer didn't give his occupation as he drained his tall glass of amber ale.

"Who wants coffee?" Minnie asked, getting up.

The Prescotts and the Fishburnes raised their hands. "Decaf for us," Jasper said. Ken and Deana agreed. The Ward brothers shook their heads.

"I'd like another beer," John said. "I can't believe we check out tomorrow. Vacation went so fast."

"It's been great fun, Charlene." Marc gestured at Charlene. "We'll be back. You have any vacancies for Halloween?"

"The most popular day in Salem!" Will said, clicking his teeth.

"I'm booked for this year," Charlene said, "but I'll take your name down for the waiting list—if you want."

The brothers exchanged a look, then nodded. "We're in!" Marc said.

"Sam, coffee?" Minnie asked. "I know how you like it

with a sweet. I should have offered with dessert, but I was too excited about the cake."

"That's fine," Sam said with a sheepish smile. "I'd love a cup of dark roast."

"My Will is the same. Sheffer?" Minnie asked their only guest who hadn't answered.

"I'll stick to water, thank you." Sheffer drummed the table with his thumb. "Got a busy day planned for tomorrow."

Charlene put her napkin over her empty plate. "Are you doing some excursions?"

"I prefer to poke around and see things for myself."

Probably didn't like anybody telling him what to do, Charlene thought with irritation.

She glanced at Sam as she got up. Would he offer to assist for a chance to flirt? He stayed seated. Hmm. "Avery, hot chocolate?"

"Yes, please. Can I help?"

"No, hon. You sit and enjoy. You worked hard this week on your school tests."

Charlene and Minnie went into the kitchen to make coffees and a hot chocolate. "I don't know what people did before the Keurig."

"I love my appliances." Minnie brought out mugs for the dark roasts and brewed a pot of decaf.

"I think our party was a success! Thanks to your cooking, Minnie. Do you think we should do a *Charlene's Bed-and-Breakfast Cookbook* for the website?"

"Oh! Well . . . I'm not talented enough to warrant a cookbook." Minnie's cheeks flushed with pleasure.

"I would disagree, along with every guest who's eaten here." Her marketing brain really liked the idea. And

Avery had a natural eye with a camera for photos of the food.

The front door slammed shut.

Charlene walked down the hall and peeked into the dining room. Sam and Sheffer were missing from the guests around the table.

Avery saw her and explained, "Sam needed some air after all the food. Sheffer offered to keep him company, being as they're both from the city. New York."

Nothing odd about that, so why did the hair on her arms raise?

She nodded, gave the closed front door a look, and returned to the kitchen. Minnie had put half of the coffees and drinks on one tray, and half on another. They each took one and returned to the dining room.

"Here we go." Charlene set the hot chocolate in front of Avery. "Extra whipped cream for doing so well on your test Monday."

"Yum!"

She passed around the coffees and put cream and sugar in the center. The Wards had fresh beers before them and were chatting with the Prescotts about England.

Charlene offered Ken another napkin. "What did you think of your trip to the police station? I thought it was very interesting, how the sketch artist could take our few details and come close to what I saw."

"I saw even less . . . I gave him the back." Ken laughed and rolled his eyes, mocking his powers of observation.

"Neither of us saw his face." She stirred cream into her coffee.

Ken shook his head.

Deana doctored her coffee with lots of sugar and extra

cream. "Mason, sweetie, why don't you run into the bathroom and wash the chocolate off your hands?"

"*Mommm*!"

"Please?" She put mom-tone into the question, meaning he needed to just do it.

"Fine." He scuffled off and Deana grabbed Charlene's wrist.

"Does this mean that Gil is the killer?" She asked the question in a whisper meant to be between them. The Wards leaned close.

Charlene moved her shoulder to block her words from being heard. "I don't know."

"Can't you ask your detective friend?" Deana stirred her sweet and creamy brew. "Sam? He's a hottie."

"Not exactly. Sam has a firm policy of not discussing an open case." Which was too bad for her.

Ken sighed. "Oh well. I don't think it could be Gil. When he passed by me, he was shorter than the person I saw running off the stairs."

"Are you sure?" Charlene agreed, but it was good to have a second opinion.

"Not a hundred percent, but I think so." Ken drank cautiously.

"We leave on Friday morning. I sure hope they catch the killer by then." Deana sipped and lowered her cup.

"These things take time," Charlene said. She'd learned that television made police work seem straightforward and fast. The reality was quite the opposite.

"You'll send us an email?" Ken asked. "When you find out what happened. Just in case we aren't here?"

"Sure." She could do that.

"What are you all whispering about?" Marc asked.

"It has to be about the dead guy." John nudged his brother's arm. "We've been thinking about Connor's death too."

"Oh?" Charlene kept an ear out for Sam and Mason. For different reasons, of course.

"Well, yeah. We partied that night with the Irish band. That Aiden dude showed up later at the pub in different clothes—not so spiffed up. Jeans. He was buying drinks for everyone like he'd just won the lottery or something."

"What if—" Marc gazed around the table—"what if he'd just killed his cousin?"

"Why would you think that?" Charlene asked in surprise. "I thought you liked Aiden."

"Nah. He was putting on a show for his mom. Good college son. Wants to be a doctor. Well, from the way he was partying, I don't think studies were at the top of his priority list, right, bro?"

John offered his knuckles for a fist bump. "Too bad we're leaving in the morning. We could meet him for drinks later tonight. You know. Find out what he's up to."

"You have his number?" Charlene stepped back from Ken to eye the Wards. Were they pulling her leg, or serious? They were jokers, so it was hard to tell.

"No," said John. "Aiden will be at Pub 36 all week. Celebrating. He didn't say what."

"It was loud and crowded, and he was the man of the hour, buying rounds—it was hard to hear." Marc shrugged.

Charlene shook her head. "Don't get too involved," she warned. "Leave it to the police. As you suggested, he might be part of this."

She gave the department credit for already questioning Aiden Best. Poor Shannon. He was not as he appeared.

The front door opened and shut.

Jack materialized behind her in a frenzy and she shivered. The shamrocks moved as if in a breeze.

Sam returned, followed by Sheffer. "Sorry about that. I was stuffed to the gills and needed a walk." He sat and clasped his hands around the coffee mug Minnie had put before him.

"Just catching up on a few things back home. I think I'll say my good nights." Sheffer waved to them all and brought his water glass to the stairs, climbing with a steady pace.

"Their 'catching up' involved an argument," Jack said with suspicion. "Something's going on there, and you should find out."

CHAPTER 7

Charlene was startled by Jack's observation. What could Sheffer and Sam have gotten into an argument about? She turned toward Sam, who was no longer smiling. "Sam, will you join me in the kitchen? I could use your help with something."

Not the smoothest segue, but Jack had put her on the spot.

Sam tugged at his mustache and shook his head with regret. "I hate to eat and run," he said to Charlene as well as the others still seated at the table, "but I can't stay. Duty calls." He touched her elbow. "Thanks for a great meal."

Her mouth parted for a quip to keep him there, but Sam was already out of the dining room to the foyer, leather jacket in hand, before she could formulate a question. The door slammed closed behind him.

"What about Rover's doggie bag?" Charlene stood and rested her fingers on her hip.

Avery jumped up and raced out of the house to wave Sam down, but she returned with a headshake. "He peeled outta here. Maybe he got news about the case?"

"That would be wonderful," Deana said, patting Ken's shoulder. "I'd love it solved before we leave on Friday."

Jack disappeared in a poof of cold air and Charlene surveyed her guests before sitting back down next to Avery.

Sheffer was mysterious and aloof. Neither Sam nor her new guest had mentioned having a history, yet there was something almost antagonistic between them. Sheffer, to her knowledge, wasn't interested in the normal tours or sightseeing, so why was he here? What was he doing in his room? What had Sheffer had in his suitcase that was so heavy?

"What's up, Charlene?" Avery tapped Charlene's hand. "You're a million miles away."

"Sorry." She laughed at herself for making something out of nothing—the argument was probably as simple as being fans of opposing football teams. Each man was very attractive and single, and that tended to bring out testosterone. "I think I'm in a food coma."

Avery laughed. Jasper stood and assisted Lila. "I'm ready for a snuggle with my lady before the fire," he said.

"That sounds like just the right speed." Lila tucked her hand in her husband's elbow. "After you." The pair sauntered lazily into the living room.

Mason bounced around his parents, full of energy. Ken rose from the chair with a longing look in the Prescotts' direction then sighed toward Deana. "How about we take our son for a walk around the yard?"

"Yes!" Mason said. "Let's go, Dad. Come on, Mom. I'll race you."

Deana groaned but joined her son and husband in getting on their jackets. "Fresh air is a good idea. Then a movie in our room, all right?"

Mason agreed.

Ken smiled and side-hugged Deana. "Smart thinking. We can wear him out and then relax upstairs."

"Can we help clear the table?" Marc asked.

"Absolutely not," Charlene said to the brothers. "We've got it. What is your plan for the night?"

"John and I decided to hit Pub 36 for our last night in town after all. Everyone's welcome to join us."

Since it was only Minnie, Will, Charlene, and Avery left at the table, the offer fell on the wrong people to party. "Take care," Charlene warned. The brothers left after more effusive thanks for a terrific meal.

Minnie and Will got up next, stacking plates to return to the kitchen. "No way, you two go home and relax," Charlene insisted. "Thank you so much for all you do. Avery and I can manage the dishes."

"You're sure?" Minnie asked, covering a yawn.

Will chuckled. "Happy Saint Patrick's Day."

Charlene walked them out to the porch with a wave, then joined Avery in the kitchen. The sweetheart already had the plates piled to the side.

"Did you enjoy dinner with everyone, or was it too boring for you?"

Her diamond twinkled at her nose. "Hardly boring, Charlene. There's always something going on here, and this was my first dinner party for Saint Patrick's Day. I can't wait to tell Janet about it. I bet she'd make the Irish cream cake for the kids next year." Her voice hitched.

What went unsaid, was that this would be Avery's last year at the teen house. Janet, a big-hearted woman in her mid-fifties, was the live-in chaperone. Charlene tied on an apron and appraised her young friend. Avery might've had a rough start in life, but she was a hard worker and smart. She was part of the family Charlene had created for herself. "You rinse. I'll load. You in a hurry to get home?"

"Nope. I've got nothing to do for the rest of the night. I've done all my tests for the colleges around here, so now it's just high school stuff. I wanted to ask Sam about going on another ride-along."

Charlene held back a smile. Avery's interest in joining the police force had only grown since Sam had taken her for a ride. Avery had sat in the back seat, plying him with questions. He had purposely chosen an off night and a safe neighborhood to show how dull his job could be. Before that, it had been Officer Bernard. Instead of discouraging her, the rides had fed a fire.

"So . . . Jenna has a boyfriend." Avery rinsed a plate and handed it to Charlene.

Jenna and Avery had been best friends all through high school. "Do you like him?"

"Haven't met him yet. Me and Brandon are gonna go to the movies with them next week. I'm excited to get an apartment with her, but kinda nervous too."

"About what?"

"Money. What if I can't do school and work?"

"You can have whatever hours you need here." Yes, Charlene had said it before, and she would say it again. She slipped a damp hand around Avery's shoulders. "You can do whatever you want. We need to continue driving lessons so you can get your license."

Avery's pulse fluttered at her throat. "I don't need a car."

"I think you need a driver's license to be a police officer. And if you get into Boston Academy, you might want to drive and have the freedom of a vehicle."

"I'm on the wait-list, which means my chances of getting in are slim. If that miracle happens, I can take the bus. But Jenna doesn't want to live in Boston." Avery passed Charlene another rinsed plate for the dishwasher.

"I love your independence, don't get me wrong," Charlene said, trying to find a place for a small serving bowl. "It's okay to accept help."

"I'm letting you show me how to drive, aren't I?" Avery scanned the full dishwasher. "I don't think there's room for more."

Charlene smiled at Avery, wanting to make things easier for her, but the teen could be surprisingly prickly about what she viewed as handouts. She pressed the button on the dishwasher, saving the good wineglasses to wash by hand, along with the platters.

"If Sam was here, we could play Clue. It takes at least three players. I'd ask the Prescotts, but I think they're dozing." Avery prattled on about how Sam had an unfair advantage in the game since he solved crimes for a living. "Who done it. Where? And with what weapon?"

Charlene carefully washed the wineglasses, then rinsed them and set them to dry on an absorbent towel. Her mind put the question of "who done it" together with Connor's death. She knew where, but not who did it, why, or with what weapon.

Avery dried the glasses and put them in the cupboard. One way Charlene could get more answers, at least from Aiden, who the Wards were going to party with tonight, would be at the pub. They'd invited everyone in a general way so it wouldn't be too strange for her to show up at the Irish bar.

"We can play a game another night," Charlene suggested. "How about I take you home?"

Avery's pretty smile faltered. "Sure. If you don't need me anymore."

"Avery, I love your company, hon . . . that's not it. But your talk about finding clues reminded me that there was something I wanted to check out."

"You mean about the Gallagher case?" Her eyes widened. "You shouldn't. You know how angry that makes Sam."

"I'll be at the pub with the Wards, and I'll be extra-careful. You know that I am. The police seem to think that Aiden might be connected, but I don't see it. I'd love to talk with him, that's all."

Charlene pressed her fingers to her brow and ducked her head. She'd sounded like Officer Tate just then. *Having conversation, that's all.*

"Tell you what: I'll let you drive to the teen house and share what happened with the police sketch artist yesterday. That might be a cool job." And possibly a safe one, done at the station.

"For real? I'm a good drawer."

"They use digital software now, but the officer also used a regular pen and pad."

They finished the kitchen, then Avery went to get her leather jacket, a Christmas present from Charlene that she'd picked out and loved.

Charlene had checked on the Prescotts, who were watching the fire crackle in companionable silence. Jack was nowhere to be found; otherwise, she would have told him her plan. She met Avery at the door and tossed the teen her keys.

"You're a good driver," Charlene said. "How close are we to forty supervised hours?"

"I need a few more before I can take the test. Janet said she'd take me too, since she's my legal guardian."

They walked to the car and Avery got in, checking the mirrors before starting the car. She chewed her bottom lip. "I understand that you want to help find the killer. Maybe *you* should be a police officer?"

Charlene's reaction was immediate. "No, thanks. I love my bed-and-breakfast. I only get involved with these cases when it touches my life somehow. I care about the people. I don't have the stamina to do that every day like a police officer does. You?"

"I've thought about that part," Avery assured her. "It's like Janet's job, at the teen house? She cares a lot for the kids she watches over. Not everyone stays on the right path, and it hurts her, you know? But she says it's worth it, to care. Even if sometimes she gets burned."

Charlene reached across the console to pat Avery's leg. "You're pretty smart, kiddo."

Avery carefully reversed out of the long driveway, the sixth time she'd practiced at night, and Charlene could see she was more comfortable. She got on the main road with no problem and drove toward the teen house.

"Will you text me when you leave the pub tonight? So I don't worry."

"You don't have to worry about me!" Charlene chuckled.

Avery snorted. "If you don't text me, I'm going to call Sam and he'll drag you home, like it or not."

Charlene smiled fondly at this bright, nearly-grown young woman in the driver's seat. "I care for you very much, you know."

"Me too. I mean, I care about you, not me." She glanced at Charlene, then returned her gaze to the road.

They reached the teen house and the light in the driveway was on. Avery parked. "Here I am."

"Say hello to Janet for me. I promise I'll text you. I bet I'll be home by eleven."

Avery jumped out of the Pilot and slammed the door to show that she was not okay with the plan.

Charlene exited the passenger side calmly. "Don't forget to log your time."

"Thanks, Charlene, I will." Avery waved from the porch stairs. "Bye."

Once again behind the wheel, Charlene read the time on the dashboard. Nine-thirty. Hopefully, she'd find Aiden, sidle up to him to assess if he could be the person who had raced past her down the stairs, and then return home to be snug in bed long before midnight. She'd met Aiden, but it was hard for her to picture his height and stature.

As in the game Clue, finding the truth meant narrowing things down. She had a mission. In, and out.

Charlene parked across the street from the crowded parking lot of the Irish bar. On Saint Paddy's Day, the place was jammed. A live band rocked the walls of the old brick building.

She went inside the dark and noisy pub. The lighting was dim, with flashing green and gold strobe lights, their nod to the Irish holiday. A couple of guys with mohawks whistled at her as she passed, but she ignored them as she was old enough to be their mother.

Booths on both sides were loaded with people drinking pitchers of beer between bouts of dancing on the enormous wooden dance floor. She glanced around for Aiden or the Ward brothers. She was too close to the door to see back at the bar, so she headed through the crowd.

She'd have something without alcohol, needing to keep her wits about her. She'd learned in her self-defense classes that being aware of one's surroundings was the best first step in defense.

A barstool opened on the end just as she reached the dark mahogany counter, so she slipped onto it before someone else did. Charlene kept her purse on her lap as the bar top and the floor were sticky.

She felt eyes upon her and turned her head. The Wards! It was a relief to see friendly faces. They looked like they were having a lot of fun, each with their arms around cute girls.

John and Marc had ditched the collared shirts they'd worn for the dinner party for tight-fitting T's that showed off their toned muscles. Faded jeans and boots completed their casual look and they fit right in, whispering in their companions' ears and making them laugh. For a couple of Rhode Island IT boys, they knew how to win over the ladies.

She fluttered her fingers and wondered if she should go over and break up the party. The bartender appeared as she was mulling it over. "What can I get ya? Draft beer is two for one all night."

Charlene didn't mind the occasional beer, but that really wasn't what she wanted. "Do you have cappuccino?"

His brow rose and he hid a smile. "Sure—got the machine with all the flavors, but I might have to brush the dust off. Got a favorite?"

"French vanilla, please."

"Coming right up." He winked and Charlene couldn't help but check him out. Blond hair, muscled but lean. Easy on the eye.

The Irish punk band jammed loud, the vocalist shouting into the mike as the drummer rattled the walls. The band reminded her of the Dropkick Murphys that she and Jared had seen live in Chicago. She missed him with a pang. What would he think of this curious side to her nature? Back then, she'd put her what-ifs into campaigns.

She swirled on her stool to scan the dancers for Aiden, but it was someone else on the floor who caught her eye. Could that be Gil? Without all that makeup it was hard to tell, but he had a slight build. More than just the face, it was his movements that sparked her attention. He kept dropping his hand to his front jean pocket as he talked with a punk rock girl. When he removed his hand, she noticed pocket change sifting through his fingers.

It reminded her of the gold in Connor's pocket. Had she told that to Officer Tate? About the chocolate coin?

Charlene left a ten on the counter for her cappuccino, then sauntered toward John and Marc, who were romancing their young friends. She beckoned Marc over. He nodded and made a comment to his girl of the moment, who glared at Charlene.

"Sorry to bother you," she murmured when he joined her.

"No worries," he said. "Glad you decided to hang out. Though, I'm surprised. This isn't really your scene."

She tilted her head and shrugged. "I was wondering if you'd seen Aiden?"

"The hot redhead bartender said he's been around. This place is a madhouse. I love it, but we may have just missed each other. He'll show up at the bar eventually. Why?"

"I wanted to ask him a few questions, that's all."

She indicated with one finger to where the man she thought was Gil stood. "Does that look like the leprechaun from the other night to you?"

Marc squinted. "Hell no. That dude had orange hair and bad teeth."

Charlene sighed. "Take away the layers of makeup and this man has a similar facial shape and the same habit of sliding coins from one hand to another with his fingers."

Marc studied the figure with more focus, leaning forward, but then he stumbled, reminding Charlene that he might not be the most reliable person to ask. She'd just have to go see for herself.

"You might have something there." Marc glanced over to John and the two girls. "Mind if I go now?"

"All right . . . thanks for your help."

He gave her a half-smile, acknowledging that he hadn't really. "You think Aiden might have offed his cousin?"

"Marc," she admonished. "I don't have an opinion about it. I just want to know why he was flashing money around. Medical school is expensive. Shannon mentioned owning an accounting firm, but she didn't seem superrich, you know?" She thought of the Camry in the AOH parking lot. Nothing flashy.

"Bummer. But maybe he has other ideas about what to do with his life. He told us the night of the party that he was quitting." Marc dug his elbow to her side. "There's Aiden now, talking with the leprechaun. Just go chat them up, Charlene."

His "girlfriend" came to claim Marc, and slipping his hand around her waist, he swung her onto the dance floor.

Aiden was quitting medical school? How sad! What did Shannon think?

Charlene cradled her cappuccino and avoided dancers as she made her way to where Aiden and Gil stood talking, feeling somewhat guilty as she listened from a few feet behind. Aiden was her height, and slender. The figure that had pushed by her the night of the attack had been thick and stocky. It wasn't Aiden. Could it have been Gil?

Gil was commiserating about Connor. Aiden, cheeks flushed with alcohol, eyes bright, slung his arm around Gil.

"Issall good now, Gil," Aiden slurred. "Lesss get more drinks! Tell Sinead to put it on m'tab."

"Aiden, how about slowin' down a bit? You've been passed out behind the bar a couple nights this week."

"It's my cousin's bar. Family safe place." Aiden smacked his palm to his jean-clad thigh.

"What would your mom think?"

Aiden brushed off Gil's arm and glared at the shorter man. "Shut up about my mom."

He stomped toward the mahogany bar and Charlene watched him stumble through the people who mostly helped him stay upright. She swiveled her gaze to the corner opposite the band.

Was that Sheffer, from the bed-and-breakfast? What was he doing here? The Ward brothers had invited everyone, but Sheffer had gone up to his room at that time. Maybe he'd heard them talk about coming out for drinks. Could be her guest was a night owl.

Sheffer was definitely on the periphery of the crowd. If she hadn't known him and had a strong opinion about him, her gaze would have passed right over him. He had a way about him that allowed him to blend in.

Sheffer kept his attention on Aiden. The young man was cheered on as he downed a large draft in one long swallow. Gil clapped him on the back as if to make sure Aiden stayed upright.

Aiden slammed the empty glass on the bar to wild applause. "Another round, cuz!"

His friends went crazy with shouts and fist pumps as a cute, flame-haired bartender slid another along the counter. Did Sheffer know Aiden? The ages were wrong for them to be college friends. Maybe professor and student. What did Sheffer do for a living?

Aiden knew Gil from the AOH—the Irish in Salem appeared to be a close-knit group. Just because their body language was tense didn't mean there was something shady. If anything, Gil was looking out for Aiden. Why had Connor, the dead cousin, gotten into a fight with Gil? It seemed like a bigger deal than no ticket for a meal.

She edged between the throng of dancing people to where she'd spotted Sheffer in the shadows. The song slowed and the dancers parted. She smiled at where he'd been standing, but Sheffer was no longer there.

CHAPTER 8

Charlene swirled in place. Where had Sheffer gone? More importantly, she wanted to know why he'd been there in the first place.

"Charlene!" John called to her, motioning her toward the bar. "Want something? Aiden's buying."

"No, thanks." She scooted closer to the long, wooden bar top and set her empty cappuccino down. The rafters on the old brick building shook from the force of the music.

She smiled and waved at Aiden, who grinned bleary-eyed at her. "Hey," he said, then he allowed himself to be dragged out to the dance floor by his friends. Gil was at the far end of the bar, drinking from a tall glass. He was an interesting character in or out of his costume.

Charlene turned to the bartender who Aiden had called

cuz. The hair was similar in shade to Aiden's and Shannon's red locks.

"What can I get for you?" she asked, wiping up a spill with a towel that she quickly tucked out of sight. "Drafts are two for one."

She pointed to her empty cup.

"Another cap?" The bartender radiated energy and glanced up and down the bar as she waited for Charlene to make up her mind.

"No, thanks." She realized that she should probably order a drink or stand out like a sore forty-year-old thumb. "Corona. Bottle is fine."

"Coming up." The young lady returned with an open bottle and lime on the side. "That everything?"

"Yeah." Charlene put a twenty on the bar, hoping to slow the bartender down with cash. "Is Aiden really your cousin?"

The young woman nodded. "The hair gives us away. All of us O'Briens and Gallaghers have it."

This close, Charlene noticed the beginnings of lines around the woman's blue eyes and placed her to be about thirty. "It's very pretty."

The bartender pointed to a photo of a group of redheads on a baseball team with the Pub 36 logo on the wall behind the taps. "My mom and sister are the only blondes."

Charlene sipped her Corona and studied the photo, but detailed features were difficult in the dim light. "Is Shannon your aunt? I met her the other day at the AOH, for the corned beef banquet."

"Oh, yeah. I had to work the bar with my dad, James. He's the baby. Mom and Gwynne were supposed to go this year. I'm Sinead O'Brien." She swiped her hand on the bar towel, then offered it for a quick shake.

Charlene smiled. "Charlene Morris. Your family owns the pub?"

"The preferred honest work for an Irishman, according to my dad. He likes to add an extra-heavy lilt to his brogue when he says it." Sinead winked.

"I've never been to Ireland, but it's supposed to be stunningly beautiful."

The band slowed, but then immediately went into an even louder, harder song with a booming beat.

Charlene sat on the edge of her stool when Sinead leaned close.

"We went on holiday after high school graduation, but it's hard to leave the bar. We're all tied to it, Mom says." Sinead shrugged. "I wasn't that impressed with the city, Dublin. It was kinda dirty, you know? The fields were nice, but after a week I'd had my fill of sheep. Gwynne thought so too."

"Are you close in age with your sister?"

"Yep. Irish twins." Sinead raised her hand to a patron wanting to order. "Twelve months apart. Be right there, Liam."

Charlene followed Sinead's line of sight. A man about fifty, but a hard-lived fifty, tipped his cap.

"Take your time, love."

"Don't want to make him wait, so I should go." Sinead glanced up and down the bar before smiling at Charlene. "Anything else?"

"No. Thanks."

The music ended abruptly and Aiden started toward them, along with his posse of freeloaders.

"What is he celebrating?" Charlene asked.

Sinead pulled out the dish towel and mopped a spill of water. "Idiot quit medical school. Poor Aunt Shannon. All she wanted was for her brilliant son to be more than a fisherman or a pub owner."

The bartender hustled down the mahogany counter to the man named Liam. Charlene strained to discreetly overhear, but it was impossible in the noise.

Why had Aiden quit school if he was so smart?

Charlene sipped her beer and waited to see if Sinead would join her again, but the woman was busy with Liam, then Aiden. She kept Gil's glass filled too.

Charlene turned so that her back was to the bar and she had a view of the dance floor.

Liam was not part of the partying crowd, so why was he here? Why did he refer to Sinead as "love"? It was a familiar form of address and the man had to be at least thirty years older. Even from down the bar in the shadows, Liam emanated menace. A cigarette was tucked above his ear.

She returned her attention to the baseball photos on the wall. Bars and taverns had always been places to hang out and be a part of a community, especially one that had a baseball team.

Though she'd only had a few sips of her beer, she was ready to go home. She'd found out that Aiden wasn't the man who'd sped past her down the stairs. He was celebrating because he'd decided to quit school.

Nothing sinister about either of those things.

"What are you doing here, love?" Liam joined her, a heavily tattooed arm on the bar top. Three gold stars, each the size of a quarter, were tattooed in a burst of color on his inner forearm.

"Enjoying a beer." She couldn't bring herself to say that she was enjoying the hard punk rock music.

He crowded close to her and her skin pebbled in alarm. She noticed a teardrop tattoo on both eyes.

"I saw you looking at me," he said in a low, growly voice.

"I . . . wasn't."

"There you are, Charlene," Marc said, coming to her other side. She'd never been happier to see a guest.

Liam exuded danger. Unlike the cousins, his hair beneath the cap was black, his eyes dark brown. Deep lines cragged his face. She pulled her gaze free from Liam. "Hi, Marc!"

She quickly slung her purse strap over her shoulder and hooked her arm through his. They headed toward the exit.

"You okay? I think you have an admirer."

She didn't look back. "Not interested."

"You telling me that he's not your type?" Marc teased. They reached the door and he opened it for her.

Fresh, cool air brushed her cheeks.

"Funny."

"You okay to get home?"

Sweet of him. "I got it. Have fun. I'll see you around noon for checkout. It's okay if you stay a little late. No extra charge."

He waved and went back inside to his pouting dance partner. Charlene got into the SUV and started it up, checking the seats and locking the doors.

Liam's dark and penetrating gaze made her feel on guard. She started the engine and sent Avery a text that she was on her way home. **All good.**

Avery sent back a thumbs-up emoji. **See you tomorrow!**

Charlene drove through downtown and was at the bed-and-breakfast in ten minutes. The inside lights were dim, as most everyone had gone to bed. Would Sheffer be home again, and awake?

She glanced up the staircase as Silva twined around her ankles in greeting, but there was no sound of her guest. Charlene hurried to her suite, where Jack waited in his favorite armchair.

"Home by midnight!" He sent her an admonishing smile. "Must not have been a great party."

"I went to the Irish pub for a beer. When did rock and roll get so loud?" She grinned to show she was mostly joking.

"Why'd you go somewhere like that without telling me?" Jack got up to pace before the television, the volume on low behind him. "It's Saint Patrick's Day and wild, I bet."

"I'm fine. I had a cappuccino and a few sips of beer. Besides, Jack, you weren't here when I left. Next time I'll leave a note."

He nodded. "Did you find out why Sheffer and Sam were arguing?"

"No. It remains a mystery." She tossed her purse to the love seat. "I went to Pub 36, the bar Shannon's younger brother James owns with his wife. I met Sinead, one of their daughters. She and her dad share amazing red hair. Her mom and her sister are the only blondes."

"Ah! It's in the family. Did you know that redheads have a recessive genetic trait caused by a series of mutations that—"

Charlene started laughing. "That sounds terrible!"

He smiled. "There's been studies that uphold the old wives' tales about redheads having shorter tempers . . . it has to do with hormones. Redheads are typically more sensitive to pain. It's a hormonal mut—"

"Stop saying *mutation*, Jack," Charlene insisted. "The hair color is just so beautiful. Oh . . . hotheaded. Do you think maybe one of the red-haired relatives lost it with Connor and decided to kill him?"

"You can't rule these things out, Charlene, but I didn't mean to imply that might be the case. I was simply sharing a bit of knowledge on the melanocortin one receptor, or MCR one. I noticed while doing business with Brandy Flint that her temper was quick to spark."

"Brandy's auburn hair is gorgeous, and I'll keep that to myself," she said, not wanting to ruin her and Brandy's truce.

He rubbed his chin and strode around her small living area. "You went for a beer, to hang out?" Jack stopped to study her. "I don't believe it. What were you really doing at the Irish pub?"

She laughed, busted. "Checking to see if Aiden could be Connor's attacker, but the build is wrong. Too slight."

"That makes more sense. I wish I could have been there, but, well, I guess my essence needed to rest a bit."

There was so much they didn't know about Jack and his abilities. She feared the day he might not manifest for her. She would lose her best friend. "You're better now?"

"Of course. Now, did you learn anything else?"

"Gil was at the bar. He and Aiden know each other well through the AOH and Shannon. I sure wish I knew why Connor left town five years ago. Why he returned. I bet I could get Sinead to tell me. She's a sweet and chatty girl."

Jack returned to his armchair, sank down, and crossed his legs. "Perfect bartender material."

"Right?" She chuckled and perched on the edge of the love seat. "Jack, Sheffer was at the pub."

"Our guest?" His voice lifted in surprise.

"Yep. Watching Aiden. Sheffer's not Irish and he's not from here, so I don't know the connection, but I feel like there is one. That man is so tight-lipped about what he does for a living! All we know is that he hails from New York City. Maybe." She rolled her eyes at Jack. "I think he might be a very good liar."

"I can search his room for you, Charlene."

"No, Jack. He's a paying guest." She raised her brow at him until he nodded.

"Fine . . . but it's not like he'd see me."

"Not the point! Our guests trust us to provide them privacy." Still, when she went in to change the towels tomorrow, she might take an extra second to see what was out on the table, if there was anything. Personal items might provide a clue.

"I heard that Aiden wants to drop out of med school."

Jack sat back with a scowl. "It's tough. Not everybody wants to deal with the grueling studies and internships before you start making money." He sighed. "It's not all about helping people get well. It requires great dedication."

Aiden had seemed nice the night of the dinner, but that was hardly enough to judge his character on. Charlene stood and walked to her closed bedroom door, opening it. She was suddenly exhausted.

"Maybe he can go into the family bar business," Jack suggested.

"I don't think that's a good idea. From the looks of it, he likes to party too much as it is. I gathered from Sinead that his poor mother wanted more for him."

Jack shrugged. "We can talk in the morning, my dear. You look beat. What's on the agenda?"

"The Wards check out. Then Friday we have a whole new group of guests checking in." She leaned back against the doorframe, grateful for a full house. The Wards leaving reminded her of Liam. "Jack, what do teardrop tattoos on the face mean?"

"Why?" He tilted his head, a curious smile on his lips.

"I met a very scary man, don't mind saying, at the pub and he had them. Marc was very cool and came to my rescue."

"Might not mean anything, but I'll look it up. Sweet dreams, Charlene."

The next morning, she woke with a start. Her dreams had been filled with gold stars, and gold coins, and teardrops.

"Ugh!" She pushed back the covers, careful not to disturb Silva, and hopped into the shower.

Fifteen minutes later her mind was cleared and the bad dreams relegated to the back of her head.

She entered her living area where Jack waited at her desk with her laptop open. "Morning," she said. "Were you working all night?"

"Time doesn't matter to me." He gestured for her to join him. "Tell me about the teardrops."

"Liam, the man from last night, had two. He was very *hard*. I don't know how else to explain it."

She stood over Jack's shoulder to read the articles he'd compiled, complete with pictures of tough men and women in orange jumpsuits with crude tattoos.

"It's a symbol of going to prison," Jack said.

She shuddered as she recalled Liam's intense perusal of her. The cigarette behind his ear. Shaggy hair. Sinead's deference to the man. "What?"

"It's true." Jack looked at her over his shoulder and raised two fingers. "Two tattoos could mean that he killed someone."

She cupped her elbows and brought her arms to her waist. Charlene wondered if she should warn Sinead. He'd called the pretty girl *love*. Her stomach clenched. He'd called her *love* too. "He had one on each side of his face."

Jack nodded. "Meaning can vary according to region, but that's the main gist. This Liam's been in jail and possibly killed someone."

Could he have killed Connor? Was there a connection somehow? He'd had a cigarette on him, though she hadn't smelled it last night. The bars in Salem were no-smoking. Liam was certainly stocky. About her height.

She would give Marc an extra thank-you this morning when she saw him for coming to her rescue.

"I don't think you should hang out at that bar anymore," Jack said, watching her closely. "Even to talk with Sinead about the case. Liam is a bad dude."

"I won't! I prefer Brews and Broomsticks anyway, with Kevin." The blond bar manager also ran paranormal tours of Salem and had become a friend.

Jack no longer grew jealous of Kevin, as Kevin had a great girlfriend, Amy. "Good. I don't worry about you when you go there. I wish I . . ." He let the sentence trail off.

They both wished he could leave the house, but he was a ghost and couldn't go beyond the property line. She smiled softly at him. "I need coffee, Jack, to go with my early-morning teardrop news. I guess Connor's killer hasn't been found yet?"

He shook his head and gestured at the news running in the background. "Not yet, anyway."

"Kay. I think Minnie just got here."

He turned his attention back to the computer. "You have breakfast and I'll keep reading. Prison tattoos. There's a whole underground language that I find fascinating. Human beings are so complex. Maybe I should have been a psychiatrist."

"You would have been a caring doctor in that field as well. It's in your nature, Jack."

He sent her a warm look and she went into the kitchen, feeling better about leaving him in the suite. She knew he missed helping others through his physician practice. He was a big help to her in the B and B, but it wasn't the same.

Later that morning, she and Minnie were cleaning up the breakfast dishes when Charlene's cell phone rang on the counter by the coffeepot.

She eyed it but didn't recognize the number. "Charlene here."

"Hello! This is Shannon Best. We met at the AOH Saint Paddy's Day dinner?"

As if Shannon hadn't been on Charlene's mind since the suspicious death of her cousin. "I remember. How are you?"

"Just *busy*, but I could really use a break. I'd like to meet for coffee if you don't mind. Lunch is impossible."

Charlene had plenty of questions, and empathy, for the accountant. "Sure. When is a good time?"

"Well . . . I have so much going on with family coming in because of Connor's wake and funeral."

"Why don't we meet after?"

"No. I need to speak with you. Today. It really can't wait."

Charlene's curiosity spiked as they arranged to meet at ten at the local coffee shop, Sips and Spells.

She'd be back in time to help with the guests. Normally she wouldn't leave until the afternoon, but Shannon had sounded, well . . . almost afraid.

CHAPTER 9

Driving to Sips and Spells, a coffee spot that was new to her, Charlene wondered why Sheffer had been absent for their morning meal. As far as she knew, he hadn't even come down for a plate to take back to his room. She didn't like that kind of secrecy in her bed-and-breakfast. It unnerved her. *Sheffer* unnerved her.

Charlene decided not to question Sam about it and possibly put a crack in the bridge they'd made. She'd agreed to keep out of his business . . . unless it was completely necessary to save herself or someone else, and to put her energy into managing her own affairs. He'd made it clear that this was the way it had to be if they wanted their friendship to remain as is, or perhaps even flourish.

Well, she did and she didn't. Living with a ghost, which Sam stubbornly did not believe in, made it awkward to move forward.

Turning into the full parking lot, Charlene surmised the place must be top-notch if there were so many cars. She waited as someone backed out, then zipped into their spot. The coffee shop was painted a light blue with white trim and had a small awning over the threshold with the name, Sips and Spells.

She walked toward the entrance and passed a white Camry with the AOH sticker in green and white. The vehicle, just a few years old, had been the only car left Sunday evening as the guests boarded the van she'd rented to return to Charlene's. She'd run to get Lila's coat and hadn't seen the car again.

Must be Shannon's. But why had the accountant been the last to leave? Had she been with Connor? Had she seen the attacker?

Charlene entered the crowded shop and searched the patrons already seated at little bistro tables. She noticed Shannon's red hair right away—swept up into a messy bun that was very attractive. Shannon wore a colorful scarf around her neck, a green sweater, and cream-colored pants as if on her way to work.

Spotting Charlene next to the door, Shannon waved and smiled, though there were shadows under her blue eyes.

"Hi, Shannon. What a cute place! Haven't been here before." Inside had a nautical theme that matched the exterior, and an outdoor deck that viewed a stand of pine trees and a burbling brook over rocks.

"It only opened a few months back." Shannon's shoulders bowed. "Thanks for joining me for coffee instead of lunch."

"No problem." Charlene shrugged out of her light blue raincoat and draped it behind her chair. It was a mild morning with the possibility of showers. She liked to be prepared.

A young waitress bounced over to their table. "Hi. I'm Alexia." She handed them both a menu. "May I get you a coffee while you decide on one of our pastries or desserts? Everything is yummy and big enough to share."

Charlene glanced at Shannon. "That works for me. Do you have a favorite coffee?"

Shannon nodded amenably. "I like the caramel iced coffee here. It's delicious."

"Make that two," Charlene told Alexia. "What would you recommend?"

"Today's special is a cinnamon and coffee cheesecake. Or a strawberry and macadamia baked brie."

"Oh, my gosh. My mouth is watering. Shall we have both?"

Shannon showed a dimple. "Sounds perfect. Why choose if we don't have to?"

"We'll take one of each," Charlene told their waitress. Alexia left with their order and Charlene leaned toward Shannon. "I shouldn't confess this, but I've already had a muffin and fruit for breakfast. And coffee."

Shannon tossed her head and laughed. "Oh, thank you for saying that. I knew we could be friends. Another confession? I only like coffee if it's cold and sweet."

"I won't go that far." Charlene smiled. "So, why are we meeting up today . . . I get the feeling that it's a bit more than a social call. I'm not sure that I can be much help, but you have a friendly ear."

"Thank you, Charlene. That means a lot. I don't have many friends . . . time is hard to come by and I've either been building my business or . . ."

Alexia dropped off their iced coffees and brie, saying she'd bring out the cheesecake in a few minutes.

Once she departed, Shannon lowered her voice and continued from where they'd been interrupted. ". . . taking care of Aiden and encouraging him. Being a mom is a full-time job. Do you have kids?"

Charlene shook her head but didn't elaborate, sensing that Shannon wanted to talk.

"It's just that I'm trying to make sense of what happened to Connor. There wasn't any love lost between him and my brother Finn. They had a big blowout a few years back, and that's why Connor left town and didn't return until Sunday. Obviously unchanged."

Her voice trembled and she used the scrunched paper napkin in her hand to wipe away a single tear.

"I'm sorry," Charlene said. "Do you think Connor returned, hoping to mend the family fences?"

"If he wanted to mend fences, he should have been sober." Shannon tossed the napkin to the table.

"Is that why they fought?" Would Finn want Connor dead? But it couldn't have been Finn that night as the attacker had thought Connor was Finn.

"I was so upset seeing him drunk and obnoxious that it made my blood boil. I—I behaved badly."

Charlene stopped her fork digging into the brie. The hair rose on her nape. "What do you mean?"

"Connor and I argued that night before I left. I must have just missed you coming up the outside stairs. I took the inside stairs and exited the ground floor in the back." Stirring her iced coffee, Shannon didn't look at Charlene as she said, "I'm ashamed to say that I was embarrassed by him. He's had a drinking problem most of his life.

Never could keep a girlfriend, a job, or find happiness. It was sad. The only one who loved him and stuck by him was Patty, his sister."

Was Shannon telling her this to get the heat off of Aiden? Why did she have to be cynical? Charlene cleared her throat. "I understand. Everyone has their skeletons. Did you mention this to the police?"

"Of course." Shannon stopped playing with her iced drink and took a sip.

Charlene slathered a piece of the warm cheese melting over the fruit and nuts onto a triangle of hard toast. She bit into the brie and sighed.

"You've got to taste this. It'll lift your spirits." Charlene pushed the dish closer to Shannon, tempting her and hoping it would ease her concern if only for a moment. Alexia dropped off the cheesecake.

The ladies enjoyed the coffee and food, the sharing bringing them close. Shannon wiped her mouth with a paper napkin.

"What did you see that night, Charlene?" Her blue eyes blazed. "Anything to help Aiden? My son didn't kill Connor."

She recalled his build compared to the attacker's. "I don't think Aiden is guilty of murder either."

Shannon blinked her thanks.

"If it wasn't for one of my guests leaving her coat behind, I wouldn't have been there. Connor was alive when I saw him," Charlene murmured, "and didn't pass on until later—as you know."

"I visited him at the hospital, but he wasn't conscious. His sister was there. God. Poor Patty."

"I don't even know how Connor died exactly."

"A brain injury. Maybe caused by all the drinking." Shannon shrugged helplessly.

Charlene could ask Jack. "Does Aiden smoke, Shannon?"

"Of course not!"

"Well, the person that rushed by me smelled like cigarette smoke. I've told the police this, so I hope they'll cut you and Aiden some slack."

"That's a big relief. Is it terrible that I'm running down the list of people I know who smoke right now? My sister-in-law Cindy. It's part of the bar scene." Shannon smoothed her hair back. "James used to, but quit."

"It's human nature, I think, to want to find answers." Charlene drummed her fingers next to her empty plate. "Do you know of anyone, besides Finn, who might not have welcomed Connor back to town?"

"That's the other thing I wanted to explain . . . my brother had nothing to do with this. He's practically a recluse. I take care of him as best as I can." Her voice deepened. "Bring his groceries, clean when he lets me past the kitchen, which isn't often." She grimaced. "He's become a hoarder and it breaks my heart."

"That must be so difficult."

Shannon sliced off a piece of cake. "I remember when we were both young . . . he was so handsome. Those blue eyes of his slayed the women and they doted on him. He liked to spend money on fancy dinners and nice wine. Champagne." She smiled sadly. "Finn was outgoing, telling jokes, and fun to be around. I see so much of Finn in Aiden."

"What do you think happened to cause the change?"

Shannon shrugged and sipped her iced coffee. "We inherited a little money, and I do mean *a little*, when our dad died. We weren't even eighteen yet. Finn got the family house. I stayed there with James, and we raised him like a family until I got married to Trey. James was in high school then. He complains that he didn't know our parents, but he doesn't realize how good he had it."

"They weren't kind?"

"Our mom took off after James was born, leaving Dad to manage things. He was a fisherman and did what he could, which wasn't much." Shannon crossed her legs. "The property's been in the family for a hundred years. It's large and used to be quite impressive, but Finn's let it go to seed. It's an eyesore, even though I send Aiden over with the mower. Finn won't let him in the back. The trees are immense and dangerous but, well, I hate to spend the little time we have together arguing."

"When was the last time you saw Finn?"

"Two weeks ago. I tried to convince him to come out for Saint Patrick's Day. He used to love corned beef and cabbage. He's lost so much weight I almost didn't recognize him. My own brother." Shannon patted her heart.

"I'm sorry."

"He doesn't talk much to anybody, except himself." Shannon was silent for a few moments. "Aiden's visited him a few times, whenever he's home for the holidays or a long weekend. He'll mow the front lawn and drop off groceries, not that Finn thanks him for it. But he's a good boy and does what he can. He'll make a fine doctor one day. I sometimes wonder if growing up with an uncle like his, if he didn't go into medicine to fix him."

Charlene nearly dropped her fork. It sounded like Shannon had no idea that Aiden was drinking like a fish and "celebrating" his leave from medical school. Passing out at the family pub. She held her tongue.

"The police keep pestering Aiden," Shannon said. "What did you hear that night? Tell me again."

How had Shannon not seen the attacker inside the AOH club? Charlene said, "The person said, *Finn, give me my share*."

Shannon's expression didn't change.

Charlene continued: "Then the kitchen light went out and the man burst by me so fast that I almost got pushed off the staircase in his haste to leave."

"I'm glad you're all right." Shannon patted Charlene's wrist. "You didn't see them?"

"No. The hoodie covered his face."

Shannon's shoulders slumped. "I know Aiden didn't do it, but he seems different lately. I can't quite put my finger on what's wrong."

Charlene rested a comforting hand on Shannon's arm. "I understand how painful this must be for you." Life could change course in the blink of an eye.

"How did everything get so complicated?" Shannon asked. "Connor never should have returned to Salem. He was supposed to be in California, living the high life. The only reason for him to come back was that he ran out of cash."

Charlene recalled the gold poking from his pocket . . . it had to be chocolate. "Speaking of money, is it possible Aiden came into a bit from somewhere?"

"No! Why would you ask such a thing?" Shannon brushed a red strand from her cheek. "He's earned scholarships for medical school and I help, but we're not trillionaires," she blustered.

As Charlene had guessed. "I don't know if you remember my guests, the Ward brothers, from Sunday? At dinner last night, they'd mentioned hanging out at Pub 36."

Shannon turned pale and jutted her chin. "My brother's bar. Go on."

Charlene bit her lip. Should she keep this information to herself, or possibly ruin Shannon's dreams for Aiden with the truth?

"What did they see?" she demanded.

"John and Marc said Aiden was buying everyone drinks. Like, a celebration."

Shannon's eyes welled, on the verge of tears. "Why? Why would he be *there* when he knows how I feel about the place? Even cheap drinks get expensive."

Charlene bowed her head. "If it's family, I'm sure they let him have a tab?"

"He doesn't have that kind of allowance to buy drinks." Shannon put her hand to her mouth. "Even on a bar tab. God, I've tried so hard to give him a better life."

"I went there last night for a drink with the Wards, and spotted Gil in the crowd . . . and Aiden was speaking with him." A stretch of the truth.

Shannon sniffed and tilted her head. "Gil was with Aiden? I don't understand."

"Gil seemed to be looking out for Aiden."

"Gil's known Aiden since Aiden was born." Shannon curled her fingers tightly into her palm, bringing tears of pain to her blue eyes. "Who else was there?"

"I met another redheaded relative of yours." Charlene smiled softly, hoping to lighten the mood. "Sinead, the bartender."

"James's daughter is a sweetheart, despite her upbringing. So is Gwynne, though she's got some snark in her like her mom, Cindy."

So, no love lost between the younger brother, his wife, and Shannon. "I liked her too. I was paying for my beer when . . ."

"Yes?" Shannon prodded.

"This menacing guy slid up beside me at the bar. I was worried for Sinead, but she was fine. *I* was spooked . . . he had a cigarette over his ear. Lots of tats on his arms and face. Short dark hair under a cap."

Shannon swallowed and touched her throat. "Did you get his name, Charlene?"

"Liam," Charlene said. "No last name. He seemed dangerous. I must have looked frightened because Marc, one of the brothers, came to my rescue and walked me to the exit of the bar."

"Liam? You're sure?"

"Yes. You know him?" Charlene observed Shannon closely.

The woman's eye twitched, yet she managed a smile. "Maybe, maybe not. Lots of Liams around here in the Irish district."

Shannon had a good idea of who this guy was, Charlene knew it. "Could he be connected to Connor?"

Shannon scanned the time on her phone. "Listen, I have an appointment with a new account and can't be late. Can you come to Connor's service? Please? It's going to be at St. Michael's Church tomorrow. Two o'clock. I'll have food at my house afterward. We can talk then."

"I can't promise. I have more guests arriving this weekend." She glanced at the bill and tossed down her credit card. Alexia took it to the counter.

"Oh—let me. I have plenty of cash, Charlene. You didn't have to treat."

"You can get the bill next time." She agreed that they had more to discuss.

"All right." Shannon blew out a breath. "I want things back to normal."

Until Shannon knew the truth, it wasn't in the cards. Charlene touched Shannon's arm once again. "Can you handle one more thing?"

Shannon flinched, then squared her shoulders with a heavy sigh. "I hope so. You're not easy on the nerves, Charlene. Is this about my son?"

"Yes." Her stomach tightened at the hurtful words she was about to deliver. "Aiden might be quitting medical school. That why he's been at the pub. I'm so sorry."

"What?" Shannon stood up so quickly she knocked over the water glass. "You're wrong."

"I'm only telling you what I saw for myself. I don't mean to be hurtful. It's just that you said you were worried, so I thought the truth—"

"I take offense at your insensitive words. Aiden is my son and he would never lie to me about something so huge. He knows what I want for him." Shannon rushed past her, tears streaming down her reddened cheeks.

Charlene's eyes smarted as she waited for her credit card. Once she had it back in her handbag, she put on her raincoat and dashed to the car, not surprised when the dark skies opened up.

It was early yet, but she already knew it was going to be that kind of day.

CHAPTER 10

When Charlene returned home, Minnie greeted her with a glance at the clock in the kitchen. "Sorry, Charlene, but the Wards just left. They said they'd enjoyed themselves and want to be on the waiting list for Halloween."

"It's not even noon yet," Charlene said with regret. "I'll send them an email. I probably should have declined meeting Shannon for coffee. Oh, well." She shook out the moisture in her hair and removed her raincoat.

"They'd hoped to say goodbye but called the cab early, wanting to get to the airport in plenty of time."

"That is too bad. You know how I like to greet my guests and say goodbye. Gives it that personal touch."

"It's more than that with you." Minnie knew her too well. "You care about your guests, not as a bed-and-breakfast owner, but genuinely. Like friends."

"Guilty as charged. But they *do* become my family for a few days or more. Not like you and Avery and Will . . . you don't come in and out the door. You're staying with me for keeps," Charlene said, putting her arm through Minnie's.

Behind her, she felt a chill. "You didn't list me? I am certainly a keeper, Charlene."

She turned her head slightly to let him know his arrival had not been missed and gave him a quick smile.

"Who are you smiling at?" Minnie mumbled, putting on her oven mitts to pull something savory from inside. She set it on the stove top.

"Silva." Charlene pointed to the cat, who was sleeping on the kitchen chair. Jack, ever so helpful, gave her tail a gentle tug.

Silva yowled and leaped down, circling Jack's legs. Her tail was up and her ears were back as she tried to connect with Jack's pant leg but couldn't. Charlene came in a far second when Silva's playmate was around . . . unless she was handing out treats or spooning a can of tuna in her bowl.

"I swear that cat is a little batty." Minnie clicked her tongue. "Made a chicken, spinach, and mushroom quiche. Just need to let it cool and then we can have lunch."

"I'm sorry, Minnie. I couldn't eat a thing. I'm stuffed." Charlene hefted Silva in her arms. In return, Silva extended her claws to Charlene's sweater. "Bad cat," she admonished, looking into Silva's golden eyes.

Silva blinked, then haughtily stretched her neck . . . almost preening until Charlene gave her a soft pat under the chin. What a diva.

"What could be better than my cooking?" Minnie poured them each an iced tea from the fridge.

"Not better, Minnie, just different. Shannon and I shared cinnamon and coffee cheesecake, and the strawberry macadamia baked brie."

"And?" Minnie put her hands on her hips crossly.

"It was delicious—we devoured every bite."

"Ha!" Minnie studied her nice golden quiche. "Can't match that. But I bet Will will appreciate you."

Charlene picked up her iced tea. "Are you talking to me or the quiche?"

"Not you, you're too fancy for me." Minnie raised her nose in the air, as snooty in that second as Silva.

Charlene dropped the cat and played into her hired help's hands. "But Minnie, they weren't as good as your baklava or lemon-drop cake. Not even close."

Minnie shook a finger at her, laughter rumbling as she said, "You remember that, my girl."

"I will! Now, who is arriving today, and when?"

"The Montgomerys from Kentucky. A family of four. They're expected between two and three."

"That's right. I remember the reservation. The woman asked about the size of the beds and I explained that each of the larger rooms had two queens. She was happy with that."

"They've got a spacious room. It's ready and waiting, with their welcome basket filled with fruit, cheese and crackers, and a bottle of the Flint's finest."

"Thanks, Minnie. I can always rely on you."

"Yes. But one more thing." Her cheeks turned pink. "I hope I didn't overstep myself."

"You couldn't possibly." Charlene crossed her arms. "What is it?"

"Having grandchildren, I figured that the siblings, a boy and a girl, would hate sharing a bed." She paused and then rushed on, "I brought a single pullout from my house with brand-new sheets. I hope you don't mind?"

"Of course not. It was a wonderful idea and I'll reimburse you for the sheets. Guess I should invest in one of those beds. There's plenty of space here to store it."

"It would come in handy. Grandkids are forever and so will your guests be, God willing."

"You are more familiar with children than me. What else would make their time here more enjoyable?" Charlene had purchased the latest Nintendo and some fun games to play, and rainy-day board games for the young and the old.

"You've done a marvelous job already. Heck, if they're not happy, they can go outside and play tag, like we used to do." Minnie skipped in place. "Or jump rope? Hopscotch? Hide-and-seek?"

"Enough, already! I don't want you to hurt yourself."

They both laughed. Charlene hopped off the stool and brushed her hands. "All right. Less conversation and more work. We have another couple arriving around dinnertime. Maybe we can have the quiche then?"

"You're the boss!"

Charlene scooted off to her rooms, hoping to have a word with Jack. She caught him playing online poker on her iPad in his favorite armchair. The television hummed on low in the background.

"Poker, Jack?" She tossed her purse and raincoat in her bedroom.

He winked and gave her a dazzling smile. "Used to be quite good. During my college days, I took most of my buddies for a ride. Pocket money."

"They were your friends! Why did they continue to play with you if you won all the time?"

He patted his chest. "Because I supplied the rum and Coke."

"Oh, you were a wild child."

He chuckled at that. "Hardly, but I found it amusing for a while, then my attention got diverted." He shut the program and floated the iPad to the coffee table.

"Guess it did." She folded her arms at the waist. "Must have been when sweet Shauna entered your life."

"Sweet nothing. More like a she-devil, but you already know that. Tell me about your meeting with Shannon."

Charlene picked up a tortoise hair clip from her desk, twisted her long hair high on her head, and secured it.

"It started fine but ended rough. Shannon didn't know about Aiden's plans to quit med school, and she was quite angry with me when I mentioned seeing him at the pub, making friends by buying rounds."

"Ah . . . that wouldn't be pleasant to hear."

"I tried to be gentle, but the truth is the truth no matter how you sugar coat it." Charlene sat on the love seat. "She asked me to go over what happened again, which I was happy to do. I got the feeling that the police questioning Aiden didn't go well."

"Is it possible that she had a reason to think Aiden had been there?"

"*She* was there, Jack. Shannon talked with Connor and then went home, she says. I saw her in the kitchen earlier and her Camry in the lot. It was gone when I drove us home that night. Is it true? I don't know!" Charlene sank back against the cushions. "I told her that I didn't believe it was Aiden who attacked Connor."

"That had to be a relief for her." Jack tilted his head as if he could discern her feelings with a look.

"Shannon is very protective of her son, as she should

be. But then add his drinking and quitting school and that could rock even a mother's faith."

He nodded. "It's probably why she was upset with you when you brought up his grandstanding at the pub."

She squeezed her hands together. "I also mentioned seeing Gil with Aiden there and that creepy guy, Liam." Charlene sighed. "I've never seen anybody backpedal so fast. I could tell Shannon knew him, but she wouldn't confirm."

"Too bad you didn't get his last name. Guess I could play detective while you're busy with your new guests. Let me rattle around and shake the family tree."

"So handsome. So wise," she teased him. "Jack, Shannon said Connor died of a brain bleed, but I didn't see him hurt anywhere."

Jack nodded sagely. "Heavy drinkers often have higher blood pressure or liver damage, which affects the ability for blood to clot. It can lead to stroke or brain bleeds." He tapped his head. "No outside blow necessary."

Charlene decided that the odd sound she'd heard was the table moving when Connor fell. "I'm going to pick up Avery since it's still pouring cats out there. Catch you later." Grabbing her coat from her room, she closed the suite door behind her.

Minnie was seated at the counter, flipping through a recipe book, completely engrossed.

"Minnie, will you listen for the Montgomerys while I run out for Avery? The rain is a deluge. I heard on the news a storm is expected later." Charlene slipped into her raincoat.

"Be careful." Minnie earmarked a page in the book. "I sure hope the couple who rented a car from Boston drive safe."

"Dylan and Janice Shelton. They'll be here a whole week. Sounded very nice on the phone." She dug her keys from the side pocket of her purse. Thunder boomed.

"Speaking of the phone, your mother called the land-line earlier. Said she couldn't get you on your cell." Minnie finally looked up from the colorful pages.

"I turn it off when I'm inside a shop. I can't stand hearing people yak so loud that everyone knows their business. I won't be that person."

Minnie straightened and swung her calf around the leg of the stool. "She asked that you call her back right away—but it's not an emergency."

Charlene parted the curtain of the kitchen window to watch the darkening skies. "She probably wants a chat, but I have new guests to entertain. I doubt they'll go out in this weather unless they cab it to a restaurant." She sighed. "We should be prepared. I suspect that a nice, cozy fire, a fully stocked bar, and whatever you're cooking will have more appeal."

Minnie shrugged. "I dunno. If you've only got a few days in Salem it might be worth braving the storm." Her gaze turned crafty. "How about that gazebo you keep talking about, maybe with a hot tub inside?"

Charlene chuckled and wagged her finger at the expense. "One thing at a time, my friend. I could suggest Kevin's place; it's less than two miles down the road. Heck, if I sell the idea, I might go with them." He managed a bar, Brews and Broomsticks, with the best hot toddy around. She needed the big van before the gazebo and hot tub, but it would go on the dream list.

Minnie stood and closed the book. "In addition to quiche, I can warm the extra chili I put in the freezer and cornbread muffins, so we're covered if they stay here."

"We have lots of options! Should be back in twenty minutes or so." Avery had gotten out of school at noon this Thursday for a dental appointment. She'd texted Charlene that she was ready to come in.

Charlene messaged her that she was on the way. It would be perfect to have extra hands on deck if they had a lot of guests in the house.

Avery, looking like Little Red Riding Hood in her red raincoat, stood on the top step of the large residential home that had been converted into a place for teens. Janet was the house mom and created a warm and safe environment. Charlene pulled into the driveway. Avery ran down the steps and hopped into the SUV.

"Holy shamoli! What an awful day! Thanks for picking me up, Charlene. Janet was going to drive me, but now she doesn't have to." She shivered and put the heater up a few notches.

"You got it, kid. But you should have waited inside until I honked. I can't have you catching pneumonia, now, can I? I'd have to make daily trips to the hospital with pots and pots of Minnie's homemade soup, and I'd never get any work done."

Avery giggled. "I might enjoy it, though. Think of all those books I could read." Grinning at Charlene, she put her hand out like a paw. "Oh, the life of leisure, being waited on all day."

"Keep dreaming, kiddo," Charlene replied with a smile.

Avery turned up the music and sang along with Olivia Rodrigo, a song called "Drivers License" that Charlene knew as well. She hoped the freedom implied would prod Avery to get her own.

The music ended as they pulled into the driveway. Sam's blue SUV was to the far right, leaving the closest spot to the porch available for Charlene.

"Ready? Race you!" Charlene said.

They both raised their hoods and ran up the stairs to the front door, which magically opened the instant they reached it.

Sam ushered them inside after they shook off the raindrops from their coats.

"Hi, Sam! Did you come out in the rain to see me?" Avery teased.

"Of course," Sam said with a half-bow. "I hear you want to go on another ride-along? Call the station and talk to Officer Ramon. She agreed to take you this time."

"Yes! Thank you!" Avery giggled and tossed her red raincoat on the coat-tree near the door, then ran to the kitchen to tell Minnie.

Charlene's mouth went dry. Sam watched her like he was a hungry wolf, and she was a rabbit.

"You didn't show up to tell Avery that news in person, did you?" He sometimes dropped by on the thinnest excuses.

Sam rubbed his thumb and forefinger down his mustache. "No. Your mother called me at the precinct an hour ago. Told me she tried to get hold of you and you didn't answer the phone. She sounded quite excitable, more than usual," he drawled. "I offered to check on you. Here I am, and here you are."

Charlene removed her coat, her cheeks hot with mortification. "That was very kind of you and totally inappropriate of my mother!" Her mom's actions were so out of line that she wasn't going to call her back until she was good and ready.

Sam wore an amused expression, but didn't seem in a big hurry to go back out in the bad weather.

"Won't you stay for a few minutes? I have guests arriving soon, but Minnie has everything ready. We could sit next to the fire." Did he have news about Connor's death?

"Don't mind if I do."

She went to the living room and sat in a brocaded chair close to the fireplace. Sam picked up the poker from the antique set on the hearth and stoked the embers.

"It's nice to see you, Sam, outside of business, I mean."

"Good to see you too." He put the poker down and stepped in front of her, forcing her to look up into his face.

"What did my mother want," she stammered. "Did she say?"

"No, and I didn't ask." He finally sat down on the edge of the seat next to hers. "Did you have fun at the Irish pub last night?" His dark eyes held hers.

"No, not at all. How did you—"

"I hear things, like you. People just want to tell me things, and I'm forced to listen."

He had just repeated her words, verbatim. Threw them back at her as if they might not be sincere.

"I'm sure that's not true. No one could force you to do anything." She folded her hands in her lap like a good little girl. He made her feel like a child sometimes. When he was about to lecture her. What was it this time? What could she possibly have done wrong? Besides crossing Aiden off her list as the attacker. And Finn. And Shannon.

A good night's work, actually. She raised her chin and met his gaze.

"I spoke with Sinead O'Brien at Pub 36—she remembers you coming in. You'd ordered a cappuccino, and then switched to Corona, which you overpaid for. Cash. That's not your kinda bar, Charlene." Sam shifted in the chair. Jack's chair. "What were you doing there?"

This sounded official. She was tempted to suggest they have this conversation at the station but decided not to push it.

"You heard Marc and John at dinner last night. How Aiden was at the pub the evening before, buying drinks for everybody." Charlene shrugged. "He'd also told John that he'd changed his mind about med school. He wanted to quit."

"So you thought you'd go ask him about it?" His brow rose in disbelief.

Her face warmed.

Sam leaned back, making himself comfortable—which put her on pins and needles. He smiled that wolflike smile and suggested softly, "Why don't you clear your conscience and fill me in?"

At that moment she wanted to show him the door. She took a deep breath. This was about finding who had killed Connor and not personal.

"All right." She told him everything she recalled about the bar last night. Gil, Aiden, Sheffer, ending with the brief meeting of the man with teardrop tattoos. "His name was Liam, and Shannon appeared nervous when I mentioned him."

Sam leaned closer, eyes bright. "Shannon Best?"

Charlene tried to stay calm beneath Sam's stare. "Shannon said Liam was a very common Irish name and got all cagey, like she was hiding something. We met earlier today. I was going to commiserate with her over Aiden quitting medical school, but then I realized she didn't even know." She winced. "Well, when I told her, she stormed out of the coffee shop."

"Where were you, if you don't mind me asking?"

"No. I don't mind. I tell you everything, don't I?" A sudden rush of cold air snapped through her and sparked the fire. Jack appeared in a stream of blue: blue eyes, blue sweater, blue jeans. Annoyed scowl.

She told Jack everything too, but he was protective of her with Sam.

"It has a cute name—very magical. Sips and Spells."

"That's Salem for you. They make money off of hocus-pocus. Ghosts and spirits and witch spells. Easy cash flow."

"As a marketing major, I think it's brilliant."

Sam made a clicking sound with his mouth, then pulled on his mustache again. He did this when he was angry or flirting, but she had a strong hunch he wasn't flirting now. "Don't buy into all of this paranormal garbage, Charlene. We've proved all crimes are committed by flesh and blood."

She shrugged, not bothering to tell him that a very real ghost was pacing behind him. Agitated.

Sam patted the armrest and glanced at the crackling fire before returning his gaze to her. "Liam. What else can you tell me about him?"

"He was a tough guy seeming ready for his next fight. Called Sinead *love*, like he knew her, but then he called me *love* too. Creepy."

"He was that close to you, Charlene?" Sam demanded.

Jack crossed his arms and paused behind Sam as he said, "Sam's got an idea of who this man is. We need to find out too."

Charlene heard Jack but didn't respond to him as she answered Sam, "Liam said he saw me looking at him." She shuddered.

Sam blew out a breath, eyes hard. "Anything else you can think of?"

"Not really—oh, he had an unlit cigarette over his ear."

"Could he have been Connor's attacker?"

Charlene considered this. The height. The shoulders. "Maybe. The guy was in a hoodie and hunched, so I don't have an accurate idea."

Sam seemed poised to ask another question when she heard the ringer on the door. Saved by the bell.

"It's my guests, Sam. We'll have to continue this another time." She wanted to tell him about Shannon saying she'd argued with Connor. Shannon couldn't have attacked him—she'd been gone, along with her car.

He frowned with an annoyed expression, but she left him by the fire to cross to the foyer. Her guests came first. She opened the door to the family of four.

Sam followed her and waited while she gushed over the Montgomery family. "Welcome!" She offered her hand. "I'm Charlene. I'm so glad you made it in when you did. The weather is expected to get worse."

"The landing was a little rough and put us about twenty minutes behind, but it was no big deal." The man closed a large umbrella and set it on the porch before herding his family into the foyer. "I'm Jason, and this is my wife, Scarlett." A dark-haired woman nodded hello. "We picked up these two munchkins along the way, Caleb and Layla. They've promised to be good the entire stay so that the witches don't get them." He tickled his kids, who just laughed.

"Salem's nickname is Witch City," Sam said from behind her. "All in good fun. Detective Holden. Pleased to meet you."

"And you." Scarlett had one hand on each child's shoulder. "Sorry, but the kids need to use the bathroom."

"Of course." Charlene gestured to the staircase. "Your room is ready if you want to use that one, but we also have a half-bath behind the kitchen."

Sam nodded at her. "I'll see my way out. And don't forget to call your mom."

CHAPTER 11

Charlene, with Avery's assistance, got the Montgomery family settled in their suite. Jason, clean-shaven and just under six feet, had an easy, pleasant manner about him even as he coordinated. He pointed to either bed. "Right or left, Scarlett?"

"Right, please." Scarlett settled a large suitcase on the luggage rack. Avery helped with a third bag while Jason plopped theirs at the end of the bed.

Minnie had placed a twin cot in the corner that looked almost as inviting as the other queen, thanks to the baseball-patterned comforter and baseball throw. Caleb jumped on the bed and plumped a small pillow behind his head. "I call dibs!"

"Where's mine?" Layla said, looking at Charlene.

"You can have this big one all to yourself," Scarlett intervened. "See all of these pillows? I bet it's super-comfy, and you'll be next to me and Dad."

The little girl didn't appear completely convinced that she was getting the better deal.

"It's as big as ours, and we can watch you sleep at night. I love seeing that sweet face in dreamland." Her dad was doing his best. Maybe a little overboard?

Avery snickered, but hid her face.

"Come on, Layla. Try it out for size." Scarlett took her daughter's hand and helped her up. "There you go. Give it a good bounce."

Layla shook her head shyly, but when she tunneled under the pillows, Charlene knew the girl could be won over. She and Avery exchanged a smile.

"I realize it's raining hard right now so you can't go out to play, but we have a closet full of games downstairs that you are welcome to try. Books on Salem and movies, if you'd like. Make yourselves at home."

She and Avery stepped toward the door in tandem.

"Can we play with your cat?" Caleb asked. "We have one too. Whiskers. Grandma and Grandpa are watching him." He ran a slim hand through his wavy dark hair, his brown eyes shining.

Avery nodded. "Silva is around. If you can't find her, I'll give you a hint: She likes to sleep in the chair by the fire."

"Don't blame her for that! I'm ready for spring and warmer weather." Scarlett turned slowly to admire the room. "This is lovely. I'm sure we will be very cozy here even if it does rain."

Avery left first and Charlene followed, shutting the door behind them. "Nice family," Charlene said.

"Cute kids." Avery pulled her phone from her pocket

and checked the weather app. "Sunny weather tomorrow. Good thing. It would suck for their vacation to be ruined."

"Blue skies equal dry skies." Charlene paused in the hall on the second floor as Avery skipped down the stairs to the foyer. Her attention was drawn to Sheffer's room. The door was shut.

Why had Sheffer been at the pub last night? When she'd mentioned to Sam that she'd seen him there, he hadn't seemed to care.

She decided to see if she could get Sheffer to talk with her and walked to the bedroom door, rapping lightly.

"Hello?" Sheffer answered, his voice muffled through the wood.

"Hi there. It's Charlene." She leaned her forehead to the panel. "Can I get you fresh linens?"

"No, no." His reply was immediate. "I told Minnie already that I didn't want to be disturbed. If I wanted this kind of service I could stay at my mom's."

Ouch. She reeled backward, disgruntled.

"Are you still there?" he snapped.

"Yes."

The door swung inward as he opened it. "Sorry about that." His eyes narrowed as he studied her. "Why were you at the pub last night?"

"I was going to ask you the same thing." If he wanted to dispense with niceties, she could play along.

"I knew you'd seen me," he said. He smoothed his hand over his styled hair, an unpleasant smile tugging at his mouth. "The Wards raved about the pub so I thought I'd check it out. Couldn't hear myself think over the music, so I came back."

Charlene scrutinized his expression. Was he lying, or telling the truth? She couldn't tell. "I see."

Amusement glittered in his brown eyes. "I gave you my reason . . . what's yours?"

As if she'd tell him! She tucked her hand in her pocket. "Oh, John and Marc invited me." They'd sent an open invite to everyone. "I had a beer and met a few people." Mostly true. Jack said a good lie should always have a thread of truth.

She'd noticed the way he'd watched Aiden without actually talking to the young man and took a stab in the dark. "How do you know Aiden?"

Wily Sheffer didn't bite. "Aiden?"

Sheffer hadn't been with them at the AOH so he hadn't met Aiden that night, as the rest of them had. Maybe he was telling the truth, but Charlene doubted it.

"He's a cousin of the pub owners," she said. "Thought you knew him, but I guess I'm wrong."

His gaze flickered with interest. "Hmm. Cousin?"

"Yes." They stared at one another in a standoff that Charlene, as the hostess of the bed-and-breakfast, had to let him win. "Well. If you're sure that I can't get you fresh towels?"

He shook his head and backed up a step. "Nope."

"Will we see you for happy hour? It's raining hard, so it's not a great day for tours. We'll have plenty of appetizers so you don't have to go out." She peeked over Sheffer's shoulder to his room.

The bed was neatly made, though covered in printed papers, loose. He had a laptop plugged in at the small desk and a portable printer. That would explain the heavy suitcase she'd lugged up the stairs.

Something cylindrical poked from his blazer. His suitcase was open on the luggage rack, empty. He'd obviously utilized the wardrobe she'd put in the room for the fancy clothes he'd arrived in.

He saw her looking and blocked her view. "Four o'clock. I might be napping."

He didn't seem like the type to nap. Energy jumped off him like electricity. He was in jeans and a sweatshirt, his feet in socks. Much more informal than when he'd shown up here. The day after Connor was attacked . . . but had he already been in town?

Her mind went there, as it often did. *Stop it, Charlene. Sheffer is an elitist jerk, not a murderer.* And yet, it was not impossible.

"Just know that you're welcome—Minnie's made a pot of chili and cornbread along with a quiche to fight off the chill."

His nose twitched. "That's the smell. I thought something was burning."

Oh!

Her reaction must have tickled him, as a wide grin covered his face. Then, rather rudely, he shut the door.

Charlene practically stomped down the stairs.

She hoped he would check out early—she'd gladly give him a refund and send him home *to his mother's*. Of all the nerve! She plonked down at the kitchen table.

"What's wrong, Charlene?" Avery asked.

She'd never been any good at hiding her feelings. "Nothing." She got up and stirred the chili on the stove. It smelled delicious. She shouldn't let Sheffer get to her . . . she'd knocked on *his* door.

Minnie exited the pantry, holding a list of things she

needed to replenish from the grocery store. She saw Charlene's stormy expression and raised a gray brow. "What's going on?"

Charlene put the spoon down and crossed her arms at her waist. "Did Sheffer ask you to not change the towels in his room?"

"Not the sheets either," Minnie confirmed. "Man wants his privacy, and as far as I'm concerned, he can darn well have it. He set all of the little shampoos in the hallway as if they weren't good enough."

Avery laughed. "Really?"

"I got that message too, loud and clear." If it wasn't against her personal code of conduct regarding her guests' privacy, she'd ask Jack to take a look. Yet that didn't sit right either. Having a ghost at her disposal didn't mean she should use him for reconnaissance—no matter how tempting it might be.

Avery lowered her voice and glanced up at the ceiling. "Tell me, tell me! What'd he do, Charlene?"

Charlene blew out a breath to calm down. "Shut the door in my face when I asked if he needed anything. Said if he wanted this kind of service he could stay with his mother." She rolled her eyes.

"What a jerk," Avery said, rubbing her back.

She lifted her chin. "When he said that about staying with his mother, I should've replied, *please do*." Charlene sighed. "My mistake."

Both of her employees laughed at that. "It's not too late," Minnie said.

Charlene relaxed her shoulders and lowered her arms. "I suppose when it comes to moms, I should sympathize. Oh, God—speaking of that! I have to call mine. I'll be right back."

She hurried into her suite, where she closed and locked the door. There was no sign of Jack, and she felt a momentary loss. She could use his soothing words and steadying company right about now.

Dialing from her cell, she called Brenda Woodbridge, who answered with a tart, "Where have you been, Charlene?"

"Running a business, Mom. Right here in Salem. Please do not *ever* call Sam again to check up on me—not unless it's been like a month since you heard from me." She heaved a sigh, hoping her mother got the message. "We just texted yesterday."

Her retired parents had been here to visit more than once and had accepted the fact that Charlene was prospering in Salem and not coming back to Chicago. Ever. Her mother was the main reason why.

"What if there'd been an emergency?" her mom demanded.

"You told Minnie it wasn't! And if it was, then you'd have left a message on my landline, or with Minnie, texted, or told Sam. Which means that you're up to something, and I'm scared to know what."

Charlene paced the living room of her suite, still fired up from Sheffer grinning as he slammed the door in her face. He'd neatly evaded answering her question about Aiden, but clearly, he knew him. Or of him. There was a story there.

"Of all the—"

She heard genuine hurt in her mother's words—they'd been working on a kinder relationship. Charlene sucked in a breath and said, "Mom, I'm sorry for not calling you back."

"Humph!"

So much for offering an olive branch. "Mom. I don't have time for games. Please tell me what you want so that I can get back to work. I have accounting to do and photos to upload to the website from Saint Patrick's Day . . ." And a murderer to find.

She stopped marching to plop down on the love seat and put her feet on the coffee table. Silva jumped up next to her with a loud purr.

Her mom also took in a breath and then said, in a calmer voice, "I know that you're busy. But I was just so excited! I won a thousand dollars at bingo last night."

Charlene straightened. "That's great!"

"I had a card that won two different ways, which doubled the prize." Her mom's voice trembled, she was so happy.

"And what are you going to do with your winnings?"

"Well, my friend Annabeth from church told me about this website that you can get last-minute flight deals, but you have to act quick."

Charlene nodded. "So, what did you pick? Costa Rica? The Bahamas?"

"No—I picked Salem, Charlene. Dad and I will be there tomorrow!"

CHAPTER 12

Charlene felt a flutter of Jack's brisk air as he joined her in his chair across the love seat. It cooled her heated cheeks.

"What's wrong? You look like you've seen a ghost," he teased.

"Worse!" She rolled her eyes to the ceiling and then focused in on Jack. "Mom's coming in tomorrow. Friday. With Dad. To stay for a week. And all because she won a thousand dollars playing bingo. Lucky her, not so lucky me."

"Don't say that. You always get apprehensive, then the visit turns out great. She wants to spend her winnings to see her daughter. I think that's wonderful." Jack folded his hands around his crossed knee. "She probably should've asked whether or not you have a vacancy, I suppose. Are you going to charge her double for the last-minute reservation?" He smacked his knee, totally cracking himself up.

She was not amused. "The tickets are a special price, which my mother loves, but nonrefundable. The Montgomerys are here, Sheffer is here, and the Sheltons will be here around dinnertime. The only room available is the middle one by the stairs that Mom didn't like. Too blue, she said." Her mother always had a contrary opinion.

"Oh, Charlene, she just wants to see you. She won't care about the room."

"This is *my* mother we're talking about, Jack. She'll care. But I won't listen to her complaints." It had been a rough day. "They'll have no choice, and neither will I. Should I give them my suite?"

"No. Nothing that drastic." Jack raised a finger. "Sheffer. You think he might move to a single?"

Anger flashed within Charlene, but she tamped it down. "We had words less than an hour ago. I asked him about being at the pub last night, but he evaded the question. I peeked into his room before he slammed the door on me. He's got stuff all over the place. A printer, Jack? I know he'd never agree. And I wouldn't ask. The sooner he leaves, the happier I'll be."

"That bad, huh?"

"Worse." She petted Silva. "We need to figure out the connection between Sheffer and Aiden. Did you notice that Sam seemed to know Liam?"

"I did. And the detective was scared for you."

She nodded. "Hey, how did the O'Brien family tree research go?"

Jack stood and rubbed his hands soundlessly together. "Want to see? I left a Word doc up on the screen."

The two moved to the open laptop on her narrow desk and Charlene sat on the chair, Jack at her shoulder.

She powered it on, smiling when she saw an email from the English couple, Jasper and Lila Prescott, with pictures, and a note to say that they'd had a great time.

"I love my job," she said. "This is what I need to focus on, not rude people like Sheffer LaCroix."

Jack hummed soothingly behind her. "Don't let him get to you. You're a wonderful hostess."

She scanned the Word doc Jack had made with two columns—one for the O'Brien family and one for the Gallagher family.

"The O'Briens have been in Salem since the mid-1900s; the Gallaghers came at the turn of the twentieth century."

"Where did you get this information?"

"I made a fake account on Ancestry.com." Jack's tone conveyed his pleasure in his online skills.

"And who are you pretending to be?" Charlene asked, not hiding her grin.

"Rory O'Brien, at your service," Jack spoke in a perfect Irish brogue.

She chuckled. "All right, Rory. What did you learn about the Salem O'Briens and Gallaghers?"

"Aiden Best is Shannon O'Brien Best's only child. Finn O'Brien had no children."

"Shannon told me earlier that she does all of her twin brother's shopping and cleaning. Aiden helps out with the lawn when his uncle Finn allows it. He was just over there before Saint Paddy's Day."

Jack gestured toward the document. "Their brother James is married to Cindy, and they have two girls, Sinead and Gwynne."

Charlene thought of all the cousins in the baseball picture at the pub. Sinead had sounded proud. Family mattered very much to Shannon as well. "Shannon invited me to Connor's service tomorrow. I guess he's always had a problem with alcohol. It caused a big rift between Finn and him."

"Are you going to go?" Jack asked.

"I don't think so." Even as she said the words, her curious nature was urging her to say yes, and watch the family dynamics in person. She credited herself for being a good judge of character. Her mind began to whirl. Would Finn show up? Had Connor returned to Salem for Finn's forgiveness? "Shannon wasn't happy with me when she left the coffee shop."

"Maybe because you're on the right track, Charlene. Sam seemed to think so."

"I just met the family."

"That hasn't stopped you before," Jack said with a chuckle.

She blushed. "I like Shannon. A lot. She did invite me, but after this morning I'm not sure the offer still stands."

"Unless she made it clear that you're not welcome, I think you should go and pay your respects. When you're observing the mourners closely, you might get an inclination as to which one of them knocked Connor off—if they did." Jack shrugged when she gasped. "It's what you do."

He had a point.

"I shouldn't!" Oh, but she wanted to.

Jack raised his brow at her.

She sighed. "I'll check the time. Mom and Dad are coming in at three and I'll have to pick them up in Boston. I might not be able to swing it."

"Make it happen, Charlene. You'll have no problem blending in."

She wasn't so sure and turned back to the Word doc and the family trees. "What about the Gallaghers? Shannon mentioned that Connor had a sister named Patty."

Jack pointed in a cold wave of air to a name on the screen. "There's a Patricia Gallagher Kane on the family tree. The news article also mentioned that he was survived by his sister, Patricia. That must be Patty."

Charlene read the line. "She married Liam Kane." Liam? No, it couldn't be the same. Shannon said it was a very common Irish name. "You don't think . . . do you? That *this* Patty is with our tattooed Liam?"

"One way to find out. Look up Liam Kane," Jack suggested.

With trepidation, Charlene put *Liam Kane* in the search bar. There were so many she couldn't choose. "It's a list about a foot long. It will take forever."

A knock sounded on her door and Minnie called, "Charlene? The Montgomerys have a question about the candy shop."

"I'll be right there!"

"Want me to help?"

She stood and offered her seat to Jack. "Work your magic, my friend. I'll be back later to see what you've found."

He grinned at her and took her chair. It didn't move as he sat. She was used to his ghostly form and the fact that she could sometimes see through his manifested body to the furniture no longer freaked her out.

"Luck, Jack!"

Charlene entered the kitchen with a smile and told the family a little about the history of Salem's oldest sweet shop, Ye Old Pepper Candy Companie, and the delicious choices available. Scarlett and Layla sat at the kitchen table while Minnie straightened the counter. Caleb and Jason were playing checkers in the study.

"Do we have time for a movie before happy hour?" Scarlett asked. She peered out the kitchen window to the dark and stormy skies. Rain pelted against the glass. "Layla's getting antsy."

Charlene checked the clock on the stove. "It's three-thirty now and we'll have it ready at say, close to five? You can always start the movie, then pause and finish it later."

She hated for her guests, especially the youngest of them, to be disappointed and when Layla's face fell, she leaped into action.

"You know what? We could make a batch of sugar cookies to decorate and add to our feast. Would you like to help, Layla?"

Minnie immediately pulled out a tub she'd premade of cookie dough from the freezer. "Great idea."

"Yes, please!"

"Go wash up," Scarlett said, giving Charlene and Minnie looks of gratitude as her daughter scampered off. "This is so hard for them. We promised witches and tours, so staying indoors is difficult. Explaining that it's Mother Nature's fault doesn't help."

Charlene smiled, washed her hands, and got out several aprons. "I understand. I don't think I ever forgave my mom for canceling my birthday party because of the flu."

That had been unfair, but then again, Charlene had been ten and hadn't understood. The party had been rescheduled, not completely canceled.

"Why do we always blame our mothers?" Scarlett

laughed and accepted an apron that she put on the table. "I think I'll supervise."

"Human nature," Minnie observed.

Layla raced back with a happy grin. "I love to bake cookies!"

"You do?" her mother asked. "I don't bake, so that's news to me." Scarlett helped her daughter with the apron and tied the strings. "There you go."

"Grandpa lets me eat the cookie dough raw," Layla said with a smug tone.

Charlene hid her amusement with a bite to her cheek. The little girl was beyond adorable. "Are you close to your grandparents?"

"Yep. I have a lot of them, but Grandma and Grandpa Montgomery are my favorite. Oops." She glanced at her mom. "Can I have favorites?"

"Well. Yes. Just don't tell the other grands or you might hurt their feelings." Scarlett shrugged. "I like Jason's parents better too."

The half hour passed in a flash and soon Layla was frosting cookies. Her brother wasn't interested in decorating, but was very happy to sample the treats when she was done.

Avery came in from dusting the upstairs and after washing up, she helped Minnie set up trays for their happy hour.

"These are great, Layla," Avery said, admiring the cookies. "The frosting is my favorite part."

Charlene took a moment to enjoy the warm camaraderie within the kitchen. Her home was filled with laughter, and yes, love. At half-past four a few of her guests arrived early, others soon after. They had congregated in the living room with her special bar and the sideboard where she placed the selection of food.

Quiche, chili, cornbread, roast beef sliders with horseradish, crackers, cheese, and of course, the wine from Flint's Vineyard.

Everybody complimented Layla's cookies.

The sweet moment burst when Sheffer arrived. He stood at the threshold as if waiting for all to notice him.

He looked very put together in his designer blazer over slacks. Italian loafers. Fresh-shaved face and subtle cologne. His eyes gleamed with cunning, like a fox. His trench coat was folded over one arm.

How had she thought him attractive? He thought so much of himself that there was no room for anybody else to admire him.

"Hello, Sheffer. Glad you decided to join us." Charlene kept her voice polite. As unpleasant as he was, he was still her guest.

"Oh, I'm not staying, Charlene." He slipped into his coat. "I have dinner plans."

She knew he would never confide any further information, so she nodded silently. Her mind still whirred with questions she kept to herself.

Was it with a female friend? What did he do? Why was he here? How did he know Aiden? What was that bulge in his coat pocket?

She stepped toward him, burning with curiosity.

"Don't wait up," Sheffer said. "And stay out of my room, please. I have cameras set up inside to see that you do."

He left, stepping to the porch. Jack appeared with a ghostly flutter and knocked out the porch light so that Sheffer was in the dark.

Jack swept the door closed.

Charlene, eyes wide, turned toward her guests. Most were in conversation and hadn't noticed Sheffer's abrupt departure or the light snuffed out.

"He's rude, that one."

Charlene raised her brow at Jack. She agreed silently.

"I need you to look at something for me," Jack said with agitation.

She gave a little shake of her head and stepped toward the sideboard of steaming chili.

Avery scooped beans and thick sauce into a bowl. "Want some, Charlene?"

"You can wait to eat," Jack said. "I need you. Just for a minute."

Layla grabbed her by the hand. "Did you get a cookie?"

"Not yet. I will in a second." She eyed Jack as she said the words, meaning them for him too.

His image shimmered.

She didn't have time to deal with Jack right now. He knew that running the B and B correctly and making her guests feel at home was a priority to her. His behavior seemed demanding.

She accepted a bowl of chili from Avery and a cookie from Layla.

The whole time she ate she could feel Jack's cool energy getting even more frigid behind her. She ignored him the best she could.

When Jason joined her to ask about Plymouth Rock, Jack exploded, not willing to wait for another instant. "I'm pretty sure Liam Kane is married to Shannon's cousin Patty. I just need you to confirm it for me, so I can move on!"

She answered Jason's questions and gave him some good advice, then waved her hand. "Excuse me for just a second," she said to the group. Goose bumps dotted her arms and she blamed it on the cold emanating from Jack—not the awareness that the bad, scary guy was somehow related to Shannon.

She ducked out of the room, Jack at her side.

"I'm sorry, Charlene. This is important. If you identify that this is the right man, I can move forward," he said.

They reached her suite.

Liam Kane's evil grin greeted her from the laptop screen and her stomach knotted in fear. "That's him. Good job, Jack."

CHAPTER 13

Charlene returned to her guests for the next hour, making sure they had plans for the evening. The Montgomerys and the Sheltons were going to play charades. To make both teams equal Scarlett had volunteered to join Janice and Dylan—against her own family. The challenge was on!

Once they were all set up with the game, Charlene went into the kitchen to help Avery, as Minnie had already left. "You did a good job today entertaining the kids during our happy hour," she told the teen.

Avery laughed like it was no big deal. "When they found out that I've lived here all my life they plied me with questions about witches and stuff. Caleb wanted to know about the witch trials."

"What did you tell them?" Charlene wiped the counter down with a paper towel.

"Just that I learned in school the girls were regular kids like us, and not really witches. I figured that was the best answer so they wouldn't be scared."

"That was very thoughtful."

"It's kinda sad how religious fanatics rounded up all the supposed 'witches' and hunted them down. Can you imagine?" Avery tucked a golden blond lock behind her ear. "If Kass had been alive back then she'd have been toast. The authorities arrested two hundred falsely accused people, which resulted in mass hysteria—as you know."

"You were paying attention in class!" Charlene smiled with approval and tossed the towel into the trash.

"I did a paper on it," Avery said proudly. "Got an A."

"Of course, you did!" Charlene patted her shoulder. "What was Layla interested in?"

"Ghosts, mainly. Wanted to know if I'd ever seen one and if they were real."

Her skin prickled as she watched Avery. "Have you?"

"Heck no." Avery rolled her expressive eyes. "Any sane person knows better than that."

Just then, Jack slid up behind Avery and blew on the back of her neck.

"Boo!" Jack said in a teasing tone.

Avery yelped and swatted her nape, where she had her spider tattoo. She scooted closer to Charlene, who had to bite her lip to stop from laughing.

"What was that?" Avery glanced around in suspicion.

"Come see me, Charlene," Jack said. "I found something else."

"A draft from the kitchen window? I felt a chill too." She shot Jack a look and he disappeared with a snap. "Are you all right?"

"I'm okay." Avery searched the space with a sense she probably didn't realize she was using. "It's gone now."

Charlene dried her hands on a dish towel. "Do you mind staying a little longer tonight? I have a pile of computer work that I need to tackle."

"Sure, no problem. I'll hang out with everyone and be their bartender."

"They can get their own drinks, Avery. You're not even eighteen, so no playing bartender for you. Just knock on my door if you need me."

"Will do." She grinned. "It'll be fun to watch charades. I've never seen it played before."

"Maybe someone will sit out and give you a chance to perform a round? Just ask. It's easy and it's not like you're shy."

Avery pulled her phone from her back pocket. "Naw, I want to observe first. See about the rules and all that . . . just let me text Janet to let her know I'm staying longer." She glanced at Charlene with her thumb over the cell phone screen. "About eight or nine?"

"Nine latest," Charlene said. "Thanks, Avery. You can drive home and log a few more minutes toward your test."

"Awesome! But I think you're more excited than I am about it."

In the back of her mind, Charlene had the beginnings of a plan that couldn't happen until Avery had her own license. "Well, if you feel that way . . ."

"Nope!" Avery dropped her phone into her pocket. "I'm glad you're helping me. Janet's been watching me park in the driveway, and she says I'm getting better."

Charlene gave Avery a high five.

"I've got this covered." Avery smoothed the wrap over a plate of peanut butter cookies to serve later. "Trust me."

"I do!" Charlene ducked into the living room to get a glass of merlot that she'd bring to her suite.

"Charlene! Want to join us?" Janice called from her seat on the floor.

"Another time, maybe. I'm going to finish some paperwork, but Avery will be out in a minute if you need anything."

"We'll be fine," Scarlett assured her.

"Can we keep the bar open?" Dylan raised his empty glass and stepped toward her.

Charlene laughed and gestured toward the bottles. "Help yourselves to whatever you'd like."

She poured a glass and left them to their games, their drinks, and new friendships. She'd love to join them if only Jack wasn't waiting for her. Curiosity hurried her steps through the kitchen to her suite.

Jack sat at her desk with a very disarming smile that made her pulse race. "How long have you got?" he asked with a brow waggle.

Charlene wasn't going to let him off the hook! "You could have scared Avery half to death with that cold air trick." She put her wineglass on the coffee table.

"But I didn't. Ghosts don't frighten her because she's got common sense." He slid one leg over the over, his blue, blue eyes dancing.

"That she does." Charlene placed her hands on her hips, but couldn't stop returning his smile. Jack was a charmer and twisted her around his finger more often than not. "What if she'd caught you?"

"Then I'd have two people to believe in me."

She sucked in a breath at that. "Jack. Don't go there."

His jaw clenched, but then he agreed with a nod.

"Okay, what did you find that you wanted to show me? I could be playing charades right now," Charlene said with a soft laugh. She sat on the left side of her love seat, closest to Jack, and faced him. "What has Liam Kane been up to?"

Jack turned back to the laptop. "To start with, Liam did a stint in Franklin State Correctional Facility."

That information fit the grittiness about the man. "I knew it!"

"Franklin is a medium-security state prison with well over a thousand prisoners." Jack tapped the screen where the website was open. "Looks like Liam Kane was in for twelve years and was just released last month."

"I bet he made a lot of friends there," Charlene answered, hunched forward. "What did he do?"

"The record says that he and an accomplice were sentenced to prison for aggravated robbery with a deadly weapon. A felony."

She blew out a breath. "Is the accomplice Connor?" That would certainly be a connection.

Jack read the notes. "It doesn't say here, but I can do more research to find out. It's a matter of public record."

She stood up to read the site for herself. "Mind if I have a peek?"

"Not if you don't mind me breathing over your shoulder." With his usual grace, Jack moved from the chair and gestured for her to sit at the desk.

"You don't breathe," she reminded him.

"See? Not a problem, then."

She laughed, loving Jack's sense of humor. When she'd first met him, he'd been a grouchy ghost, but that had changed. Neither of them was lonely anymore.

"Liam was married to Patty, or Patricia, who happens to be Connor's sister. Perhaps he and Connor had a deal that went wrong." Charlene got excited as she typed *Connor Gallagher* into a separate browser.

Jack said, "Connor had DUIs but no prison record."

"If Connor was an accomplice to the robbery, that would have angered Liam, wouldn't it have? I mean, Connor's going about business as usual but Liam's doing time. Makes sense that all caged up, his resentment grew so on his release he found a way to kill him!"

"That's very logical . . . but why wouldn't Liam give up Connor's name to the police, if that were true?"

Charlene suggested, "Loyalty among thieves?"

Jack frowned. "I don't think that's really a thing outside of the movies."

"Connor didn't seem very reliable. According to Shannon, he was supposed to leave town and not come back, yet he did."

"Addiction changes behavior, so I don't think it's unreasonable for Connor to return to his roots when he's down on his luck. Especially if his cousins own a pub with unlimited alcohol."

Charlene continued reading the arrest record for Liam Kane. An accomplice had also been sentenced, in a different prison. She typed in the date that Liam had been arrested and added *known associates*.

"Look what we have here, Jack." Charlene grinned up at him. "Patrick Hennessy. Arrested in New York City on a petty theft charge. Patrick Hennessy was a person of interest in the aggravated robbery with Liam Kane, but also had other priors . . . he was sentenced to fourteen years."

"Which means he still has two years left to serve, at least," Jack said.

"Darn it. He's in jail. Also, neither man is connected in a criminal way to Connor." She exhaled and pushed back from the desk. "I hate it when things don't fall in line."

"We don't know that for sure," Jack advised. "The connection isn't through the courts, which we've found so far."

"Good point."

"Let's create a list of what we know." He levitated a pen toward her. "It helps you think when you doodle and I like to see how your mind connects the dots and squiggles."

She caught it in midair with a furtive glance to the closed and locked suite door, then found a piece of paper. Jack was right—it helped her think.

"Who first?" Jack hovered near her shoulder to read.

"Aiden. Suddenly spending money like he's rich. Quit medical school. Shannon was devastated when I told her."

Jack ruffled her hair in a show of empathy. "It was the right thing to do."

She wrote Shannon's name down. "I hate to even think it, but Shannon might have been involved. Not that I believe it for a second, but if Connor had anything over her son, she'd fight with her last breath. She and Connor argued that night before his attack in the kitchen at the AOH."

Tilting his head, Jack looked at the ceiling as if answers were to be found in the ivory paint. "What other relatives could gain from Connor's death?"

She drew circles within circles. "What about Patty? Shannon told me that Patty is Connor's closest family. But if her brother had something to do with her husband being locked up, well, she might want revenge against her brother."

"Or," Jack said, "she might look the other way if Liam wanted Connor gone. Write her name down."

Charlene patted her lip with the pen, searching her memory for anything that might help. She doodled stars within the circles and gasped when she realized what they reminded her of. "Jack! There's something else about Liam. It wasn't just the teardrops below his eyes, he also had tats on his inner arm."

"What did they look like?"

She tapped her paper and the drawings. "I only got a glance, but I'm quite sure there were three stars. Think that could have any significance?"

"I'll look up the meaning to see if I can find something online. Like I said, it's a language all its own. I'd love to know more about Liam's life before incarceration. Any connection that ties him with Connor. Anybody else?"

Charlene added Finn to the list. "Shannon's twin is connected to Connor over a fight they'd had. It was why Connor left Salem. According to Shannon, Finn has become a recluse and a hoarder. Still, they all grew up together. It seemed they were close but then something changed."

"I'll search crimes around the same time that Liam and Patrick went to jail."

"It's a shot." She glanced at her cell and stood up. "I've gotta get Avery home, then visit again with the guests. You've been a big help as always, Jack. Thank you."

"As usual, the pleasure is all mine." He unlocked the door and opened it for her as she sailed out.

* * *

Charlene and Avery were halfway back to the teen house, a silent trip mostly as Avery concentrated on the dark, damp roads. Charlene was very proud of her for staying calm even when a big truck swerved into their lane.

Avery turned off the music and glanced at Charlene. "Can I ask you something?"

"Sure." Charlene spread her arm out and accidentally knocked her knuckles against the dashboard. "Ouch. Anything. This about college? Or boyfriend trouble?"

"I wish." Avery stopped at a red light and checked her mirrors.

"You still have a double date lined up for tomorrow night?"

"Yeah. Jenna is so into her new guy. Me and Brandon are just . . . I mean, it's high school. Not love."

The light turned green and Avery waited to make sure the intersection was clear before pressing on the gas.

"Just wait until you're in college. I think those years are the best in a girl's life." She'd met Jared in college, but her first two years had been parties and dates and fun without real responsibility.

"You can't be serious?"

"Of course!" Charlene laughed at the disbelief in Avery's voice. "It's the first time you'll be on your own and have a certain amount of freedom. Once you're married, that's gone."

"I'm not getting married, Charlene. The idea of college is hard enough." She blew out a breath that ruffled her bangs.

"I said the same thing to my parents, believe it or not.

Then I met Jared. Anyway, the college years are a time to look forward and make something of yourself. Dream big and work hard, that's the key to success."

Avery gave her a half-smile as she pulled into the driveway of the teen house. "You're one of the most optimistic people I've ever known. No, scratch that. You're number one."

Charlene shrugged, but she was pleased that Avery thought so. "I try to choose to be happy, every day. Even when it's hard. Like dealing with Sheffer's rudeness. I'm not perfect, but I try."

"Janet says that's the most important thing."

The outdoor porch light was on, but only a few upstairs bedrooms showed others inside. The pair got out of the vehicle and met at the stairs. Charlene could see that Avery had more on her mind.

"Okay. Out with it." She rested her hand on Avery's shoulder and looked her in the eye. "What did you want to discuss with me?"

"I—what if I don't want to go to college?" Avery's glance slid to the stairs of the teen house. Charlene did her best not to react. Was this really worrying Avery? "I just don't think it's right for me. It's a lot of money and then I'd have student loans when instead I could be earning a living. Even sharing an apartment with Jenna will be expensive."

Charlene kept her hand on Avery's shoulder. The poor girl had no parents acting on her behalf. No nest egg waiting for her when she finished high school. No support of any kind.

Her parents had funded Charlene's schooling and she'd only had to work for pocket money. Gifts from graduation and grandparents had allowed her to buy a car.

No loans to pay back. Once she'd graduated, she'd gone straight to work at the ad agency with no debt.

There was a world of difference.

Charlene reached for Avery's fingers. "Avery, I'm not rich by any means, but I will help you the best I can. If you stay locally you can continue to work for me. Or if you go out of state, you can stay with us for all your holidays, including the summer months. You'd have a summer job and be able to save. You know how much Minnie and I would love to have you."

"What if I didn't go to college at all? Would you be disappointed?" Avery held her gaze. "It's kind of like driving. *You* want me to do it."

Was she pushing too hard? The last thing she wanted was to have Avery feel about her the way Charlene had about her mom. But she had to be honest too. "I will support you no matter what, all right?"

Avery sniffed and nodded. "But?"

"No buts. Facts: Without a college degree, you might have to work harder for less money to get the same financial stability as your peers. A minimal requirement for job seekers these days is a college degree or trade certificate, as you know. You've done the research, hon."

Avery's shoulders slumped.

Charlene didn't want to lose the open communication between her and Avery. "Your situation is much different than mine, but that doesn't mean you can't have the same outcome. Independence. If you don't do college, what other options are there?"

Avery turned back toward Charlene with a skeptical expression. "Fast food."

"That would bring in money, yes, if you didn't want to work at the B and B."

"Online courses, so I could work full-time and do classes on the side. I have to pay for my share of the apartment with Jenna."

"Yep. A lot of adults find that to be a good solution." Charlene kept her tone calm. It was important for Avery to go over her choices and understand that Charlene cared unconditionally. "It means you won't have the college experience, but if that's the route you choose, maybe we could ask Sam if there's a job at the station you could apply for, to pay the bills."

Avery's face lit up. "You would do that, Charlene?"

"Well, I hope I haven't spoken out of turn." The relief evident in Avery's body language made Charlene realize that she had to walk a fine line between being supportive and being pushy. "I don't know what positions are available."

"I'd mop and clean toilets if that gave me an in," Avery assured her.

Charlene lifted her chin. "I think we can hope for better than that. There's also a police academy, isn't there?"

Avery laughed. "That's a lot to consider! You're always looking out for me, Charlene."

She pulled the girl close for a hug. "And I will always have your back, all right?"

Avery climbed the stairs and put her key in the lock. Before going in, she waved and tossed her a kiss.

It was like she'd been tested and had passed with flying colors. Charlene smiled all the way home.

CHAPTER 14

When she arrived home, the Montgomerys had retired to their rooms and a note from Janice Shelton was placed on the kitchen counter.

Her guests were free to come and go, but this was sweet just the same. Sheffer might want to take notice.

Charlene, the rain has finally stopped so Dylan suggested we walk into town. Don't know when we'll be back, but don't wait up! We had a fun night, thank you!

They were such a nice couple. Dylan was a pharmacist and Janice worked in a dance studio for younger children. They had an eleven-year-old daughter named Hailey staying with the grandparents, as the little girl was in school.

They really missed her and Charlene wouldn't be surprised if they decided to leave early.

Charlene turned off a few lights, then entered the living room to collect glasses and check that the fire was banked.

She could see the shape of a head in Jack's chair and rushed over to tell him about Avery. But when the man turned, she was looking at Sheffer instead. Her warm feelings curdled.

"Oh! I thought no one was up," she said politely. "Did you enjoy your dinner?"

"I did." He steepled his fingers together at his crossed knee.

"Where did you go? Salem has a surprisingly high number of quality restaurants to choose from. Being so close to Boston doesn't hurt."

"Turner's Seafood." He added drolly, "I had the rack of lamb."

She chuckled, determined to find out more about this enigmatic man. "What? You're not a lobster lover?"

"Depends. Tonight I was in the mood for a very rare rack of New Zealand lamb."

"Do you mind if I pour us both a drink and chat awhile? This is one of my favorite parts of being a hostess."

He didn't say yes or no, just, "Scotch neat for me, please."

Charlene selected a crystal tumbler for Sheffer and poured the amber scotch two inches. Her dark red had a similar oaky scent as she filled a glass of cabernet for herself.

He stayed in the chair by the fire, his hooded gaze

watching her. She gave him his tumbler. He wore no rings of any kind.

She kept her voice light. "I've been here two years and never had dinner there. Lunch a few times, but . . ."

He lifted his glass and said, "Cheers." She did the same, but they didn't clink, just sipped.

"I'm sorry for getting off on the wrong foot earlier."

He nodded.

"Tell me a little about yourself." Charlene settled back on the sofa. "What kind of business are you in?"

"The none-of-your-business kind." His mouth lifted in a smile that didn't reach his eyes. "Sorry."

She bit her lip. The man was beyond rude. Why stay at a bed-and-breakfast if you wanted a motel experience? And avoided your mother's. "I didn't mean to be nosy. Just making conversation. Most people like to talk about themselves."

He chortled at that. "True observation. I'm not one of them."

Hmm. How to draw him out? She could share a little about herself, she supposed, and hope to lower his guard.

"My parents are arriving from Chicago tomorrow. That's where I'm from, born and raised."

He sipped his drink and watched her over the rim.

She squirmed a little.

Nothing ventured, nothing gained. She lobbed an arrow in the dark. "My guess is that you're an auditor and with tax time coming up, you probably need to visit places of business and make sure everything is on the up-and-up."

"You think I'm a tax auditor?" He snorted with laughter. "Tell me why?"

"You don't talk about yourself. You don't seem to care about the tours in Salem, which is the main draw for most people."

Sheffer raised his hand. "All right, all right. I am not a tax auditor. This could be a fun game, Charlene." He got to his feet. "Thank you for the drink."

"Night."

She shut everything down, but left a few lights on in most of the rooms. She would never let people come in at night in the dark. Hers was a welcoming place.

Charlene went to her suite, eager to catch up with Jack. Her ghost wasn't around so she went to bed, where Silva waited for her. She fell asleep but dozed with strange dreams. No, *nightmares*. Her mother rifling through her room, searching for Charlene's secrets. Jack watching, amused. If her mother ever suspected the bed-and-breakfast was haunted and that Charlene saw Jack, Brenda would have Charlene committed.

Sheffer waiting with a predator's grin, demanding an audit.

Would this night ever end?

Her nose twitched as sunlight peeked through her blinds to say hello. She stretched and yawned, feeling relieved that it was morning at last. What was that smell?

Silva pounced on top of her with a mouse squirming in her mouth.

Charlene let out a scream and pushed both cat and mouse off her bed.

Minnie pounded on her door. "Are you all right?"

"Come in," she called, stepping gingerly around Silva, who seemed happy torturing the poor little mouse. Like a Tom and Jerry cartoon, except it turned her stomach to watch.

"What is it?" Minnie asked.

"Silva caught a mouse." Charlene retrieved a broom and dustpan, along with a trash bag, and returned to her room. Silva purred in satisfaction, one paw on the mouse tail.

"What happened to her bell?" Minnie fretted, wringing her hands.

"That cat got out of her collar again. She's Houdini with that thing."

Minnie opened the door leading to the back porch and garden. "Try to get them out this way," she suggested.

Charlene positioned herself behind Silva, who had the mouse in her mouth again. "Go, go, go!" She shooed the Persian toward the open door.

Minnie helped the fat cat out, then slammed the door closed.

"Oh, that bad cat! Minnie, I'll need to get a new collar today. Again." Charlene peered out the window to see Silva staring at her with wide yellow orbs, swishing her tail as though she deserved praise, not punishment. "She's not even sorry!"

Minnie laughed. "She's a huntress, wanting to give you gifts."

"Well, I'll be out in a few minutes. I need to wash the remnants of the gift off. Ew!"

"That's fine. Mr. LaCroix was down early. The Montgomerys are upstairs but awake, and I haven't seen head nor tail of the Sheltons."

"They went out last night so might have gotten home late."

"Take your time!" Minnie walked out of the suite and shut the door.

After a quick shower, Charlene put her hair into a

ponytail, then slid into her best blue jeans and a white T, followed by a flannel shirt left open. If she decided to go to the funeral service it wasn't until eleven. Her mind was not made up as she walked into the kitchen—no Jack in her suite.

"We heard a scream!" Layla jumped up from the table when Charlene entered the dining room. "Were you hurt?"

"No, sweetheart!" Charlene didn't want to share about a mouse in the house, so she settled on a white lie. "I had a spider in my room. I'm a big sissy when it comes to spiders!" She made a frightened face and the parents laughed. "Who won charades?"

Layla said, "The Sheltons!"

"Did I hear my name?" Janice smiled as she and Dylan took their seats at the dining table.

"We were just complaining that you won last night," Jason said.

He tossed a bagel toward Dylan, who caught it, smacked it on the table, and called, "Touchdown!"

They'd become fast friends and Charlene felt a little regret when Dylan informed her that they'd decided to take a night flight home.

"Our bags are packed and we figured we could take in a few tours, have an early dinner, and catch the flight to Michigan that leaves at eight."

Charlene nodded. "I know you spent five days in Boston before coming here, so you must be anxious to get home and see your daughter."

"We are." Janice glanced at her husband. "First time away for a week's vacation and we thought we could handle it, but it was a little too much. Hope this isn't a problem for you, Charlene. Your place is stunning. It's just—"

Dylan stepped in. "Hailey started to cry when we spoke to her last night. It's time to come home."

Minnie popped her head in. "Sorry to intrude, but the two ladies who were expected at ten are running late."

"Thanks, Minnie." Charlene stood. "Janice and Dylan, have a great day. You're free to leave your luggage in the foyer behind the stairs if you'd like."

"That would be a huge help. Thank you!" Janice said.

"Not at all. We hope to see you again someday—and bring your daughter!"

Charlene went into the kitchen to speak with Minnie about the suitcases. And the church service. "Should I go, Minnie? I was staying to check in the ladies, but if they aren't here, I have time to go and pay my respects."

"That's important," Minnie said. "Especially if you want to make a friend of the woman accountant. I'll get the blue room ready for your parents. With the Sheltons leaving early, that gives us an extra suite if someone calls."

"And that single room. We usually just have the one." Charlene had an idea about that, but she wanted to talk to Jack. She eyed the time on the stove: Nine.

"I'm going to the service, Minnie."

"Good! I can handle things here."

Despite the best of intentions, Charlene was running late. At least it wasn't raining. She dressed in black pants and a blazer, suitable for the church where the service was being held. The funeral at the cemetery would be directly afterward, with food at Shannon's. She had no intention of being there for that or she'd be late to pick up her parents in Boston at three.

After the conversation with Avery in the car, she

couldn't stop thinking about offering Avery a room permanently.

"Jack?" she whispered from her living room. She hoped he hadn't expended too much energy helping her with the Gallagher and O'Brien investigation.

What would he think of adding to their household? She knew he considered Avery one of the team. Would Avery even accept?

Since she and Jack were permanent roommates, she had to ask first. He cared for Avery, just as she did. She left the suite in a rush.

"Finally out the door, Minnie," she said as she stepped into the kitchen.

"I made you a to-go cup of coffee. Isn't the service in twenty minutes?"

She accepted the steaming metal cup. "Yes. Thank you."

"Welcome. If you get held up, we can send Will for your parents. Just let me know."

"Thank you, but I'll manage. My mother wouldn't forgive me if I wasn't there."

Minnie patted Charlene's arm with a commiserating *tsk*. "Their last visit in the summer was really lovely."

"I kept Mom too busy to complain." They'd done a lot of tours and fun things that Charlene had also enjoyed. Summer in Salem was gorgeous.

Charlene shouldered her purse and swept out of the house to her car, juggling keys and coffee. She counted it a miracle that she didn't spill anything on her suit.

She drove around the block twice and then lucked out with a spot across from the church. The church parking lot was packed. From what Shannon had said, Connor wasn't popular, so this must be the Irish community banding together to send off one of their own.

Charlene counted many redheads in varying shades, from strawberry blond to auburn among the mourners as she filed inside. She chose the back pew, as it was the best place to observe the crowd. At least a hundred people were packed inside.

She spied Shannon in the second row, sitting with Aiden. On Shannon's other side was a man who greatly resembled the deceased Connor, though his longish red hair had faded and was thin—just like his frame. He had the same pale skin as Shannon. The same nose.

Finn, she guessed.

Shannon must have coerced him into leaving his home somehow. Had Connor returned to Salem to apologize to Finn? Maybe Connor wanted to make amends for whatever had happened five years ago.

Would Finn have agreed to see his cousin and forgive whatever trespass he'd committed? Shannon seemed to think that Finn was in the right. Why had Shannon and Connor argued at the AOH?

Finn's jaw was clenched and perspiration shone on his forehead as if the man was uneasy—which could be from being in public after so long alone. Charlene had done a paper on agoraphobia in college. Maybe Finn suffered from a form of mental illness that could be helped if he saw a professional. Shannon could have her brother back if she could get him to therapy.

Shannon whispered something to him. The man nodded and bowed his head. Aiden studiously ignored the proceedings, and the coffin in front of the church, by reading his phone.

Behind Shannon sat Sinead and a blond girl who was probably her sister. She assumed the red-haired man sitting next to the older blond woman was James, the youngest brother, and Cindy, his wife. They owned the pub. James and Cindy had the splotchy skin tones and veined noses of those who liked the nightlife, which was in deep contrast to Shannon's porcelain skin.

In the fourth row was Liam Kane. Charlene shivered.

A woman with red hair partially covered with a black scarf viewed Connor in the coffin. She studied Connor's face and smoothed her finger over his forehead. She pressed her knuckle beneath her nose, sucked in a quivering breath, then sank into the first pew. She kept glancing around nervously—especially at Liam, who glared at her. Sad blue eyes were set in a worn face. She clutched her purse in her lap.

Shannon leaned forward over the pew to speak to her. The woman continued to cry, and Finn offered her a tissue from a box.

Was that Patty Gallagher Kane?

A man in a dark-green checked fedora passed by the coffin and stopped to bow his head at Connor's body. Dark brown hair, short, was visible above a pale nape. Finn stared at the figure in confusion and watched as the man in the leather coat went around to find a seat in the center of the church.

The next person she recognized at Connor's body was Gil. His thin brown hair had been slicked back. He sat behind Aiden.

Finn rose to look into the pews, his face red, but Shannon pulled him down.

A tall man in a black trench coat also walked around to pay his respects, studying Connor before moving on to the other side of the church. Sheffer LaCroix. What was *he* doing here?

"Can I sit with you?" a masculine voice rumbled.

Charlene's heart jumped to her throat. It was Sam. *Of course*. She'd seen him observe services before.

"You may," she said, scooting closer to the woman on her right. "Have you found the killer?"

"I wouldn't be here on a Friday morning if I had," he murmured. Sam looked very handsome in a dark gray suit. His brown eyes settled on her and his mustache twitched.

"What?" She folded her hands primly on her lap.

"Your sweet expression doesn't fool me, Charlene. I saw you checking out the family. Who do you think did it? They might be here right now."

"I'm sure I don't know," she answered softly. *Yet.*

Sam sat back against the pew and murmured, "Do you know the players? O'Briens and Gallaghers."

And Liam Kane. "I've met some of the family, yes."

"Is that the official reason you're here?" His brow rose. "For a certain member of the family."

Charlene could hardly take offense, since he was right on the money. "Shannon invited me."

"Shannon Best. Aiden's mother."

"That's the one. She's worried that you still think Aiden is guilty or connected somehow. Also, she was an O'Brien before she was a Best. Connor's cousin."

The woman to Charlene's right scowled at them over her prayer sheet. Connor's face was on the front. Pale skin, blue eyes, bright red hair.

"Aiden Best remains a person of interest." Sam lifted the prayer sheet from the pew to read the inside. "I know you cleared him from being the attacker."

Which meant that there was more to the story that Sam wouldn't share. What did she expect?

Charlene turned to Sam. "Hard to believe that Connor and Finn were only two years apart. Finn seems ancient."

"Finn O'Brien is here?" Sam rested his arms on the pew ahead of him and whispered, "Where?"

"I think that's him in the second row, sitting next to Shannon. I've never actually met him."

Sam peered around the full pews to see up front. His forehead furrowed. "I've been trying to get an interview with the man but he never answers the door."

"His sister says he's a recluse." Charlene shifted on the hard pew bench and lifted the prayer sheet from the shelf in front of her, next to the Bibles and songbooks. "I guess he used to be friendly, but now he doesn't like to leave home."

"She hasn't mentioned that to me. I just have a few questions that he might be able to answer. He can stand on his front porch for all I care."

"Like?"

His gaze turned crafty when he faced her. "You won't be catching me out like that, Ms. Morris." Sam had the audacity to wink at her when she gave an involuntary huff. "Something to do with an old case."

She hefted her chin, refusing to be charmed by his flirty refusal to share information. "If it's an old case, what can it hurt?"

He smoothed his mustache and continued to survey the crowd.

"I saw Sheffer here, Sam. I don't like the man and I think he's up to something. Do you realize that he told me it was none of my business when I asked what he did for a living?"

Sam covered a chuckle with his fist, then scanned the crowd. "Sheffer's here?" He shook his head. "I don't see him."

"See? Who would come in to view the body and then leave? That's weird, you have to admit. I don't care if you are both Yankees fans."

"You wound me, Charlene. I'm Red Sox, through and through." Sam sat back and pulled his phone up to read the screen before dropping it back in his suit jacket pocket. He wasn't wearing a badge.

"Well?" she prodded. "He was at the pub the other night, watching Aiden. When I told you that, you didn't care, but I think something's fishy."

"Listen, I know you get yourself involved in these situations, and I know by now that you won't stay home or stop asking questions. Trust me when I tell you that I am close to finding who attacked Connor, so you don't need to worry."

Charlene fidgeted, admitting to herself that there had been times when her curiosity had put her in danger, and Sam didn't like it. Would he admit that she'd helped him solve his cases? Oh, no. She was tempted to go sit in another pew, but they were all full.

Sam tapped her arm with the prayer sheet. "Will you be at the cemetery?"

"I hadn't planned on it. My parents are coming in this afternoon."

"Oh?" His grin stretched from ear to ear. "Too bad. I was going to offer you a ride."

She searched his face—was this Sam, offering to share information? Or was he suggesting it because he figured she'd say no? Well, the joke was on him. "In that case, I would love to go."

He tilted his head in mock disbelief. "Going to have Brenda and Michael take a taxi? Charlene. Shame on you."

"They don't get in till three. I can make it." She peered at him with suspicion. "What do you really want from me?"

"Let's not go there," he suggested, eyes flashing with mirth.

Their conversation was halted when the priest began the service. The woman to Charlene's right sniffed to show her disapproval of their chatter.

Charlene, not Catholic as Connor had been, went through the motions of the service with prayers of her own for Connor and his family.

Sam's jacket pocket vibrated with his phone and he slipped out of the church to read the text.

Had this to do with the case? Would he still go to the cemetery? By the end of the service, Charlene was one of the first out and she searched the sidewalk for Sam's dark brown hair. Around six foot six, he was easy to see.

She waved when he caught her looking.

"Car's over here," Sam said.

She got inside the dark blue SUV and buckled up. "Everything all right?"

Per Sam's usual style, he told her nothing about the text message. "I'd love to pick your brain on who else you knew in the church."

"Other than Shannon and Aiden?"

He pulled into traffic headed toward the cemetery. "Yeah."

"Well. Gil, the guy who dresses up as a leprechaun every Saint Paddy's Day at the AOH. Sits on a big pile of gold. You've already questioned him."

Sam peeked at her, then returned his attention to the road.

"What?"

He shook his head.

Typical. He wanted information from her but wouldn't give her any. She sighed. She couldn't take it personally—this was about finding who killed Connor so that Shannon and her family could have peace of mind.

"Tell me about this pot of gold Gil protects."

"It wasn't real," she laughed. "They were plastic gold medallions mixed in with chocolate coins. The little boy staying with me that night was so excited. He wanted to catch the leprechaun because then he would have a never-ending supply of gold."

"Is that how the legend goes?"

"We Googled it. You catch a leprechaun, then you can barter his freedom for his gold—or some say that you can get three wishes."

"What would you do? Take the wishes, or take the gold?"

She sat back in consideration. "I'll have to get back to you with my answer. It's too much to think about right now. I mean, gold is great, but what could I accomplish with three wishes?"

Sam grinned at her.

"What about you?" She lobbed the question back at him.

"I'd take the pot of gold and convince you to give up your life as a bed-and-breakfast owner to travel the world with me."

"Sam!" Her heart skipped. Sam followed the road, at ease behind the wheel. She wanted to tell him about Avery and thank him for his help, but not now while he was in investigator mode.

"Luckily for you, there is no such thing as a leprechaun," he said. "Now, could Gil be the attacker?"

"I don't think so." She held up her hand to around the five-eight, five-nine mark. "He's too small."

"Aiden Best, then. Five-ten and a half."

Charlene looked out the window to the slow traffic heading toward the cemetery. "Too tall. And slim. Not bulky enough."

"Bulky? Is that a real descriptor?" He dimpled at her.

"Don't mock me, Sam, or I won't tell you another thing." She kept her tone teasing, but she wasn't really. Those dimples were a secret weapon.

"I'm sorry." He sounded contrite, so she nodded.

She pushed her luck a bit and asked, "Did you find out from Gil why he and Connor argued?"

He rubbed his smooth chin as if thinking, then tossed her a bone. "Yes. Over Connor being drunk and demanding a meal without a ticket."

"Shannon said that Connor had left Salem five years ago after an argument with Finn. I got the feeling it was due to his love for booze."

"Shannon wasn't the only one to mention Connor's drinking problem." Sam snickered. "Aiden stressed that his cousin had many enemies."

"But you think Aiden is trying to take the heat off of himself."

"Exactly." Sam tapped his thumb to the wheel.

"I'd love to know why Aiden wanted to drop out of med school." Charlene shifted on the seat to get comfortable.

Sam glanced at her to see if she was serious. "Told me yesterday afternoon when I dropped by their house with a few questions that he needed money."

Charlene frowned. "He sure was spending it at the pub a few days ago. Then again, his uncle James owns it, and his cousins bartend, so . . ."

"I don't believe it," Sam said, skillfully maneuvering through traffic. "When he gave that excuse, Shannon's jaw dropped in surprise. No, I think he knows something but he's being very tight-lipped. The entire family is hiding secrets. Starting with Finn."

Family secrets. Maybe all families had them.

People would do a lot to protect those secrets.

"I found out the scary Liam from the pub's last name. It's Kane."

Sam blinked but kept his gaze steady on the road. "Who?"

Charlene realized he was covering. "Liam Kane," she repeated. "Connor's sister Patty's husband. It's possible he had something to do with Connor's death. I—" She stopped herself from saying that she and Jack had found out he'd been in jail.

Talk about a secret that needed protecting!

"Can you confirm Liam as Connor's attacker?"

"No." Charlene rubbed her arms. "I find him terrifying, that's all. He's got prison tattoos." She tapped her upper cheekbone by the eye.

"You never fail to surprise me," Sam drawled. "How do you know that?"

"I looked up what tattoo teardrops meant online. There's an entire prison subculture on television too. *Orange Is the New Black*, *Making a Murderer*—"

"I get it!" He scowled at her. "Stay away from anyone in real life with those kinds of tattoos."

"Not a problem." She crossed her ankles. "Anyway,

Liam was at the service. Pretty sure his wife was too. Patty. She didn't sit with Liam. Finn gave her a tissue."

Sam didn't comment. Charlene hated how he was able to keep his cards close to his chest. Unlike her.

He parked and removed the keys from the ignition, facing her. "This is why I wanted to be with you at the funeral. I want you to tell me who is who. I knew you'd know, Charlene. You usually do."

CHAPTER 15

Charlene crossed the grassy lawn of the cemetery, her heels sinking into the damp earth. People milled around the burial plot where Connor's coffin would be lowered into his final resting place. Sam's hand rested at her back to steady her.

The priest was tall and thin with a full head of white hair that looked premature on his younger face. His hands were folded in front of him, eyes to the ground as he navigated through the small group of mourners braving the windy weather. He held a Bible and was speaking to the family as they waited for all the mourners to gather.

Shannon held a tissue to her eyes. Finn patted her arm and Aiden chatted with Sinead. Chairs were on the side of the open grave. Patty, Connor's sister, slung her purse onto one. Tears trickled down her cheeks. Liam approached her, but she turned her back on him.

A large arrangement in a cross shape hung next to Connor's picture. A green-and-white banner with *AOH* was visible.

"I bet Shannon took care of the flowers," she murmured to Sam. "She's the accountant for the Irish club."

Sam looked down at her with a twinkle in his eyes. "It impresses me how quickly you get to know people. Want to give our condolences to the family? I'd love to meet Finn."

Friends and family were clustered around Shannon and Patty. James joined them with his brood.

"Should we wait until afterward in the receiving line? The priest looks like he wants to get started."

Sam eyed the overcast sky as a raindrop fell. "Probably before it starts to pour. You're right. I need to speak with him, that's all."

Charlene watched as her Realtor made his way through the mourners, stopping to chat with almost everyone. Ernie still wore an awful toupee, although his brown suit was better tailored than what she remembered. He had a veiled dark-haired woman on his arm. Had he married since the last time they'd talked?

The couple turned toward her and Sam. Charlene smiled brightly and waved her fingers at them.

"An admirer of yours?" Sam teased.

She nearly choked as she swallowed her laughter. "Not in this life. That's Ernie Harvey, the Realtor who sold me the bed-and-breakfast."

"They seem to know almost everyone here." Sam stroked his mustache. "He must be successful."

She thought of how he'd sold his mother's old house to build a gas station and made millions. "Yes, but he's also a bit of a snake."

"Was he shady with you?" Sam narrowed his gaze at the Realtor and tucked his hands in his pockets. She missed the warmth of his touch on her back. "Let me know and I'll see what I can do."

Charlene thought about Jack and couldn't answer honestly. Sam didn't believe in the paranormal, therefore ghosts and her haunted mansion were off the table. "It's nothing."

Ernie patted the hair of his toupee as it fluttered in a breeze. He took a bouncy step toward them and flashed a toothy smile. His companion was at least six inches taller than Ernie, and she had her arm locked through his as they made their way across the grass. Her long black skirt trailed behind her.

"Come on, Charlene. I can tell you don't care for him and I trust your judgment."

She peered up at Sam in surprise. "You do? All right, then." Charlene shifted so her shoulder was to Ernie. "The day he handed me the keys to my home, he was very skittish and would hardly come into the foyer. When I asked if anything was wrong, he just said that it was nothing. The house had been empty for the past couple of years, so I might hear it settling. I asked why it had been empty, and the little weasel told me it was haunted. Then he ran out!"

"Leaving you alone in a strange place after that ridiculous bombshell? He's a worm. That must have been very frightening."

"It was. I won't ever forgive him."

Sam put a large hand on her shoulder in commiseration. "I remember how sweet and innocent you were when you first moved to Salem. Yet you were spunky too. Still are."

"A lot has changed, hasn't it? I've made Charlene's into the classiest bed-and-breakfast around—despite Ernie." She saw someone else talking to Ernie and smiled. "Oh, there's Archie."

Sam turned so they both faced the couples. "Do you know all the men in town?"

"Of course not. But he owns the secondhand shop, Vintage Treasures, where I bought a lot of my antiques. The mirror over the fireplace, the telescope for the widow's walk, and the shell that sits on a pedestal next to the front door. He's really helped me fill out the décor."

"Who else do you know that might be a player in Connor's death? What about the blonde?"

"The older one is Cindy O'Brien. She's married to James, Finn and Shannon's younger brother. They own the pub where I met their daughter Sinead. She was very sweet and talkative. It's also where I met Liam Kane, who is hovering around Patty by the graveside."

"I met Sinead when I interviewed her the other day."

Charlene gestured with a tilt of her head to where the family gathered with the priest. "See Aiden? He's talking to Sinead, and the younger blonde is probably her sister, Gwynne."

Cindy shouted at James, then shoved his shoulder in anger. "You ask your brother or sister, or I will!"

"Stay out of it, Cindy," James yelled.

Sinead grabbed her sister's arm and hitched her chin toward where their parents screamed at each other. The girls side-hugged in tears and Charlene's heart went out to them. What could be so important that James and Cindy would put on such a distasteful scene in front of everyone?

Charlene and Sam exchanged a look and Charlene

shrugged. Despite Sam thinking she knew everything, she had no idea what they were arguing about.

The priest, Bible in one hand, arm outstretched, approached the couple and spoke quietly. Cindy flounced off and James stood there, his face flushed, speaking with the priest, who put a hand on his shoulder before moving on.

Cindy joined her daughters, who embraced her in comfort. Was this something that happened often in the O'Brien household? James stayed next to Shannon, who murmured something, but he shook off her hand.

"Let's begin," the priest said to those gathered around the trees. "If the family will be seated."

Two rows of white chairs took up the small lawn between them and the casket to the side of the hole. Patty reluctantly sat next to Liam, on the far end. Shannon was by Patty, and Finn and Aiden were on Shannon's other side. James, Cindy, and their daughters sat in the row behind Shannon. James tried to take Cindy's hand, but she jerked it away.

Charlene and Sam moved closer to hear the priest and she again noticed the ruddy complexions of James and Cindy. Like Connor had. And so would Aiden if he carried along this path of partying too hard. Gil stood behind the row of chairs with others who wore pins of the AOH on their lapels. A man in a checkered fedora stayed near the oak tree as if to pay his respects without participating fully.

She elbowed Sam and nodded toward the leather-jacketed figure on the edge of the mourners. "Maybe an old drinking buddy of Connor's?"

The gathering of around forty or fifty people fell silent as the priest took his place at the head of the plot. It was a gorgeous casket of polished maple with dark brass hinges, and when a streak of sunlight rested upon it, it gleamed like gold.

"Wonder who paid for that?" Sam asked. He remained by her side as he pulled dark sunglasses from his jacket pocket and put them on. All the better to spy with? She wished she had a pair. "Does Shannon have money?"

"She has her own accounting business, but I don't think they're superrich."

"Patty, then? What does she do? Look at the size of her diamond wedding ring." Sam squared his shoulders and clasped his hands loosely at his hips.

Charlene squinted to make out the sparkly gold ring, distracted by the cruelty in Liam's face, his clenched fists, and the hard looks he was giving Patty. "Could Liam have stolen it, before he went to jail? Maybe it was part of a heist."

"Anything's possible." His mouth twitched. "Did you just say *heist*?"

"What did he go to jail for, then?" Charlene countered. Would Sam tell her?

"It's public record, Charlene. As you know. I'll save you the time of looking it up—he served his full sentence for aggravated robbery in New York. Liam Kane is a bad dude."

"Thanks." She shifted as her heel partially sank into the soft grass. "Was that so painful?"

"You have no idea."

Ignoring Sam's caustic reply, Charlene studied the people saying goodbye to Connor. Liam was a dangerous man, but did he have a reason to kill Connor? Patty refused to look at her husband, even though he sat right next to her. She was angry at him and didn't care who knew it . . . though Charlene gave credit for them not having a loud shouting match as James and Cindy had done.

Shannon peered at the priest with an expression of duty stamped on her face. That familial sense of doing the right thing had missed Aiden, who kept nudging Finn and blowing into his ear.

Finn smacked at the side of his head, then realized it was his nephew and growled at the younger man to stop it.

"Are you watching Finn and Aiden?" Charlene asked in amusement.

Sam turned slightly toward the front row. Finn, in an attempt to distance himself from his annoying nephew, moved his chair closer to his sister. Without missing a beat, Aiden leaned toward Finn and said something that angered the recluse enough for him to get up even as the priest was clearing his throat to begin the ceremony.

"Finn!" Shannon tugged her brother back down to his chair. "You need to stay. This is family."

"Tell your son to leave me alone," Finn complained. "I've had enough, Shannon. You've spoiled him."

Shannon changed seats with Finn so that she sat between her son and her brother. Aiden smoothed the lapels of his black jacket and marched off, but not before stepping on Finn's toes.

"Aiden!" Shannon said to her son's stiff back.

What was going on in that family?

Gil followed Aiden and talked quietly to the younger man. After a strained moment, Aiden returned to the chair in the front next to his mother, and Gil went to his spot standing behind the rows. The man in the checked fedora must be a member of the AOH too, Charlene thought, as he stood behind them. Something gold was in the hat's brim.

"Let's get closer," Sam suggested in a near-whisper.

"Go ahead. We can split up and compare notes afterward."

His mustache twitched and he gave her a light chuff on the chin before leaving her to her own devices.

A feeling that someone was watching her trickled up and down her spine, making her skin tingle. She spun around. Not far from where she stood, maybe twenty yards, was Sheffer LaCroix. He had on black jeans and a trench coat and held a pair of binoculars to his eyes as he scanned the crowd.

When he caught her staring back at him, he lowered the binoculars and drifted away. She waved at Sam to get his attention, pointing to the tree where Sheffer had been.

Of course, when Sam looked, Sheffer was gone.

Where did he go? Why was he here? That was suspicious and Sam had to agree to dig into the man's background.

Charlene rounded the outer edges of the mourners to Sam, eager to let him know her instincts about Sheffer were correct.

"Don't touch me!" Patty shrieked to Liam. She tried to jump up but didn't get out of her chair.

Liam, the ex-con and bully, towered over his wife, his hand clamped to her shoulder. "Sit."

Patty quaked up at him in obvious fear as he glared at her. Liam's body was stocky. Could he have been the one on the stairs?

Charlene's stomach clenched.

She met Sam's gaze. He was behind Liam. Would he intervene and stop yet another argument at Connor's graveside?

Sam nodded to her and stayed in place. He would handle it if it went too far. Charlene excused herself between the friends and family watching Liam and Patty.

"This is horrible," she murmured to Sam when she reached his side.

"I know. They should be comforting one another instead of tearing each other apart. This doesn't make my job any easier."

"What do you mean?"

"They all have tempers. Who here has the most to gain by Connor's demise? That's the question I need to answer."

"Get out of here, Liam, until you can cool off," Shannon said.

"Don't interfere," Liam shouted. "You are not in charge." His gaze flicked to Finn, who stood to defend his sister.

"Calm down, Liam," Finn said in a strong voice, the opposite of his thin frame.

Liam spat down at Finn's feet. "Coward."

Patty shoved Liam back. "Please, Liam? We can talk afterward, just the two of us, all right?"

Liam raked his hand through his hair, took the cigarette above his ear, and shoved it unlit in his mouth before stalking off behind the trees.

The whole crowd seemed to sigh in relief.

It took a few minutes for the priest to get things under control. "Let's be seated, everyone. Is this what Connor would want? His family at odds? Peace, my flock. Peace."

Shannon sat down, as did Patty. Aiden grabbed the corner chair. James took Liam's seat in the front row. Finn was the only one of the family standing.

Sam surveyed the mourners and the trees in the old cemetery. "I don't see Liam or Sheffer."

Just then a strange noise whistled through the crowd. A firearm with a silencer? Charlene didn't have time to speculate as a loud *thwap* hit Finn with a sickening crack. He gasped and reached for Shannon, then stumbled backward against the casket.

He fell into the open hole meant for Connor.

CHAPTER 16

Charlene gasped in disbelief as Finn toppled out of sight, dragging with him the spray of gladiolas for Connor's coffin.

Sam held her close at his side so she didn't dart into the chaos. "Wait," he said softly. Charlene watched helplessly as Aiden peered down into the open hole, then dropped to his knees to try and pull his uncle up to the grass. His black jacket split at the seams from his effort. Shannon shrieked in horror, her hands to her mouth.

Gil appeared and grabbed Finn's other arm. Finn seemed to weigh a thousand pounds as the pair grappled with the unconscious man. Charlene was close enough to notice a giant red welt on Finn's temple. The recluse's eyes were open and his mouth slack.

James, realizing that something was very wrong, rushed to assist but ended up knocking Aiden into the hole. He backpedaled like a cartoon character but managed to grab a hunk of grass to keep from going all the way in himself. At last, all three men, and Finn, were on the grass. Finn was on his back. The three men panted around him.

Sinead broke into nervous giggles and her sister Gwynne elbowed her to shut up.

"Oh, no," Charlene murmured.

Sam whipped off his sunglasses and jammed them in his suit pocket, nudging her toward the priest. "Stay here out of danger, Charlene." He strode to the mourners gathered around an unconscious Finn. "Everyone, be calm."

"What's going on?" Shannon shrieked at James in a guttural keen. Her youngest brother wrung his hands, then reached into his suit jacket pocket for a flask, but returned it at Shannon's glare.

Sam took charge of the scene, dropping to his knees beside the fallen man. "Everyone back up. Nobody leave. Charlene, call 911."

Charlene immediately dialed for help and gave the information in a shaky voice.

She searched the crowd for Sheffer and spied the leather-jacketed figure in a checked fedora hustling away from the throng, against Sam's orders to stay. As the person ducked out of sight, she was reminded of the night someone had hurt Connor. Were those shoulders the same? He stuffed something into his back pocket as he hurried into the distance.

"Hey!" she called. "Come back!"

He didn't, of course. Should she chase after the person? The way he'd stood behind Gil she'd assumed he was part of the AOH.

Did someone have a vendetta against the O'Brien and Gallagher family? She had no time to ponder the situation as the ambulance arrived within moments. She waved to the driver and escorted the paramedics to Connor's grave-side.

Sam rose to make way for the medics. "No pulse. Visible injury to the temple but could be secondary from when he fell. No obvious bullet wounds."

Charlene went to Shannon's side as the woman gave a keening sound of grief. "Impossible," Shannon cried. "He didn't want to come out today. I forced him to do it. Said we had to support the family. He's the oldest by five minutes and he never let me forget it." Her shoulders shook with grief.

"Why didn't he want to come?" Charlene patted Shannon's arm consolingly.

Shannon seemed to realize what she'd said and clamped her lips together.

"He's a hermit," James told Charlene, leaving Finn's side as he was edged out of the way by the medics getting Finn on the gurney. He put his arm around his sister and squeezed her in a hug. "They'll help at the hospital, sis. Doctors work miracles every day."

That was true and Charlene prayed they'd be able to do it today for Finn. The paramedics trampled the funeral flowers in their haste to get Finn to the hospital.

"What a waste." Aiden watched the ambulance speed off, disappointment clear on his young face. "He could have had it all. Us too."

"Don't talk like that, Aiden. I mean it. He'll be fine," Shannon insisted. "He has to be." She covered her heart with her palm.

"He better be fine," Liam growled to Shannon. He'd returned at the commotion and who was going to stop him now? He wasn't doing anything legally wrong.

Sam spoke with the officers who'd arrived on scene, telling them to interview everyone at the cemetery.

"Not now," Patty said, in a show of bravado as she chastised her husband.

Liam lifted his hand as if to backhand her for talking, but realized where he was when Patty pointed to witnesses.

"Go ahead," she taunted. "You'll go right back to jail. I sleep a lot better when you're behind bars."

Charlene patted Shannon's trembling shoulder, but kept quiet so as not to draw attention to herself in the middle of the family drama.

Cindy stood next to James with anger in her eyes as she addressed the circle of family. "I think whoever killed Connor just took out Finn. Who is next, eh? You got an answer for that, Shannon?"

Shannon's knees shook.

"Why would our family be in danger?" Sinead asked, blue eyes wide as she locked arms with her sister.

"Shut it, Cindy," Liam said with a grunt.

"Or what? I agree with Patty." Cindy sneered. "Jail is the best place for you."

"And then who would save you?" He smacked his chest. "I did my time. So did Patrick. The only one of us who didn't was just hauled off to the hospital. You all better hope he stays alive long enough to tell me where—"

Shannon stood abruptly and shoved her finger into Liam's chest. "Quiet, Liam. No wonder you end up in jail. You jabber on like an idiot." Shannon didn't look at Charlene as she walked away from her family, her gaze on the road, where Finn had been taken away by ambulance. "I'm going to the hospital. Aiden, drive me, son? I can't bear it."

"Sure, Mom." Aiden picked up his mother's purse by the chair where she'd been sitting and slid her keys from the side pocket where she kept them.

In a strong voice, Shannon said to those gathered closest to her, "Sinead, Gwynne, tell the others. I've got all of the food prepared at the house. You all might as well come over and eat as planned."

The family mumbled assent.

Shannon allowed her glance to rest on Charlene. "Family only. You understand."

"I do." Charlene stepped back from the grieving woman, having seen a hardness that she hadn't before.

Beneath the sweet exterior was a woman with a spine of steel.

Charlene had come to the cemetery with Sam, so she had to stay while he was speaking with his officers. She joined Archie and his wife—the couple was with Ernie and his companion, who'd lifted her veil to reveal a youthful face and pretty smile. The ladies were in spirited conversation.

"Sad turn of events," Archie said when Charlene approached.

"It is." Who would want to kill the Irish family? Who was Patrick? Did this have to do with Liam's time in jail? How was Connor involved?

Ernie introduced the woman at his side and Charlene banked her questions for later with Jack. "Meet Moira McKenzie," the realtor said. "My fiancée. She's good friends with Patty Gallagher."

That would explain why he was there at the funeral. It

was much better than her fear that he was canvassing for real estate clients. She wouldn't put it past the slick salesman.

"Have you met Sandy before?" Archie asked. "My wife."

The older man was a flirt with a stream of silver-haired admirers at his antique shop. "I haven't had the pleasure," Charlene said.

Sandy and Charlene shook hands.

"Nice to meet you." Sandy exuded confidence despite her gray hair and extra padding. "Archie told me that your bed-and-breakfast is lovely."

"I think so . . . I've appreciated Archie's eye for just the right pieces. You're welcome to visit any time."

"Oh, how wonderful!" Sandy looked at Moira. "Want to come along to visit Charlene's? She's got that mirror I secretly coveted."

"It wasn't a secret," Archie said with a snort. "It didn't go with our house."

"Your house is too small," Ernie declared. "You let me know when you're ready to sell and we can get you something brand-new."

"I don't want new." Archie scoffed. "I like old."

Sandy rolled her eyes but took his hand with an affectionate squeeze. "Me too, darling. Good thing."

Moira laughed. "You two." She smiled at Charlene. "If you don't mind us coming by, truly? I'd hate to be an imposition."

"My house is my business. You're welcome." Charlene smiled back. "What do you do?"

"Oh, my dad owns the coin shop in town. I've known Archie and Sandy forever, it seems. Archie sends over the coins he finds. Dad keeps his eye out for antiques. They go to estate sales all the time."

Archie nodded while Ernie appeared faintly bored as he adjusted his toupee. Moira seemed closer to fifty while Ernie must have been at the far end of the decade, but there was no accounting for love.

"Do you know the Gallaghers and O'Briens well?"

Moira patted her shoulder-length hair. "Sure. The families are mainstays in the Irish community."

"Ernie mentioned that you're close friends with Patty. I'm so sorry about Connor. She must be devastated!"

And now Finn was in the hospital. Patty's brother, and Shannon's brother. The two attacks had to be tied to the families somehow. She glanced toward the mourners around the grave for Liam but didn't see him. She wouldn't be surprised if he'd decided it was better for his freedom to leave.

"She is, not that her louse of a husband will give her any sympathy."

"Are Patty and Liam—"

"I wish she'd divorce him," Moira said. "But he refuses to grant her one."

He'd been violent right here at the funeral. Why wouldn't Patty cite grounds of abuse to get a divorce without his consent?

"I see what you're thinking," Moira said, "but trust me. He'd kill her if she divorced him and she knows it. I tell her, he's gonna kill her anyway. Might as well be a free woman before she dies, right?" She chuckled at the morbid joke that wasn't at all funny.

"Can we go now?" the Realtor asked.

"Let's say goodbye to Patty." Moira looped arms with Ernie. "She's talking with Cindy."

Charlene glanced over at the few people who remained. The priest was comforting Sinead and her sister, Gwynne. There would be no funeral service today for Connor.

James was gone. Maybe he'd raced to the hospital to be with Shannon and Finn. Shannon had told her that the three siblings had grown up with the two cousins.

Sam strode across the grass in her direction. She stepped toward him with a small goodbye smile to the foursome she'd been with, and reached her hand to Sam.

"This is a mess, Sam. I can get a ride back to the church, so don't worry if you need to stay here." She'd left her car there, not thinking it would be an issue.

He frowned. "Officer Finch, Rodney, can take you on his way back to the station."

"You don't have to pull an officer away for my sake."

"I'm not." Sam unclenched his jaw. "I suspected something might happen, but not this—the man I wanted to interview is probably dead. The way things were going, I was thinking a brawl. You learn a lot from family fights."

The things one needed to know as an officer . . . Would Avery fit in, with all of the drama and violence? Charlene would worry every day that Avery was on the job.

Sam rubbed the top of his head. "I can't believe that Shannon and Aiden left. James too. I want to question that kid."

"To the hospital to see Finn. You don't suspect Aiden of this?" She put her hand on Sam's forearm. "He was right in front of you the whole time."

"Arguing with his uncle, who is now incapacitated. What about?"

"Don't know." Charlene tucked both hands in her jacket pockets. "Shannon had Aiden drive her to the hospital to be with Finn, in case he rallies. She said that Finn didn't want to be here today. And now . . ."

"Charlene, I hate to be harsh, but Finn is dead." Sam looked at her so there would be no misunderstanding. "I want to know what and who killed him." The skin around his eyes crinkled as he narrowed them. "I'm headed to the hospital to check on that body."

Sam was already stepping away as he spoke.

What was Sam searching for?

As she stood still, buffeted by the cool gray breeze, she recalled Connor also lying so still. She hadn't seen a wound on him.

Shannon had said brain injury. Jack had agreed that heavy drinkers had thinner blood, which could lead to brain bleeds. A stroke might equal death. Could Connor have had a head wound too? Charlene hadn't noticed at the time. Patty had certainly studied his face at the church. Had she noticed something off?

Charlene walked to the edge of the grave, studying the footprints and crushed flowers. The dirt was soft, which was why Finn had fallen inside. Connor's casket shone from where it waited to be put into the ground, on the other side of the hole.

Gold within the hole caught her eye and she peered closer. Was that a button, or something from the flower arrangement? No. It was round. A coin?

There'd been a gold chocolate coin in Connor's pocket. It was unlikely this would be chocolate. This medallion had a different, brighter sheen than the coins on Saint Patrick's Day. It had an eagle on it.

She backed up and reached for her phone, calling Sam as he reached his car parked on the street.

He answered with a curt, "Yeah?"

"Come on back and bring an evidence bag. Sam, there's something gold in Connor's grave."

She watched him look up from his car to where she stood, his gaze hard. "No joke?"

"No. I think it's a coin."

"Don't touch it. Don't move away from it. This might be the break I needed. Don't let anybody see it!"

Sinead started to walk toward her, wiping her eyes. Charlene ended the call. Cindy was speaking with Archie and Sandy. And there was Patty, leaning against her friend Moira. Ernie talked with a policeman.

Charlene shifted, torn from wanting to steer Sinead away from the shiny object in the hole and staying put as Sam had ordered.

The detective strode toward her with crime tape and stakes as well as a clear bag.

"Don't I know you?" Sinead asked in confusion after stopping right before Charlene. If the bartender glanced down, there would be the coin.

"Yes." She held out her hand, stepping one foot away from the edge. "I'm Charlene Morris. We met at your family's pub on Saint Paddy's Day."

"Oh yes. I remember now. I just hate it when I see a face and can't place it. It was when Aiden was stupidly celebrating quitting med school. Idiot."

"I thought he'd won the lottery or something. Lucky scratch ticket, maybe?"

"How would I know? If he did, I wish he'd pay his tab. The roof on the bar needs to be fixed and beer specials don't cover extras. Dad says the pub is me and my sister's inheritance, but we don't want it."

"Speak for yourself," her sister said, arriving at Sinead's side. "I'm Gwynne."

"Hi." Charlene stepped away from the hole as Sam arrived and placed the crime tape and stakes around it.

"What's going on, sir?" Gwynne hooked her blond hair behind her ear. Freckles were sprinkled across her nose and cheeks.

Sam peered up from where he knelt on the ground and opened his jacket to reveal his badge. "Detective Holden." He stood and took pictures of the area around the grave. "Charlene, isn't this where Aiden fell in?"

Oh no. Did Sam suspect Aiden of having the coin? It might have fallen from his pocket when he was trying to get out and his jacket split.

Gil and James had been near the hole too, James almost a third person to fall in.

She didn't think Aiden was guilty of killing Connor or Finn, but maybe he was involved somehow. And she wanted an explanation for why Sheffer had been around.

"Yes. You're right." She cleared her throat and leaned down to him to whisper, "Sam. Don't just focus on Aiden. Maybe look at Sheffer too."

Sam rolled his eyes and descended carefully on top of the mangled gladiolas from Connor's casket. He put on gloves and reached for the gold disk. Charlene tried not to be offended at his dismissal.

Sinead and Gwynne both looked into the hole. The rest of the people waiting at the funeral had gathered around them to see what was going on.

"Is that a gold coin?" Sinead asked.

Moira and Patty hurried to the scene. "It sure is," Moira said with assurance. Of course, she would know— it was her family's business. Patty gasped and clung to Moira.

Sam quickly put the bag with the coin in his pocket as if he wished he could make them all forget they'd seen it.

Fat chance of that, Charlene thought, surveying the folks around the open hole. They all wore expressions of curiosity.

Only Patty wore stark fear.

CHAPTER 17

Charlene pulled her gaze from red-haired Patty, a pretty woman even with her tears, as she cried into Moira's shoulder. Sam climbed from the hole and raised his hands. "If you haven't already given your statement to the police, please do, and then you will be free to go."

"What about Connor?" an older man asked. He wore a suit jacket and one of the AOH pins on his lapel. "Are we just supposed to leave him here?" He gestured toward the casket with a look of distaste.

"My officers will be in touch with the funeral home," Sam said. "And stay with Mr. Gallagher until the director arrives. Have you given your statement?"

"No," the man said, affronted as he spread his hands. "I don't know anything."

Sam gritted his teeth and Charlene felt sorry for him, trying to control a situation that defied logic. A man killed at his cousin's funeral. "I'll take your statement so you can leave."

A few of the men mumbled together but they formed a line and gave Sam their information that he duly recorded in an old-fashioned notebook he pulled from his pocket.

Moira passed a teary-eyed Patty to Cindy. "Call me later, darlin'," Moira said to Patty before leaving with Ernie, Archie, and Sandy.

Charlene walked around looking for an officer in blue with the name tag of Rodney Finch, but couldn't find him anywhere. Two officers, both female, remained at the cemetery. One spoke with the handful of people left, and the other woman stayed by the casket.

Sam caught Charlene's eye. "Where's Finch?"

She shrugged. "I can't find him. It's okay, Sam. I can walk or call for a ride."

Sam pulled out his cell phone and typed in a text. He signaled her forward, then raised his voice to the people drifting away. "This is an active investigation, everyone. We thank you for your cooperation."

The last of the people at the funeral dispersed, except for the police officers.

Sam touched Charlene's arm, but kept a professional distance. "I'll drive you to your car." He checked the time. "How did it get to be two? With any luck, you'll be at the airport with moments to spare to meet your parents."

"Don't you have to stay? I hate to put you in this situation."

"Nope." He glanced at her. "You didn't. Officer Finch is going to hate it a lot more." He unlocked the SUV from a few feet away with the key fob.

"Maybe I should flag down a cab to take me to the airport." She double-checked the time on her phone. She cringed, imagining her mom's reaction to Charlene not being there with bells on. "That might be the best solution."

"We're all good. I'll get you to your car and give you a police escort to the airport to make sure you're not late."

Her eyes widened. "A police escort? No way. My parents will have to pick up their luggage, and they don't move as fast as they used to. I'll text Dad so they know to wait outside their terminal."

"You'd deprive me of being the big shot with my siren blaring the whole way?"

"Sam. Thank you, but no." She opened the passenger door of the SUV and climbed in. "Who could predict a bunch of people falling into Connor's grave? Not your fault."

Once inside, Sam shut his door on the driver's side and started the engine. "Well, even if you are a little late, at least you'll have an excuse. Your parents will be entertained on the ride to your bed-and-breakfast."

"Good point. Mom loves all this crime stuff and whodunits. It will give her something to gloat about to her friends back home. Dad's different. He prefers more peaceful pleasures like art and museums and wanting me to keep safe."

Sam gave her a long look. "I agree with that."

His phone dinged with messages that he answered through Bluetooth as he drove. He organized a call to the funeral director regarding Connor Gallagher's unburied casket, had an officer head to the hospital until he could arrive for Finn, and instructed Officer Bernard to track down Liam Kane for further questioning, all as he navigated the small streets of Salem to the church where her SUV waited.

Charlene was very impressed, as she was not often privy to his quick decision-making. Jack would be completely surprised when she told him how capable Detective Sam Holden was in action. Jack liked to compare Sam to Inspector Clouseau from the *Pink Panther* movies. Though Charlene found Jack humorous, she always heartily defended her friend.

Friend? Was that what she and Sam were? It was all they could be so long as she lived with her sweet, clever Jack who never made her feel alone.

Sam pulled into the parking lot and parked next to her SUV. Charlene turned to face him, her hand on the door.

"I've been to a few awful funerals since I've been in Salem, but this one takes the cake."

He ran his fingers through his thick mustache, his dark eyes twinkling. "You've got to stop kickin' up so much trouble everywhere you go. Life used to be sane around here until a smart and sexy, and very *curious* female moved in."

Charlene lowered her gaze as a smile flitted around her mouth. "I shouldn't laugh but after poor Aiden fell in, then James—it was like a Shakespearean comedy."

She raised her eyes. Something warm simmered between them that she had to deny. One way to ruin this moment would be to ask about the gold coin he'd bagged for evidence in the hole.

Unable to do it, she opened the car door instead.

"Say hello to your parents for me."

Her mother and Minnie were Sam's biggest supporters, and he knew it. None of them knew about Jack. "I will."

"And no speeding! I'll put out an APB to make sure that no gorgeous brunette goes over the speed limit."

She gave him a light smack on his arm. "You wouldn't dare!"

His gaze suggested otherwise, and she blew out a breath as she slid from the car.

"I'll drop by in the morning, Charlene. Tell my favorite gal, Miss Minnie, not to go to any trouble."

Charlene partially closed the door, watching him as he watched her. "As soon as she knows you're coming, she'll start making the pastry for baklava."

Sam patted his flat belly. "That's the woman I should marry."

"You'd have to kill Will first. He loves her devotedly." She winked. "You don't want to spend the rest of your life in a cell with a guy like Liam."

Having gotten the last word, Charlene slammed the door before Sam could think of something else. His disgruntled expression made her smile as she got into her SUV and drove a measly three miles over the speed limit to the airport.

Charlene lined up in front of the terminal and sent her dad a text. She was glad that she'd beaten them outside.

I'm here!

Us too. Pop the hatch?

Charlene checked the sidewalk and sure enough, there were her parents, each dragging a small suitcase. She hopped out to help her mom and dad with their luggage and tossed it in the back. They all kissed hello then got inside.

"It's so great to see you both!" Charlene was surprised that she truly meant it. Had they aged in the last few months since she'd seen them? Was there more gray in her dad's hair, and was her mother's slightly whiter? "Did you have a good flight?"

"Yes. Except they didn't serve the nuts that I like," Brenda Woodbridge complained from the front passenger seat.

Dad leaned between them from the back. "I snoozed for an hour, it was such a smooth ride. The flight attendants looked like they'd just graduated high school rather than the old birds past retirement age."

"Hey!" her mom said. "You're no spring chicken, Michael."

Charlene chuckled at the image her dad painted. "It's good to know they can handle the exits in case of an emergency, instead of the passengers having to assist *them* off the plane."

Her mom snorted. "I'm not carrying some old crone. If she can't do her job, then, maybe it's her time."

"Mom!" Charlene left the airport and took the entrance toward Salem. Her mother never failed to get in a jab at someone.

"Brenda." Her dad shook his head, still leaning forward and slightly between them over the console. "You promised to be nice."

"I wasn't being mean," she tittered. "I just love the word. I read it in one of those books of yours on our last visit. An old witch is a crone, or an old woman."

Charlene didn't point out to her mother that her mom also fit the bill. "And yet Brandy's mother, Evelyn Flint, is a professor of history and very beautiful by any standard. She's a crone, according to her Wiccan community."

"You could probably join them, my dear," her dad said playfully to her mother. "They might give you an honorary membership for life."

Brenda huffed and swatted his arm. Michael gave Brenda a kiss on the cheek, then he sat back out of swatting range.

"Nothing's changed between you two," Charlene observed dryly. Now that she understood them more, it made her happy that they were happy.

Her mom patted Charlene's shoulder. "I've turned over a new leaf. You will be so pleased with how nice I can be." Brenda adjusted her sunglasses though the sky was overcast.

What could that mean? Charlene glanced in the rearview mirror and met her father's eyes. He gave her a wink and she smiled back at him, deciding not to pry.

"How was the funeral you went to?" her dad asked. "You weren't at all late."

Charlene gave them a recap of the funny bits, not wanting her parents to worry too much. As expected, her mother was full of curiosity.

"What an exciting life you lead, Charlene. A handsome detective with a mad crush on you, just waiting for you to say the word. Your bed-and-breakfast business is booming. You've made new friends." Brenda sighed and touched her rounded bosom. "I envy you a little."

The admiring tone in her mother's voice took Charlene by surprise and she swayed into the other lane.

"Charlene!"

At her dad's shout, Charlene righted the car and

avoided possible calamity. Her mother began a one-sided conversation about her church friends as Charlene mused over what had just happened.

Had she really heard admiration in her mom's voice? Charlene thought of the many junior high plays or soccer games when she'd looked for her mom's approval. Not once had she gotten it.

Instead, her mother's barbed observations struck her heart. Brenda would ask why Charlene had forgotten an important line after practicing for hours. Her mother would repeat it without a flaw. Why, Brenda asked, had Charlene come in fifth during track when she had longer legs than the others? And this one still stung—her mother's cool remark that if Charlene hadn't kicked the soccer ball into her own team's net, her team would have won.

Since Charlene's move from Chicago to Salem, she and her mother had made strides in their relationship and she hoped that this would be another inch or two forward.

When they turned into her driveway, Charlene let the old hurt go. This bed-and-breakfast belonged to her and nothing her mother or anyone could say would change her love for the place. They got out of the car and Charlene glanced at her mom, bracing herself.

Brenda strode to the white porch and gazed around the lawn. "Your plants are beautiful, honey. Did Will do the spring planting already?"

Hmm. Charlene relaxed her shoulders. "I wanted some marigolds and daffodils in by the porch and trees for Saint Patrick's Day since we had a full house. I love flowers. The weather will turn for the better soon and it will bring up our perennials."

"I hope we didn't put you out by coming here last-minute," her father said, carrying the suitcases to the porch. Brenda took one of the handles.

"It was perfect timing, actually. It's not the room with the view of the oak tree, though." Charlene opened the front door. The house smelled like lilies and blueberry pie.

As soon as her dad passed the threshold with bags in tow, Avery was on him. "Mr. Woodbridge! It's so good to see you again!"

"Call me Michael, Avery. We're way past formalities, aren't we?" Charlene squeezed her dad's shoulder in appreciation. That meant a lot to her and Avery.

"Sure, Michael . . ." Avery blushed as Brenda brushed past her. "Hello, Mrs. Woodbridge. Welcome back."

"Thank you, dear." Her mom paused by the bottom step to speak directly to Avery. "Do you mind helping us upstairs with the bags?"

Minnie came out of the kitchen, wiping her hands on a dish towel, cheeks rosy. "Hello again—you're just in time for happy hour. Why don't you go freshen up? You're in the blue room. Avery will show you the way."

"I don't need to freshen up," her dad said. "I'd love a relaxing drink."

"Have you seen the new bar?" Minnie asked.

"New bar?" her mom asked. "Where would you put it?"

Charlene had one hand on her mom's suitcase to bring upstairs with Avery, but was torn in wanting to show her parents her new accessory.

"I had Parker design it for us, especially for that nook in the living room. Minnie, why don't you show them while I get the room opened up?"

"I've got this," Avery said, taking the suitcase from Charlene. "Everything's ready for your parents."

Michael hooked his arm through his wife's while Avery easily handled both suitcases and rushed upstairs with the energy of a teenager. He kissed Charlene's cheek. "It's good to be home."

Her mom laughed. "Let's unpack and come back downstairs together, to see Charlene's new bar."

"You got it, my love!" Her parents walked up the staircase, side by side.

With a light heart, Charlene returned to the kitchen. "Everything looks amazing." She glanced at all the appetizers and plates and leftover Saint Paddy's Day napkins. "As usual."

Avery joined them. "Your folks are all settled, Charlene. Your dad gave me a ten-dollar bill."

"Start saving, my girl!" Charlene felt blessed as she smiled at her bed-and-breakfast family with her real family upstairs. "You know? I'm going to enjoy having them."

"Me too," Avery said. "At least your dad," she said in a lower voice with a guilty glance toward the stairs.

"Mom says she's a changed woman," Charlene murmured, "but let's wait and see."

Minnie snorted and gathered trivets for the hot food. Avery grabbed the forks.

"How was the funeral?" Minnie asked. "We can start happy hour if you want to change first."

Charlene realized she was overdressed. "Oh, just wait until I tell you what happened. Sam will be by in the morning, but it has to be a story for later, okay? I do want to get out of this suit."

Their eyes gleamed in anticipation. They both knew by now that when she made an announcement like that, it would be a story worth hearing.

Jack wasn't in her suite when she entered. She'd have to tell him later about Finn and the funeral. She shed her formal attire for casual jeans and a sweater, then hurried through the kitchen to the living room with the roaring fire, and the sound of laughter and conversation.

Charlene came to an abrupt halt when she spotted Sheffer in conversation with her father. What in the world was that man up to? Spying on Connor's funeral and then disappearing.

And yet her father was smiling, seemingly enjoying whatever Sheffer had to say.

She poured herself a glass of wine, then breezed up to them. "Hi, Dad. Sheffer. I see you two have already met." She gave Sheffer a long, hard look. "Heard you both laughing. Tell me what you have in common."

Her dad grinned as if Sheffer was a friend. "Told him how we'd run off every Saturday when you were a kid to crawl around the museums and investigate every nook and cranny. Never got tired of it, did we?"

Charlene relaxed at her dad's enthusiasm. "No. I miss doing that with you." He'd saved her from a lot of her mother's barbed comments that way.

"Sheffer here shares another love of mine—collecting government coins."

Her hand shook and the red wine splashed. Her dad collected quarters from each state and had books of them saved. Why did she think of the coin in the grave? Sheffer was also a collector?

Her dad took the glass out of her hand and offered her a napkin, then wiped her glass off with another. "Don't want to spill a red this good. Brenda and I were hoping to see the winery this trip."

Sheffer and Charlene continued to stare at each other.

He was connected to the coin and Connor's death somehow. She knew it.

"Sure, Dad."

"I'll go mingle," Sheffer said, turning away.

"Want to come with me, Dad?" She didn't trust Sheffer and would speak to her father in private later.

"Nope! There's your mother." He wandered toward Brenda like a homing pigeon to his roost. She and Jared had been like that.

Two ladies smiled at her and Charlene deduced they were the scholars from Rutgers, Carol and Linda, who she hadn't met because they'd arrived late. "Hello! Are you enjoying your visit?"

"We are so much!" the shorter one said, speaking for them both. "I'm Linda." They each had dark gray hair and wore no makeup. Eight inches separated them in height.

Charlene led the women to a smaller seating area next to the window. "Tell me about Rutgers! I considered it for a while." She took a sip of her wine without spilling a drop. The company was better, that was sure. "What brings you to Salem?"

"We're doing some research." Carol glanced at Linda. "We became friends when we met in the library one day. We're very interested in a new perspective on the witch trials."

Linda nodded. "I'm writing a book about the studies of the unknown. What exists all around us, another realm or reality that most people don't believe in. With my research, I hope to broaden people's minds to accept that what we see is only one dimension in multiple layers of consciousness." She pressed her fingers together like a pinch of salt. "A tiny thread to the mystery of life."

What would Sam make of these two women? In another time, would he have burned them at the stake?

"I find this fascinating," she confessed. She could tell them a lot about that unknown something, but she would never reveal Jack's existence. "And you?" Charlene looked up at Carol, who had to be five-ten.

"I'm doing this for my PhD. I need documented facts, but a new slant on this information that has never previously been published."

"It sounds so exciting," Charlene said. "And you're in the right place. Salem is loaded with history. If you need to stay longer, please do! I'm so interested I'll give you a great price."

They laughed. "We can't, but we'll definitely come back. What we're working on might take years."

"Then consider this your second home." Charlene stood up as she saw her mom behind the bar. "Can I get you ladies another drink?"

"Scotch and water for me," Carol said, passing Charlene her glass.

"And white wine would be great!" Linda kept hers. "We can help you, though—gives us a chance to mingle. It's an interesting group you have here."

"There's never a dull moment."

From the corner of her eye, she saw Jack motioning to her. Too bad she couldn't bring the two women over and introduce them to that new dimension they talked about. What a conversation that would be!

CHAPTER 18

Sometimes a group just really gelled, and such was the case with Charlene's guests tonight, except for Sheffer, who'd disappeared rather than go out to dinner with them all. Her parents were still entertaining in the living room with a last cocktail before bed.

Jack had heard about Finn's death on the five o'clock news and wanted to discuss details of that and the funeral. Charlene pleaded fatigue and joined her ghostly roommate in her suite around half-past ten in a state of shock.

"I can see why my dad fell in love with Brenda Woodbridge. She's sharp-witted and amusing without drawing blood." Charlene shook her head at Jack. Her mother had been kind and a lot of fun to be around. "Where was that woman all my life?"

Jack chuckled. "I'm sorry to pull you away. I couldn't

believe it myself just now. When Carol and Linda were going on about spirituality, that's usually a hot topic for your mom—her faith is the only faith—but no, she smiled and asked questions."

"I literally pinched my wrist to see if I was dreaming." Charlene showed the red mark to Jack, who brushed a cool, wavery finger over it as if to make it feel better.

"I wonder what happened to create the change?"

"I'm scared to dig too deep," Charlene admitted. She gestured to her open laptop. "What are you looking at?"

"It might be nothing." Jack shrugged. "Have a seat. It's been a long day and you didn't sleep well last night."

She perched on her chair with a grateful smile to Jack. Cindy and James O'Brien were in the open tabs on the screen. "Does this have to do with Pub 36?"

"Yes, and the research on James and Cindy you wanted," he said.

She sighed. "They were at Connor's funeral, fighting like mortal enemies rather than husband and wife in front of all the mourners. It was a fiasco. The priest had to step in."

"What on earth happened?" Jack crossed his arms and leaned his hip against the desk. The image didn't quite match, but she didn't mind. Charlene quickly brought Jack up to date while his eyes grew larger in surprise.

She shared about Finn getting attacked, the sound she'd heard, but there'd been no bullets. Sam's certainty that Aiden knew something regarding Connor's demise.

When Charlene reached the part about Aiden and James falling in Connor's grave, trying to get Finn out, Jack burst out laughing, his body shaking with mirth. He was so loud she feared someone might hear them, but then she remembered that he was a ghost.

Nobody heard him but her. "Shh," she said anyway.

With a flick of his fingers, he raised the volume on her television just enough to mask her voice. He liked to trick her into giving herself away. Minnie and Avery both thought she had a bad habit of talking to herself, something she'd invented as a cover story.

"I still think Sheffer is involved." Charlene believed Sheffer needed to be questioned. He exuded sneaky vibes and had been at the funeral with binocs and he'd disappeared before Finn had been killed. His comment to her dad about coin collecting raised all kinds of red flags to her. Her dad had said he'd brought up the subject, but she'd bet Sheffer had manipulated the conversation.

"You have good instincts, and Sam should listen to you. Don't ask me how—" Jack's brow wriggled, which meant he might have accessed a site that wasn't *exactly* legal—"but James and Cindy just filed a bankruptcy petition."

"Oh no!" Charlene vacillated between wanting the information and violating someone's privacy. "You didn't get into their bank records?"

"No. This will all be public eventually. And recent . . . as of two weeks ago. The first step is to file with the bankruptcy court, which they've done. They've gone to credit counseling and listed their debts. This is in the early stages, so it hasn't been approved or discharged yet."

"Sinead and Gwynne think they're getting the pub as their inheritance. Maybe their parents didn't tell them? Poor girls. This would explain why James and Cindy were arguing. That's a lot of pressure."

"We've learned that couples fight about money. Financial strain is the number-one cause of divorce," Jack said.

Charlene hoped their troubles didn't lead to that. She

read the petition of assets they wanted to reaffirm and keep. Home mortgage, yes. Car loan, yes. Business. Willing to sell the assets to pay off the debt.

She summarized, "They own the property the bar is on, so a sale could cover the debts that have accumulated. It says they owe money to just about every liquor distributor within sixty miles."

"Keep reading to the end. In the attorney's notes," Jack said.

She skimmed the document, and her heart froze in her chest. "Liam Kane gave a cash offer for the bar?" How on earth would a man who'd been in jail for the last fourteen years have a quarter-million dollars?

"This is very suspect," Jack said. "Don't you think?"

"Yes. I do." Charlene drummed her fingers along the edge of her desk. Did Cindy believe, as Aiden did, that Finn had money he wasn't sharing with the family? Cindy had demanded that James speak with Finn or Shannon. About the bankruptcy? Liam had told Cindy to shut her mouth, and asked who would save her . . . was he talking about the money for the pub?

Shannon was an accountant and could have helped them. Would the sale save the family from filing bankruptcy? Could Finn, as head of the household, have done more for them?

Charlene typed the name *Finn O'Brien* into her search bar, but nothing popped up. She turned to Jack behind her. "I think you should use your gift with cyber investigation to find out how Finn supported himself. Shannon said there'd been a tiny inheritance with the house, but that would have been over thirty years ago." Her brow scrunched. "Would Aiden inherit, if Finn died?"

Jack smoothed his chin. "I'll work on it tomorrow

morning. Liam offering to save the pub just rubs me wrong. What do we know about him besides the fact that he's a felon?"

"Well, he and Patty Gallagher are still married. She's got quite the rock." Charlene touched her bare wedding finger. "He's abusive—he threatened Patty in front of multiple witnesses today. I thought Sam was going to lose his cool. Patty seems nice enough. She's friends with Ernie's fiancée, Moira McKenzie. Her father owns a coin collector shop and is tight with Archie, at the antique shop. I met his wife too. Sandy."

"Sounds like a social event rather than a funeral. A coin collector?" Jack appeared thoughtful. "Interesting."

"Before today, I wouldn't have thought so." Charlene stood from the chair, ready to unwind. "There was a gold coin in Connor's grave—it must have dropped when the guys fell in—but out of who's pocket?"

"Aiden, James . . . who else?"

"Finn's. He was the first man in the hole. I'm sure it must tie in with the coin I saw on Connor the night he died."

Jack scowled. "The chocolate one?"

She held his gaze. "What if the one in Connor's jeans wasn't chocolate?"

Jack shimmered beside her. "What are you thinking?"

"I'm not sure. Two gold coins. I'd sure like to see them. Are they collector's items?" She wished she'd gotten a better look before Sam had scooped it up and put it in his evidence bag. "Dad collects quarters, and Moira's family owns a coin shop, so coin collecting must be a lucrative business. I always thought it was sketchy."

"I had a patient who collected buffalo nickels," Jack said. "You'd be surprised at what people are into. Coins don't have to be gold to be valuable. There used to be conventions. Course now, people probably just do most trading online."

A loose strand of hair tickled her cheek, so she tucked it back. "Buffalo nickels?"

"My patient said his collection was worth half a million, but he wouldn't sell for a full million. It was the joy of collecting that he loved." Jack grinned and rubbed his hands together. "Not a bad hobby."

"I guess not! Makes me want to empty my change jars."

"My hobby was wine."

"I prefer that to coins any day!" They shared a laugh. Charlene crossed the few feet from her desk to the love seat and sat down, facing the television. It was almost time for the eleven o'clock nightly news.

"Me too. Especially considering I had no family to leave my fortune to. I'm glad I drank most of my collection." His tone was borderline teasing, but she knew the hurt was there as he thought of how he'd died.

"I'm sorry, Jack." Charlene reached toward him, yet didn't touch him. She'd learned her lesson that his essence was bone-chilling the hard way.

They watched TV for a few moments in companionable silence. Charlene thought of Cindy and James. Aiden. Finn. Shannon. She must be overwhelmed with grief. Had Moira recognized what kind of coin Sam had retrieved?

The eleven o'clock news started with the familiar musical intro and Topaz Browning, news anchor, welcomed them with a bright smile.

"Welcome to your eleven o'clock news," Topaz greeted. "Another Irishman is dead in Salem. Finn O'Brien was at his cousin's funeral when he collapsed with what mourners thought was grief."

Charlene sat forward on the cushion as the news-woman panned over the cemetery yard. Headstones and moss-covered oaks. A hearse.

"Watch this clip here from a friend who happened to be recording for the family." Topaz's eyes gleamed with excitement as she pointed to the shaky cell phone video enlarged for the TV viewers.

"I can't believe this," Jack said. "Who would record a funeral?"

"Just watch." Charlene folded her hands together, eyes locked to the bouncing, grainy images. Would she be able to see what happened to Finn?

Finn and the others had been standing up, arguing about Liam. The priest was speaking to Shannon. Finn was in the center, with Shannon on one side and Aiden on the other.

Finn, head bowed, his hands in his jacket pockets. He fiddled with something in his left pocket, reminding her of Gil with his gold.

Topaz used a yellow highlighter on the screen. "Watch. This isn't grief, but an attack on Finn O'Brien!"

They used slow motion to show Finn's head jerking back as if he'd been hit and then his eyes widened and he fell forward, against Connor's casket, knocking the flow-ers off and into the hole. White gladiolas and roses, blue iris, green fronds, gone. Charlene recalled the smell of roses that she'd forgotten at the time.

The person stopped filming with a shriek and they must have lost their phone, because the recording was of the grass for the next few seconds and then the person continued recording the chaos before clicking off to call the police.

Charlene snapped her mouth closed.

Someone had murdered Finn O'Brien in front of his family.

Topaz faced the news camera and squared her slender shoulders. "If you have any information on this heinous attack in broad daylight, please phone the Salem police department right away."

Charlene swallowed over the lump in her throat.

"I can't believe it. I mean, I know that he fell . . . I heard this strange sound."

"You did?" Jack turned toward her from his place on his armchair. "What was it like?"

She shrugged. "A twang? I don't know. There was no blood. Not with Connor, either."

"Shannon said Connor had a brain bleed," Jack said, sounding like the doctor he used to be. "There is a vulnerable artery in the head—a blow to the temple can cause a brain hemorrhage that leads to paralysis or death."

"And Finn was hit in the temple. What if Connor was too?" She concentrated hard on the night. What she'd heard and smelled. Seen.

"The doctors knew Connor was a drinker, so maybe they attributed the bleed to thin arteries when it's possible he was knocked in the head. The temple, specifically." He tapped his.

Charlene scooted forward, feeling like they were onto something. The sound she'd heard was just out of reach. "With what?"

Jack got up from the chair to the TV as if to peer closer

at the video, but Topaz had moved on in her newscast. "I want to get a look at that recording. See if there's bruising or a red mark . . . not that it matters. The coroner will do a thorough inspection of the body."

"Sam believes Aiden knows something about Connor's death. The coin fell into the grave after Aiden was inside it—but James helped, and so did Gil."

"Could have belonged to any of them, as you said. This means that they were in sight the whole time and didn't kill Finn. Are you sure that Aiden isn't connected somehow?"

"No." She glanced at him from her comfy seat, her legs tucked to the side as she covered them with her blanket.

"Your heart wants him to be innocent," Jack surmised.

"Yes. Shannon adores her only son."

"We know that mothers can be fiercely protective." He crossed his ankles and gazed at the TV.

"We do." She shivered as she recalled her first weeks in this house where a mother's protective actions had led to disaster, and Jack's death. What could she do to prove that Aiden was innocent? Find the guilty party. Like it was so easy.

She shared with Jack Avery's latest troubles and fears for her future. "What do you think of inviting her to live here, Jack?"

"It's a great idea! Avery's a good human being." He grinned. "We get to be parents in our old age."

Charlene laughed so hard tears came to her eyes. "You always make me feel better, Jack. I'll ask her. Just to let her know that she's not alone."

"So . . . what is your plan for tomorrow?" Jack fluttered her hair to make her smile. "I see the wheels turning in your mind."

She lifted a shoulder and let it drop, guilty as charged. "Saturday will be a full breakfast with the guests. I'll have my dad strike up a friendship with Sheffer to see if he can crack what the man is doing here—in Salem. He's not like the other guests who want to visit the sights or know about the witches."

"Your dad is easy to talk to. I think that's where you get it. But warn him to be careful."

"I will. Next, I'll take Mom to Archie's and ask about the coin shop. From there, we can track down Moira and ask if Patty had mentioned a coin collector in the family." A piece of the puzzle shifted into possibility. "I want to find out if *Finn* was a collector."

Jack stilled and watched her with narrowed eyes. "That would explain a lot—from why the family thinks he has money, to not wanting to leave the house."

"Sheffer was very interested in my dad's quarter collection. More than just being polite."

Jack got up and took a few steps to the right. "I'll add that information into my searches tomorrow while you are out with your mom. I'll keep an eye on your dad and Sheffer."

"Perfect."

She also rose and folded the afghan on the corner of the love seat. "Maybe Moira can tell me a little more about Patty, and Liam. Does Patty know that Liam wants to buy the pub? Where did they get the money?"

"What does Patty do for a living?" Jack asked.

"I'll ask Moira. Maybe Patty's got a lucrative career

and that's where Liam got the cash to buy. She might want to help her family, her cousins." Charlene nodded. "I can see that."

"That's a big financial risk, paying cash for a bar that's in the red."

Charlene placed the folded blanket on the arm with a pat.

"I agree, Jack. The O'Briens and Gallaghers have family secrets . . . let's find out if killing their own is one of them."

CHAPTER 19

Light filtered through the window as Charlene opened her bleary eyes. Last night's sleep had been no better than the evening before, filled with coins and shamrocks and evil leprechauns. Silva purred at the crook of her knees. No dead mouse. That was a plus. Her parents were here and her mom was a different woman, also a plus.

Charlene didn't dawdle as she got ready, quickly washing her face and brushing her teeth. She pulled on jeans and a gray, long-sleeved T. She would get answers today as well as entertain her parents.

With a bounce in her step, she hurried to the kitchen. Brenda and Michael were each seated on kitchen stools at the counter, drinking coffee and laughing with Minnie.

"Hey sleepyhead," her dad greeted her. "It's after eight."

"Good morning," she said, cheerfully giving her mom and dad each a big hug. "Morning, Minnie."

Minnie handed her a steaming mug of coffee, fixed exactly the way she liked. "I'm surprised our laughing didn't wake you up," her housekeeper said with a sparkle in her eyes. "I told them all about Silva and her hunting skills."

Charlene grimaced and sipped her coffee. "She's a huntress and gets out of her collars like magic."

Her mom wiped a tear of mirth from her eye. "That cat!"

"I brought a new collar for us to try on her today," Minnie said, gesturing to a shopping bag on the kitchen table.

"You're the best, Minnie." Charlene turned to her parents. "Have you been up long?" Her father wore a navy pair of sweatpants and a white, long-sleeved T. His hair was mussy, as if he'd forgotten to comb it and there was scruff on his jawline. She found him endearingly handsome.

Her mom, in beige slacks and a maroon top, had on full makeup. Her almost white hair framed her oval face. She looked pretty with a smile on her face instead of the usual frown.

Brenda took a sip of coffee, then put her mug down. "Dad always gets up earlier than me. He came down for two cups of coffee and returned with a tray. Fresh fruit and two muffins and the best-smelling coffee I've had for some time. Maybe it's time for us to get a new coffee maker."

"Or buy better coffee," her dad joked.

Her mother was in a rare good mood as she glanced fondly at Minnie. "It was very kind of you to have pastries ready and here you are creating a breakfast feast."

"It's always my pleasure." Minnie swiped a dish towel across the counter, catching a drop of coffee. "Linda and Carol also popped down for a tray to take to their rooms," she told Charlene. "They're doing a few tours later today, but had some notes to transfer this morning."

The Montgomery family arrived with the kids flying down the staircase, laughing and dashing in front of each other while the parents followed behind.

Charlene smiled at Scarlett with amusement.

"Kids," Scarlett called. "Behave." She stuffed her hands into her cardigan pockets. "They were betting each other who could find Silva first."

"I can, I can," Layla said, scooting around the kitchen floor to search for Silva.

"No way. I know where she's hiding!" Caleb took off for the dining room.

Charlene knew exactly where Silva was—her suite. Should she let the cat sleep or allow the kids to play with her?

Silva scratched at the door separating Charlene's rooms from the kitchen, answering the question. She cracked open the door and the silver Persian peered at her cautiously.

"Come on out, girl. You have children to play with while I get your breakfast."

Silva's tail curled upwards while her golden eyes stared at Charlene with recrimination for having food—er, fun, without her.

"I have a can of tuna fish with your name on it." Charlene stepped toward the pantry and the frisky feline followed. Both kids made a grab for her. Silva evaded them as Charlene opened the tuna and put it in the cat bowl, leaping onto the kitchen chair to survey the situation.

Charlene opened the bag of Silva's favorite treats. "Here, kids. Get a few of these and whoever Silva comes to will be the winner of the game. Then we can all sit down and eat."

They both opened their hands while Charlene poured an equal amount in their palms. Once loaded with their weapons of temptation, Caleb blocked Layla, who pushed him back. Silva blinked at them and didn't come down from the chair.

"Ah, she's not hungry," Caleb said, his lower lip jutted.

"She's finicky," Charlene said. "How about we try again later? You can put the treats in her bowl."

The children did as asked. "Who wins?" Layla said with a sniff.

"Everybody wins!" Jason clapped sternly. "Go wash up and then come to the dining table." The kids grumbled a little but obeyed their father.

As soon as the children were out of the kitchen, Silva jumped down from the chair and went to the bowl with a satisfied purr. Breakfast, treats, and no rowdy kids.

"Brat," Charlene told her cat.

Minnie chuckled. "Diva. Want to get the meat platter? I'll get the frittata."

"Sure." Charlene brought the oval dish filled with perfectly browned sausages and crispy bacon slices to the dining room table and set it in the middle with serving tongs. Minnie put her frittata made with vegetables and cheese on the left side, and French toast with syrup, strawberries, and whipped cream was on the right, within easy reach of the children.

"Please help yourselves," she announced. Charlene took the chair at the far end of the table, with her parents on either side. Minnie refreshed coffee cups and brought in a chilled pitcher of fresh orange juice before returning to clean up the mess.

Everyone had a plateful of food, content to eat. Sheffer poked his head into the dining room. He looked quite handsome today, relaxed and informal. She smiled from her seat, forced to be polite even though she didn't trust him. "You're welcome to join us."

In the few days he'd been at the bed-and-breakfast he'd mostly brought a light breakfast to his room. Would he visit?

"No, thanks." Sheffer chose a large plate and scooped up eggs and sausage. "Good morning, everyone," he said pleasantly, nodding to Jason and Scarlett, then her parents. "I have work upstairs."

Charlene wondered what kind of work. Why wouldn't he just share, as the other guests did? What could be so top secret?

"We missed you last night at dinner," her dad said. "We come to Charlene's and it feels like we do nothing but eat. I love it."

Her mom laughed and ate a bite of frittata. "It's true. It's nice to have a change from our routine."

Charlene glanced at her mom in surprise. Since when? She kept the response to herself.

Sheffer, with a full plate and a coffee, said his good-byes and returned upstairs. Charlene turned to her father and said in a low voice, "If you get a chance, I'd like to know what Sheffer does for a living. He won't say and I think he thinks he's clever. It's annoying me." She half-smiled, but it was no joke.

Her dad lifted a slice of bacon. "I can find out for you, or at least try. I'll challenge him to a game of chess."

"Perfect."

After everyone finished breakfast, Charlene and her mom brought the empty dishes to the kitchen. Minnie scraped plates into the trash while Silva watched eagerly. Her mom picked out two nice pears from the fruit basket and set them aside on a napkin.

"Do you have plans for today?" Charlene asked her mom. "You didn't say."

"I was hoping to spend some time with you. I know Dad wants to take the three of us to dinner, if that works into your schedule." She gave Charlene a quick glance to read her expression. "We don't get to see you often enough."

"Oh . . . I think that will work out okay." Charlene provided happy hour, but the guests were on their own for dinners. "I have a few errands this morning if you want to come along?"

"Sure!"

Charlene began to rinse as Minnie filled the dishwasher. Her mom sat on the edge of the stool, not in a rush to go back to the room. "The breakfast was delicious, Minnie. What did you add to the French toast to give it that flavor?"

Minnie smiled with pleasure. "Thanks, Brenda. Nothing special, just a little trick I learned from the Food Channel. The key is to use good bakery bread. I like brioche and slice it thickly, about three-quarters of an inch. Add cinnamon, vanilla extract, nutmeg if you want, half a cup of light brown sugar, and heavy cream in a large bowl of a dozen eggs. If you want to get fancy you can also add pecans, golden raisins, and confectioners' sugar for dusting, but I skipped all that."

"So, it's all in the spice." Brenda folded her hands on the counter and leaned forward. "Sounds easy enough.

I'll try it out on Michael when we get back home. He'll be surprised."

So it wasn't just Charlene . . . she'd have to get to the bottom of this mystery.

Charlene went back to her room to get ready for the day. As she was brushing her hair, she noticed a couple of gray threads in the part line, almost hidden in the otherwise thick cocoa hair.

What the heck! She was only forty-three!

She opened her cosmetic bag, grabbed her tweezers and plucked the little devils out. Her mother had been completely gray by the time she was sixty. But she was not her mother and a little Clairol never hurt anyone.

What was the matter with her mother? After years of putting her through misery, why the sudden change? OMG! What if she was *dying*? Was this act of kindness her final farewell?

Impatient now, she quickly brushed on a dash of bronze-colored eye shadow, a brown eyeliner, and a swipe of apricot blush to her cheeks. A light hand with the mascara and pale lipstick, and she was good for the day. She entered her suite and whispered, "Jack?"

"You look lovely this morning," a melodious voice sang around her.

"Jack! Oh, Jack! I think my mom might be dying!"

He materialized at her real fear with a look of concern. "Charlene, why would you think that? Brenda Woodbridge is in perfect health."

She trusted his years of being a doctor and his unnatural ability to see things clearly now that he was dead, so her racing heart calmed.

"It's just that she's acting so nice, and after thirty-five years of her constant criticism I can't help but wonder why." She bit her bottom lip, tasting gloss. "Most people don't have a personality switch unless . . . could she have a brain tumor or something you can't see?"

"Highly unlikely. Tell you what though: I'll give her a once-over, all right? And put your fears at ease."

"Thank you." She crossed her arms in front of her body. Something had changed and she had to find out what. "I suppose I could just ask Dad."

"That's a great idea. Go to the source." He smiled at her. "Are you still planning on a trip to Vintage Treasures today?"

"Yes, of course." She glanced at Jack and patted the top of her head. "I just found two gray hairs so I'm also going to the pharmacy to buy some hair coloring."

He chuckled. "You're beautiful, Charlene, just the way you are."

"You think so?" she asked, feeling pleased.

"I do." He floated her notepad to her. "Do you remember your plan from last night? You can write it down."

She tapped her temple. "Got it right here. Archie, Moira, Patty, Liam."

Jack made the pad disappear with a snap of his fingers. "Your wisdom is showing," he said with a smirk. "I'll work on the O'Brien-Gallagher inheritance angle and see if I can find out more about the bankruptcy."

She nodded. "Try and rescue poor Silva from the children, would you? They amuse her for a while, but then her claws can come out."

"Like your mother's? Be careful today and don't lower your guard too much."

"You make a good point." Charlene crossed her fingers, the TV running in the background. "Catch you later." She left the suite.

"Good luck."

Charlene walked through the clean kitchen to the living room. Minnie wasn't around and neither was the Montgomery family or her mother. She found her dad in his favorite chair near the fireplace, absorbed in a book.

"Hey, Dad. Whatchya doing?"

He looked up with a startled blink. "Oh, just flipping through this old book. You have quite a collection, Charlene. A lot on the occult, demons, and spells. Are you getting caught up in Salem's craziness—a Chicago girl like you?"

"Not really." She shrugged. "But since moving here, I've expanded my perception. I've met modern witches who use potions and make spells. Weird, right?"

Her dad just listened, as was his habit.

"But they aren't evil; they do spells for good. Like healthy crops and prosperity and love. They have a strong connection with Mother Nature and can directly connect with the divine source energy."

His brow lifted at that last line.

She laughed at his expression. "At least, that's how my friends Brandy Flint and Kass Fortune explain it to me."

He gestured to her inviting living room. "It's obvious to me that you're doing well. As long as your friends' beliefs don't do harm, I suppose it's not a bad thing."

"It's not." She knelt by his chair and put her hand on the armrest to look into his eyes. "Dad. I've got something to ask you. It's about Mom."

"What's about Mom?" Brenda entered the room with one of those unnatural smiles on her face. "I heard you talking about witches—do you suspect me?"

"Nope." Charlene stood and brushed her hands together. "I mentioned a few errands, earlier, Mom. Want to go with me to Vintage Treasures?"

"Sounds great."

"And Dad, you can join us or check out Evergreen Bookstore, if you want to come along. The bookshop is right across the street. Then we could all do a light lunch. Mom said that you wanted to go out to dinner tonight?"

Brenda glanced at her husband, who set the book aside. "Michael, are you up for that?"

"Yup. Guess I am." He stood and told Charlene, "I tried to engage Sheffer in a game of chess and conversation, but he was in a hurry to leave."

"I don't suppose he mentioned where?" she asked wryly.

"Nope, sorry."

"Thanks for trying, Dad. Okay. The Honda express will be leaving the station at precisely ten-thirty. Twenty minutes from now."

A half-hour later Charlene dropped off her dad at the bookstore and she and her mother headed for the antique shop.

Archie was delighted to see them both again. He took her mother's hands in his and gushed. "Well, aren't you a sight for sore eyes, Brenda! I swear you get younger every time I see you."

Charlene rolled her eyes when she noticed her mother blush.

"As do you," she said brightly. "Doesn't he, Charlene?"

"Yes, you do look well, Archie. And it was so nice to meet your wife Sandy yesterday. At Connor Gallagher's funeral?"

"Oh yes, I remember. Such a sad business. What can I

help you lovely ladies find today?" Archie tugged his brown vest over his protruding tummy in an attempt to hold it in.

"We're just browsing. Mom, why don't you have a peek around and I'll be with you in a minute?"

"Sure," she said without a hitch.

"Always a pleasure to chat with you," Archie told Charlene. "How is that telescope holding up?"

"Just fine. It didn't get too much use during the winter months, but that will change with the nicer weather."

He peered over his glasses at her. "Is there something specific you want to ask?"

"Yes. You know me too well."

"Not possible," he answered and her cheeks warmed. Married man or not, he was a definite flirt. With grandiose hopes.

"At the funeral, Moira McKenzie mentioned that you and her father have been friends for a long time. He owns a coin shop?"

He leaned his elbow on the counter. "Does this have anything to do with the coin from Connor's grave? It was all Moira talked about on the way to our cars. Sandy thinks we should add coins to Vintage Treasures, but we don't have space."

She took note of the overfilled shelves and crowded walkway. "I agree with you. Listen, I wanted the address to the coin shop if you don't mind?"

He took a step back, gaze filled with speculation.

Charlene didn't cave, but it was hard not to give a reason.

At last, Archie said, "Let me get that information for you."

While he searched a stack of business cards in the desk

drawer, her mother returned and plopped a wooden planter shaped like a wagon on the counter.

"What on earth are you going to do with that?" It would cost a mint to ship to Chicago.

"It's a house gift for you," her mother said, smiling wide. "You plant seasonal flowers in it and can place it outside in your back garden or on the front porch. I'll help you while I'm here—it'll be a little project for the two of us!"

A project for them? Jack had to give her mother a physical and find out what was wrong with Brenda Woodbridge.

"Mom! Thank you, I love it." She hugged her mother, patting her shoulders to see if she'd lost weight, but her figure was the same.

Archie handed her a business card where he'd hand-written the phone number for the coin shop. "It's just a few streets down."

She nodded her thanks. Should she drop in and see if Moira could answer her questions? If only she didn't have her parents with her.

Charlene wrote a text to Sam to make sure he was checking the coin collector thread. It just might buy her a brownie point or two.

That would break the rules of their friendship, so she deleted the message.

CHAPTER 20

Charlene pocketed her phone and smiled at Archie as he rang up her mom's thoughtful purchase for their joint project.

"What kind of flowers should we plant?" Brenda asked.

"Bright blossoms," Archie said, winking, "to match your bright faces."

Her mom giggled and stepped back to allow Charlene to lift the awkward planter. She hid an eye roll and carried their prize out of the store to the SUV.

"This will be fun, Mom." Should they skip the coin shop and go to a garden nursery instead?

"Your dad texted for us to take our time and shop— he's having fun at the bookstore."

"Oh, really?" She closed the back hatch.

"Where to?" Brenda asked in a chipper tone.

Charlene waited for a smart remark on *time a wastin'* but there was no comment after her perky question.

"Well, do you mind if we drive to the coin shop?"

"Not at all!" Brenda swung her near-white chin-length bob and opened the passenger-side door. "What for?"

They each got in. Charlene started the engine and read the address.

"I met the daughter of the owner at Connor's funeral yesterday. Who better to tell me about coins and local coin collectors, than the proprietor, right?"

Her mom rubbed her hands together. "I agree. This is about the gold coin you saw?"

"Yes."

"How well did you see it? Could you draw it?"

Charlene shook her head and drove the few blocks down the street. "Not that close at all. It was gold."

She wondered if she really was just wasting time.

"I'm sure that the owner will prompt questions," her mother said with assurance. "Here we are!"

She wasn't used to her mother's unwavering support and snuck another peek. Her mom was smiling as she looked out the window. Her pink-cheeked complexion exuded good health.

They parked on the street before a storefront with a worn exterior and Charlene feared nobody would be there.

Her mother had no reservations as she tugged on the metal knob of a heavy glass door with metal bars and a blinking sign in the window that flashed COINS. COLLEC-TIBLES. COINS.

A gray-haired man with pale skin and a broad smile, Moira's smile, greeted them.

"Welcome! I'm Oscar McKenzie. And how may I help

you today?" He tapped the glass counter above rows and rows of cellophaned coins in assorted shapes and sizes, as well as colors.

Moira slinked out of the backroom office in heels and a silver dress. Her black hair was loose to her shoulders. "Hello, Charlene. Archie just called to say you might be on your way. We are happy to help, but I'm not sure how we can. This is about what happened yesterday, Papa."

"Did you get a chance to see the coin?" Brenda asked. "I'm Brenda Woodbridge, Charlene's mother."

"Not really. That hunky detective nabbed and bagged it before I could get a good look." Moira shrugged and leaned her elbow on the counter, standing next to her dad.

Charlene wasn't that surprised Archie, the gossip, had already called ahead. Two murders in Salem, one at the funeral of the other, was sensational news. "It might be nothing, but I was also wondering if any local families were collectors of gold or rare coins?" Like the O'Briens, specifically.

"As I told Officer Bernard earlier this morning when he dropped by to see if I could identify the coin," Oscar began.

Charlene sucked in a breath. Sam was already on the right track, thinking the killer could be a collector. Her mom stepped to the counter, white brow arched encouragingly.

"Yes?" Charlene joined her mom. "What did you tell the officer?"

"That was not a collectible coin at all, but a common Gold Eagle. The banks use them as currency all the time." Oscar splayed his open palm. "No big deal."

Moira turned to her dad, her gaze annoyed. "You didn't mention that you'd already spoken to the police, Papa."

He jammed a hand in his pocket. "You were so busy telling me what to do that I didn't have a chance."

Tension simmered between father and daughter.

"Papa! I was only saying—"

"I know how to run my business, thank you."

Charlene stayed put, though she wanted to dash for the door. They sounded just like her and her mom, in the old days.

"That's good news then, right?" Charlene asked. "If it's a common coin, then it's not worth killing someone over." Finn. And Connor. Both dead. "Or two someones."

Moira graced her with a brittle smile. "A lot of collectors are crazy. They think that their treasure is valuable because *they* value it, and so they go to great lengths to protect it. Other people might not agree with their perceived value."

"Speak English, Moira!" The man crossed his arms and inched back from his daughter to eye Charlene and Brenda. "She's talking about a gent who saved carved walnuts. These things were delicate and one of a kind. He got it into his head that someone wanted to steal his walnuts, and he became a complete recluse."

"It was awful. He died alone," Moira said. "No family. Nobody wanted his ridiculous nuts. He had other coins and trinkets that were given to us to put a price on. We donated the walnuts to Archie, and I think he eventually found a buyer. Were they worth losing his family over?" She patted her dad's shoulder and shook her head. "Family is the most important legacy we have, right?"

Her dad relaxed and the tension eased between them. "You're right, my lamb."

Brenda nodded. "I couldn't agree more, Oscar. Now,

my husband collects state quarters. What do you have in stock?"

"Oh, if he's a collector he probably has them all in pristine condition. I tell you what quarter is worth money? A 1965 quarter that was made on the wrong metal. Instead of copper-clad, they used silver!"

Moira and Charlene moved down to the opposite end of the counter as their parents discussed quarters.

"I can't believe Papa already talked to the police." Moira swept her dark hair from her faintly lined brow. "He usually tries to keep his distance from the cops with a 'don't know, don't tell' policy."

"Why is that?"

"He grew up in a different era. You don't snitch to the cops. But murder? I'm a good friend of the family and this is just awful."

"If the coin in the grave is common, then that's a good thing, right?"

"I sure hope they find who is responsible." Moira tapped her fingers against the glass.

"How is Patty doing?" Charlene decided to take advantage of one-on-one time with Moira and asks a personal question about her friend.

"Oh, she could be better." Her eyes welled.

"I'm sure. Losing her brother must be terrible." Charlene bit her lip, wondering if Connor's death had been a financial boon to Patty, his closest living relative.

She hated to think that way, but she couldn't deny that she'd learned most suspicious deaths were committed by those closest to the victim.

Not just Patty would benefit if Connor had a legacy to leave. So would Liam, as Patty's husband.

Was it a coincidence that Liam had gotten out of jail, at the same time that Connor had resurfaced in Salem, and now Connor was dead? Finn, too.

Now *Liam* had made an offer for the O'Brien's pub. Cash. Had he gotten money from Patty, through Connor's death?

"Patty's broken up," Moira said, breaking Charlene's train of thought. "Crying one minute, determined to live life to the fullest in the next. I've never seen her moods swing like this before."

Charlene sighed. "It's just so sad, with the cousins dying. Shannon told me that Connor and Finn used to look like twins but at the funeral, Finn seemed older by at least a decade."

Moira nodded. "He didn't age well, that's true. All the cousins have that bright red hair except Finn. His was faded and straggly." She shuddered.

"Do you know why Connor had left Salem?"

Moira glanced back at their parents, still deep in conversation as they peered down into the counter at the various coins. "Well. I think it had to do with Connor drinking like he did. I guess he tended to talk to the wrong people about the wrong things when he got loaded."

"Like what?" Charlene put her hand to her throat. "I mean, could that be why he was killed?"

Moira exhaled and smoothed the silver sequins on her dress. It was more appropriate for a nightclub than a day at work, but to each their own taste. Maybe she was trying to convey wealth but was off by a mile. Ernie hadn't seemed to mind, though. There was somebody for everybody.

At last, Moira said, "I doubt anything that serious. I know when I've had a few, I get too loud. I would hate for someone to kill me over it." She shifted her weight, balancing on her high heels. "Patty told me that all the cousins got into some trouble in high school."

Charlene could see it with the boys, but not Shannon. "Even Shannon?"

"Don't look so shocked," Moira laughed. "Even precious Shannon, superwoman of Salem, had a wild streak. She's been doing penance, to my way of thinking. Taking care of her brother the way she does. Er, did."

Moira blinked watery eyes clear.

Charlene patted her wrist. "Were Shannon and Patty close, as kids? What did the family think of Patty marrying Liam?"

Moira twisted two fingers together. "Liam and Connor were tight as brothers once upon a time. Connor was Liam's best man for his wedding."

"Then Liam went to jail . . . but not Connor."

"Liam was a bad apple, but Patty told me she was in love. And love made her stupid and blind to his faults. With Connor giving his approval, well, she thought she'd be protected from the crime he was involved in. Then Liam heads to jail and Connor was kicked out of Salem by the family. Patty was left alone to fend for herself. I guess Shannon helped but she was kinda snarky about it."

Charlene had seen a hardness in Shannon yesterday. "What happened to Shannon's husband?"

"He died," Moira said. "Went out fishing and drowned in a storm."

"That's awful!" The family had suffered one tragedy after another.

"None of the cousins liked him, that I know for a fact. Trey Best thought he was better than everyone else. He was a psychologist."

"That must be why Shannon encouraged Aiden to be a doctor? If the rest of the family is . . ." Charlene trailed off. Content with middle-class vocations, she thought, but couldn't find a nice way to say it.

"Not aspiring so high?" Moira laughed. "You're right on the money there. But yeah, that sounds correct. Not that I know the rest of the family as well as Patty. I've met James, Cindy, and the girls at the pub." She grinned. "I especially love happy hour."

Who didn't? But Charlene's version of happy hour was much different than dollar shots of Jäger. "And now Patty and Liam will own it."

"What?" Moira blinked.

Charlene wished she hadn't let down her guard like that. *Think, think.* "I'd heard Patty and Liam want to own a pub?" She scrambled and hoped the tiny falsehood would lead to the truth.

Moira fluttered her fingers dismissively. "Oh, Shannon probably told you that. Well, she's discouraged Patty every step of the way, so she shouldn't be sharing the news."

Her shot in the dark had hit a bull's-eye. Now to find out details. "Are we talking about *another* pub besides Pub 36?"

Did Shannon know that her brother James's bar had gone bankrupt? That her cousin had bought it? Cindy had told James to ask for financial assistance.

"Nope. Salem doesn't need two Irish pubs competing against each other." Moira tilted her head. "I agree with Shannon about that. Patty wants to invest in a business that makes immediate money. Bars are lucrative when run properly."

Would Patty and Liam have killed Connor for his assets to buy Pub 36? "That can't be cheap."

Moira snapped her mouth shut and eyed Charlene cautiously. "I don't mind telling you, since Patty doesn't keep secrets, but when Liam got out of jail, she cashed out her 401(k) at the bank to invest in a turnkey property. For their future as man and wife, together. But I worry about her. They didn't look lovey-dovey yesterday."

"So, Patty works at a bank?" That made more sense than Liam earning money in jail. "It's great that she wants to give them a chance." If that were Charlene, she'd take the 401(k) and start a new life, without Liam.

"If Liam doesn't ruin it. I suggested a bakery or a coffee shop rather than a bar, considering the clientele an ex-con might attract."

It would be a harder crowd than what the O'Briens had going on now, with their pretty daughters at the counter. "Maybe Shannon can help with the business end." Why wouldn't she have helped her brother James with the finances?

"Shannon offered to do the accounting at a family discount." Moira chuckled. "Patty says Shannon is like an annoying older sister who just won't stop interfering, though you've grown up already."

Charlene nodded and kept a neutral expression as she tried to make sense of what she'd learned.

Was Patty lying to her dear friend Moira? Patty didn't keep secrets. Ha. Charlene doubted that very much. A woman couldn't be married to a jailbird without knowing the value of keeping secrets close to the chest. And Moira hadn't said for sure whether or not Patty still worked.

Brenda paid for something at the register. "Michael will be very surprised by this—thank you, Oscar."

Charlene and Moira raised their heads.

Her mom walked toward them. "I'm so glad we stopped in at this shop. Did you mention an older sister? Charlene is an only child. After many prayers, we were blessed."

Charlene couldn't believe her mother's change in attitude.

"I'm the youngest of three." Moira smiled at her dad. "The only girl. I didn't get away with much. That's why I love Ernie. He encourages me to be myself."

"Ernie's all right," Oscar said begrudgingly. "He loves you and that's what matters most. As a parent, Brenda, you know what I mean."

"Oh, I do," Brenda said with all sincerity. "All you want is for your child to be happy."

"Even if they are over fifty," Oscar remarked.

"Papa!" Moira exclaimed.

"Is there anything else we can do for you?" Oscar asked as his daughter spluttered.

"I don't think you ever did say if there were local families who collected coins." Charlene looked from Oscar to Moira.

"Of course there are!" Oscar exclaimed.

"The O'Briens, or Gallaghers?" Charlene pressed.

He clicked his tongue behind his teeth and gave a shake of his head. "Now, I can't tell you that without betraying confidences. If I talked as much as my pal Archie, then I wouldn't be in business much longer, right?"

Moira peered up to the ceiling, then at Charlene. "I warned you, didn't I?"

Charlene chuckled at Moira's exasperation, but it was clear she loved her dad and he loved her.

"You did. That's okay . . . you've been an immense help. Thank you."

Charlene and her mom left the shop. "How was that helpful?" Brenda asked. "He didn't answer your question."

"He told us that the coin was a common gold coin, so it doesn't really matter if either family is a collector."

They got into the car and Charlene started the engine, smiling at her mother, who gave her a confused look. "I don't understand."

"Finn and Connor weren't killed over a coin collection."

"Ah," Brenda said, still confused. "So who did it?"

"I don't know yet, but we are one step closer to the truth."

CHAPTER 21

After leaving the old coin shop, Charlene texted her dad to say they were on their way. Just over an hour had passed since she'd dropped him off at Evergreen's and he must have been wondering what happened to them.

Her dad waited on the sidewalk, one hand in his pocket, the other holding an Evergreen Bookstore bag. She pulled in front and he hopped in the back seat.

Her mom turned to welcome him with a smile. "Sorry, dear. We just got busy! Hope you didn't mind waiting. Did you find any interesting books?"

Dear? Her pleasant voice and sweet concern? Sparks were flying between her parents.

"I bought a book about Plymouth Rock and the *Mayflower*. You know me. I'm a sucker for history."

"Dad, I am *soooo* sorry for leaving you so long. We

spent some time at the antique shop, and Mom bought me this wagon planter to fill with blooming plants for the garden."

"That's nice, Charlene. I'm sure it'll be beautiful."

"Our little project together." Charlene snuck a peek at her mom. "Then we made a quick stop at a coin shop because I've been like a dog with a bone. Coins have been appearing in the most unusual spots, which could be an important link to the men's deaths."

"That sounds interesting. You know your mom is very good at piecing clues together in her books and nailing the guilty party early on."

"Thanks, dear," her mother chirped, sending Michael a kiss from the front passenger seat.

"I had a nice chat with Lucas. The store wasn't busy so we sat and had tea." Her dad laughed. "He was telling me some pretty wild tales of when he and his wife were younger." He chuckled. "The pair were quite adventurous, not like you and me, Brenda."

"Never too late to change, Michael. We're still young yet. Annabeth says seventy is the new fifty."

Charlene's head swiveled to see her dad wink at her mom.

Words failed her. Clearly, this "change" in her mother worked favorably for her father too.

"I'm glad he kept you entertained, Dad. But it seems that I was wrong about the coin collections. Turns out that gold coins are quite common and not worth killing for."

"Well, that's good news, isn't it?" he asked, placing his bag of books beside him on the seat.

"Yes," she said. "But no. It brings me no closer to figuring out who wanted the cousins dead. It must be a relative, right? There is a lot of animosity and bad blood between the Gallaghers and the O'Briens. Add in Liam Kane, family by marriage."

Her mom rubbed her hands together. "Charlene! I'm very impressed. Logic is the way to narrow down too many suspects. I'll help if you'd like."

"Uh, how about lunch?" She kept her gaze on the road and watched the speedometer. Speeding was her only sin. Well, almost her only. "I haven't been to Cod and Capers for a while and we're in the neighborhood. Does that sound good? Or Sea Level? We visited there on your last trip."

"Whatever you like, both are very nice," her mom said. "What was the name of that redheaded woman at Cod and Capers? The one who runs the place?"

"Sharon Turnberry is the manager." Charlene remembered their first meeting. "Brandy recommended the restaurant when I was at her winery, asking if she could create a special brand for my bed-and-breakfast."

"You had just moved here at that time." Her dad nodded. "We were missing you so much and Mom was calling you every day, annoying the daylights out of you, I imagine. You had a lot on your plate back then. Sharon was one of your first friends here, wasn't she?"

"Yes, she came to my opening. Lately, we seem to have lost touch." Decision made, she turned into the parking lot of Cod and Capers, next to the wharf. "It's time to say hello. She'll enjoy seeing you again."

They were greeted by a young woman around twenty once they'd entered. Wasn't she the same girl who had waited on her when she was here with Sam?

Charlene swallowed a lump in her throat, not wanting to go there.

"We'd like to be seated by the window," she told the waitress, seeing plenty of tables empty. The nautical décor was painted in grays and blues, with hanging nets and painted lobster traps. It was a perfect tourist spot that also had great food.

"Of course." The waitress grabbed three menus and escorted them to a table with the finest view of the harbor.

As they took their seats, Charlene said, "Is Sharon in today?"

The waitress nodded. "In back."

"Could you please let her know that Charlene and her parents are here? We'd love to say hello."

"I'll do that. May I take your drink orders while you have a glance at the menu?"

Her parents both had an ale and she asked for an iced tea, with plenty of lemons.

A few minutes later Sharon came flying out of the kitchen, pink-faced, hair tied up in a knot on the top of her head and wearing the big, warmhearted smile she knew so well.

"Charlene, great to see you! I remember your mom and dad, Brenda and Michael? Is that correct?"

"You have an excellent memory," her father said. "Couldn't come to Salem and not pay a visit to you and the finest restaurant around."

Sharon beamed. "What a pleasure—I'm going to bring you folks a little something to enjoy while you're deciding on the menu. How about a bottle of pinot grigio—light and fruity white?"

"No need, Shannon. I'm driving, so iced tea for me. And the drink order is in, but thank you! You're so sweet."

Undeterred, Sharon returned ten minutes later with a platter of six fresh oysters on a half shell and six baked clams with spinach and melted cheese.

"That's way too much," Brenda told her, picking up her fork. "But it does look wonderful."

"We'll enjoy it and have a smaller lunch," Charlene suggested.

They settled on two lobster rolls split and French fries. Her dad couldn't resist a cup of clam chowder.

The appetizer was gone by the time her dad's soup arrived. He tasted it and then again. "This is excellent," he said with a grin. "But nothing can beat that *pasta e fagioli* that Bella's used to make. Shame that little gem of a place changed hands. Darn good food."

"Yes," Charlene agreed. "David was a decent man and a good manager for all his faults."

"We all do the best we can," her mother intoned.

The lobster rolls arrived. Her parents ordered another beer each and Charlene's iced tea was topped off. They reminisced about things from the past and more recent memories, enjoying each other's company, in perfect harmony for the first time Charlene could recall.

"Oh, honey! I forgot to give you my little present!" Brenda pulled the coin from her handbag and handed it to her husband. Oscar had nicely wrapped a small white box in purple netting tied with a gold ribbon.

"What is it?" Undoing the ribbon, Michael looked expectantly at his wife.

"Nothing much. Just something that I picked up at the coin shop while Charlene was asking her questions." Brenda shrugged her shoulders. "It wasn't expensive."

"It will be priceless to me," he said, making Charlene's heart squeeze with a longing of her own.

When the gift was removed from the box, her dad studied it like it was a jewel right from the Arabian desert. His pleasure was so endearing even her mother blushed.

Her father insisted on paying the bill, then they said their goodbyes to Sharon and promised to come back soon.

On their way home, her mother asked if they could stop at a garden shop for the plants to begin their project together. "Do you mind, Michael?"

"Not at all. You might not know it, my love, but I'm quite experienced with gardening."

Brenda glanced at her husband. "You are?"

"Well, who do you think has been doing it all these years?"

Charlene snickered.

"I don't know." Brenda flushed. "Figured you hired someone, I guess."

He laughed. "You're learning a little more about me day by day, aren't you, dear?"

"You bet I am. I like it." The twinkle in her mother's eye told Charlene more than she needed to know.

Ten minutes later they pulled into the parking lot of a large garden store. Within half an hour they left with not only plants for the wagon, but for the front stairs and porch as well.

Spring plants always made her smile. Tulips, daffodils, and potted geraniums. Will might think he was fired, so she'd have to give Minnie a heads-up and let her know she was only doing this for her mom and dad.

Once home, they removed the plants from the hatch of the Pilot and positioned them where they should be planted. They went inside to change into their work clothes. At half-past one, all the guests were out for the afternoon.

Except for one.

Hearing a cough from the living room, Charlene headed there to see who had remained behind. She spotted Sheffer, no surprise, leafing through the books on the shelves next to the reading area and games nook, slightly away from the fireplace, but still in plain view.

"Hello, Sheffer." She stopped to offer her assistance. "Can I help you find something?"

"No." He slid the hardcover he'd held back into its slot before she could see it, but the volume was where she kept the historic books on Salem. It was also where she'd put the book on the underground passageway instrumental in solving a previous crime. Salem was fascinating, way beyond witches. "What an eclectic selection."

"It's a gorgeous day. Are you interested in going out?" Charlene kept her tone light and cheerful. "I'm about to change, then my parents and I will do some planting."

He raised a brow as if to say, *And what does that have to do with me?*

This profession was making her a mind reader. She was definitely learning that the world was made up of the most interesting characters, not cutout cookie shapes. Sheffer presented a challenge to her. She wanted him to be happy in her home—if he wasn't a killer.

"Why don't you take a book and go outside on the back porch?" she suggested. "You'll have some rare spring Salem sunshine and quiet."

"Charlene, I thought I made it quite clear that I have my own agenda for being here. My interests are no concern of yours. I assure you there is nothing criminal about what I'm doing. I ask you again to keep out of it."

Her back straightened. What an unpleasant man.

"My mistake. Do as you wish." She turned and walked away. Like, why didn't he go down to the wharf and look for a mermaid or something?

"Charlene . . ."

She kept walking—not hurt or furious, but curious as to what he was really up to. A moment later she was in her suite with the door locked. Charlene sat on her love seat and Silva purred in her lap. Jack materialized before her. "I only have a minute, Jack, but the cousins were not killed for their coin collections."

"How do you know that?"

"Because Mom and I stopped at the coin dealer, Oscar McKenzie. He's Moira's father. Moira is engaged to Ernie, the Realtor you remember so fondly."

Jack scowled at that. "I can't believe anybody would want to marry Ernie."

"Moira is actually very nice. Anyway, Officer Bernard was already in to talk with Oscar, who told the police that the gold coin found was not a collector's item."

Silva purred, rubbing her wet nose under Charlene's chin, wanting the attention she focused on Jack.

"Back to square one?"

"Yes. Pretty much. Look, I've gotta change. I'm supposed to meet Mom and Dad outdoors. Mom bought me a planter in the shape of a wagon and we're going to fill it with potted flowers. It'll be pretty. Come and watch if you like."

"I might. I'm interested in seeing the difference in your mother."

"Do a health check, would you?" Charlene laughed and closed the bedroom door while she quickly changed clothes.

Before going outdoors, she cornered Minnie, who was doing laundry. "Let Will know that he'll be back in charge once my parents are gone."

Her housekeeper tossed her head in amusement. "I don't expect he'll take it too hard, but thanks for caring."

An hour later Charlene was hot and dirty, but the plants looked wonderful. She had first thought the wagon should be in the backyard, near the swing, but she loved it so much it ended up on the right side of her front stairs. Two other pots offset it across the path: Attractive and welcoming for her future and present guests.

Jack had given her the occasional hint on what to plant where, but it was her father who surprised her most of all. He had an eye for gardening. Her mother was best at refreshing their plastic lemonade glasses. Jack said Brenda was in the pink of health.

She ran back inside to take a shower while her mom and dad sat in the Adirondack chairs on the front patio, sipping a refreshing gin and tonic that Minnie had brought out for them.

With the physical labor done, Charlene's mind went to work. The bankruptcy, selling out to an ex-con, even if he was kin, just didn't seem like the right thing to do. What had Cindy meant about asking Finn or Shannon for money?

What had Liam meant to Cindy, about saving her?

She got out of the shower, hoping to talk to Jack, but he wasn't there. Would anybody else in the family be in danger? Why had Connor and Finn been killed?

There was only one way to find out. She called the pub and found out that Cindy would return from her break in fifteen minutes. Face-to-face conversation was needed.

She had to go, so she left a note on her television for Jack that read, *Off to the pub to see Cindy.*

She told her parents that she had to run out for cat food and would be right back. Her dad reminded her about dinner, asking her not to be too long.

Charlene arrived at the Irish pub and opened the door. It was dark compared to the afternoon light behind her. She stepped inside.

There were only about a dozen patrons in the place. Four friends, both young couples, were standing on the dance floor while one of the men fed the jukebox. The two girls were attractive, wearing skinny jeans and stylish jackets. One had long, flowing blond hair; the other a short, jagged cut, black with purple streaks.

At one end of the bar, two men were drinking beers and eating big, juicy hamburgers. They were both overweight, wearing baseball caps and old shirts. The bigger guy wiped the grease of the burger onto his jeans.

Charlene's eyes adjusted to the darkness and she noticed the woman on the other side of the counter was Cindy, in a bar apron. There was no sign of James or Liam.

She took the stool and leaned her elbow on the mahogany bar top.

Cindy smiled in recognition, deep lines around her mouth and eyes. She sipped from a draft beer. "Hey, don't I know you from the funeral?"

"Yeah. Charlene Morris. I was hoping we could talk?"

"About?" Charlene rested her elbow on the bar top.

Saving the O'Brien marriage was none of her concern, but the O'Brien girls might be in danger if Liam took over the bar. She wanted to make sure that Cindy knew Liam's background before signing on the dotted line. "You can tell me it's none of my business—it wouldn't be the first time!" She lowered her voice. "I heard you were letting this place go." Charlene glanced around. "I can see it's not busy now, but wow, the weekend nights are packed. Seems like a breadwinner to me."

Cindy shrugged. "I suppose. Why, are you interested in buying? We have a taker already." Her laughter caught in her chest. "Could be a bidding war for this dive."

"Uh, no. I have enough on my hands running the bed-and-breakfast."

Her brow arched and she patted her apron pocket. "I hear things too," she said. "Your B and B is supposed to be pretty fancy."

"I love it, but there's huge upkeep to a big place, as you know. I'm doing all right but it's not a gold mine." She moderated her tone to invite Cindy's opinion.

The bar owner/wife/mom took another drink of her draft beer. "Sometimes dreams come true *after* a lot of elbow grease. Sometimes dreams die."

Ouch. Charlene paused, hearing Cindy's pain. She decided to say her piece. "Word is that Liam Kane is taking over the pub, and I was concerned for your girls."

Cindy reached inside her pocket for a vape pen that smelled like vanilla. "You don't have a filter at all, do you? Just ask any old questions that you want, without a care if it offends anyone. Shannon told me what you said about Aiden."

Charlene bit her lip and opened her hand on the bar. "Sorry. Guess it's only-child syndrome, where you fear that if you don't speak up, no one will hear you."

"I was an only child." Cindy blew out a stream of vanilla smoke. "What are you worried about? You don't know Sinead and Gwynne."

"Your daughters are beautiful and Sinead is a natural behind the bar. I fear that the clientele Liam might attract

will be a little rougher than what you currently have."
Like, prison rough.

"I know what you're implying. Matter-of-fact, I'm
thinking about taking the girls and getting the heck out of
Dodge. Start over somewhere new and far away from the
bar scene. I need to talk to Shannon about it. Patty can
have this place." *Puff, puff.*

"What about James?"

"What about him? He drank the profits away and now
we have to scramble out of debt." She wiped a tear away
and sniffed. "Used to be a good man, but he's not strong,
you know what I mean?"

"I think I do. But . . ."

"But nothing. He couldn't even go to his own brother
and ask for a loan. Rather than go bankrupt. What a fool.
That old miser Finn had more money than the pope. Hid it
somewhere. Least that's what everyone supposes. Didn't
even spend it, what a waste!"

"Hid it? Why?"

"Don't know. James won't tell me. Connor knew, and
Shannon. I think Aiden, but screw them. They can all fry
in hell for all I care. Look what's happened! They're
cursed, each and every one!"

CHAPTER 22

"What makes you think that Finn was loaded?" Charlene asked once Cindy had calmed down.

"Family mumbling and rumors, not that Shannon would ever tell the truth." Cindy pursed her lips and made as if to lock them up, then mimed tossing a key.

"What does James think about it? Does he believe his brother is rich?"

"He *knows* it. But he won't ever demand more from Finn or Shannon, which is just plain wrong. He refuses to let me do it either. James married me and that made me family, but nope. He don't trust me. That really burns, you know?"

That would be hurtful. Hurtful enough that Cindy just might decide to take on James's family, and kill them off?

But no . . . Cindy had been in plain sight at Connor's funeral the whole time.

Charlene left a twenty on the bar and wished Cindy luck.

"Where are you off to now?" Cindy asked, as if daring Charlene not to answer after Charlene had been so, well, personal.

What could it hurt to tell her? "Shannon's." She wanted to find out how the woman was doing after Finn's death, and perhaps discover more about Finn's possible wealth. Money was often a motive for murder. "I hope to catch her at home."

"Waste of time. I'll tell you this so that you can go pester her, like you did me." Cindy snorted and slapped her vape to the bar.

Charlene's polite smile slipped.

"Saturday afternoons are spent at the AOH. Shannon runs her life by a schedule. Being an accountant is the perfect career for her. I bet it really chapped her hide to have a medical school dropout for a son. I wish I coulda seen her face when you told her."

Charlene decided not to touch that. "I just want to convey my condolences over Finn."

"Shannon and Finn were twins and very close." She twisted two fingers together. "James was kinda left out of the club, being younger and all. He told me stories of how they could actually know each other's thoughts."

"Like mind reading? That's interesting."

"Yeah. Cool, unless you're the sibling that can't do it."

James had been left out of the family dynamic from the sounds of it. Had that made him bitter?

Like Cindy, he'd been in sight the entire time. He was too tall to be Connor's attacker.

She wished she knew what had hit Finn. Had it been a pellet of some kind, like a rubber bullet? Maybe Sam had found something around the gravesite, not that he would tell her.

"Well, thank you. And I do wish you all the best, Cindy. You and your girls."

"Thanks. I'd appreciate it if you don't blab to Shannon about me and James being on the rocks. She'd say it served me right or something."

"All right. I won't. But doesn't she know about the bankruptcy?"

"Yeah." Cindy pocketed the twenty.

"As an accountant, maybe she could have helped you."

"Shannon looked down on James and me. Thought she was better than us, with her accounting office and new house. I can see why you two would get along."

Charlene held her tongue.

Cindy sent a shameful glance toward Charlene. "Could be that we already borrowed money once from her and didn't have the chance to pay it back yet."

Now that made more sense with the kindness that she had seen in Shannon. Then again, she'd also seen a hard center. "That's too bad. I really hope things turn around for you and James."

"James and Connor had drinking in common. Like I said, a family curse."

"There are places to go for treatment . . . as I'm sure you're aware."

"I know. He knows." She drained her beer. "Don't matter."

Charlene slung her purse over her shoulder and stepped toward the door. It was time to go before she got mired in Cindy's depression. The pub was like a black pit.

She opened the front door and breathed in deep of the cool March air. The blue sky had disappeared behind a curtain of gray. Rain threatened and she shivered into her lightweight jacket.

The AOH was a few blocks from the pub and Charlene decided to walk and clear her mind.

Would Shannon be as forthcoming as Cindy had been? Would she see Charlene's visit as sincere, or as none of her business?

Only one way to find out.

She entered the main door into the lobby and the office, which was open.

Shannon sat behind the desk, typing away.

"Hello," Charlene called.

Shannon shrieked and put her hand to her chest, lowering it when she saw Charlene. "Oh! You scared a decade off my life just now."

"I hope not!" Charlene closed the door behind her with a *click*. "You were very into your work."

"Weekly accounts. I love a spreadsheet that matches." She scrunched her nose and laughed. "No wonder I never remarried."

Shannon was a beautiful woman with porcelain skin and red hair. Blue eyes. Charlene doubted her affinity for math would keep away any potential suitors.

"I keep asking, but you keep turning me down," a male voice said.

Charlene turned and her gaze dropped to Gil, who was a few inches shorter than her. He had plain features, but his face lit up when he smiled.

"You don't mean it, do you?" Shannon challenged.

"I would if I thought you'd say yes, but I've got to protect my heart." He covered his chest with his palm. His fingers and wrists glittered with gold rings and bracelets. A gold watch too and gold chains adorned his neck.

It took Charlene a moment to realize he was wearing paint coveralls over a short-sleeved black T-shirt and work boots.

"You are a flirt, that's all," Shannon decreed, glancing from the computer screen to Charlene, to Gil.

"Charming to a fault, my mom would say."

"She'd be the only one," Shannon lobbed back.

It was obvious to Charlene that the two were old friends and this was familiar banter.

"I think we've shocked Charlene," Shannon admonished Gil with a tiny smile.

Gil half-bowed. "Apologies."

"None necessary!" Charlene assured them. "I'm here to see how you're doing, that's all. I didn't mean to intrude."

"You're a pleasant distraction from these accounts, but I need five minutes and then I am ready for a tea break." Shannon pointed to Gil. "Why don't you show Charlene around the place? The building has historic points of interest. It's been here a hundred years."

Gil nodded. "Happy to."

"I'll meet you both upstairs in five." Shannon's fingertips bounced along the keyboard, her attention already back to the numbers.

"This way," Gil said, leading Charlene from the office.

"You don't have to entertain me." Charlene stayed on his heels. Gil had been here the night of Connor's attack. He'd been cleared by Sam and the Salem police. He wasn't as big in stature as Connor's attacker.

She'd lost sight of him at the funeral, but did that matter? The attacker had to be the same person for both men.

"Don't mind at all. This old building means a lot to the Irish families in Salem. Most of us can trace our roots here to the 1920s, or earlier. The O'Briens arrived in 1870 and have documentation to prove it."

"I'm sorry about Finn, and Connor."

"It's a shame. It's tearing Shannon up. First her cousin and now her twin brother."

Charlene nodded encouragingly.

Gil hooked his thumb around the buckle of his coveralls and glanced back at Shannon in her office.

"They were very close, always, growing up. Finn had the family house, you know? Inherited from their parents."

She'd heard the same from Cindy, only Gil didn't sound resentful like Cindy had. "Oh! Will Shannon move into that now? Or Aiden?"

"I don't know what will happen to the place. Shannon was barely keeping it going what with Finn being so . . . quiet, these past few years. It would need a ton of work both inside and out to make habitable."

Charlene understood that Gil was being protective of Shannon.

"Were you friends with Finn too?" She followed him across the lobby to the first large open area where he'd sat on the giant pot of gold, dressed as a leprechaun on Saint Patrick's Day. It felt like a year had passed and not just a week.

"When we were kids, yeah. I'm a few years older than Shannon and Finn."

"I saw Finn at the funeral . . ."

"He looked like an old man. Hard to believe we all used to chase girls together, before getting jobs and caught up in the real world."

"Time passes, doesn't it?"

"Yep." Gil stopped before a row of pictures hanging on the wall. "This is our gallery of mug shots."

"What?" Charlene exclaimed.

"Just kidding!" He grinned as he pointed at a group of youngsters, mostly redheads, around a Christmas tree in this very room.

She noticed that not much had changed. Same white walls with dark wood trim. Laminated wood floor.

"This is forty years ago, give or take," Gil said.

Charlene peered closer and found Shannon. "Who is she with? Connor?"

"Nope. That's Finn. The cousins were exactly alike. Red hair, blue eyes."

"Aiden too and Sinead. Patty."

"Yep." He took a few more steps, searching the gallery of photos.

"Who are you looking for?" Charlene stayed on his bootheels.

"I'm trying to find a picture of Finn before he became homebound. You can see for yourself what he was like."

Charlene nodded eagerly. "What happened to him?"

"I don't know," Gil said. "Shannon is like a mama bear and never said. She just started taking on more responsibility. Made excuses for him not coming to the festivals, or AOH club dinners."

Charlene studied the pictures that Gil pointed to. "Is that Finn? With two guys. No way. Is that Liam Kane?"

Gil squinted and scratched the back of his head. "Yep. And the other guy is Patrick Hennessy."

Like Liam, Patrick had dark hair. Finn, around twenty-five, if she had to guess, was the only redhead.

Liam had said Patrick's name at the funeral, saying they'd all done their time. Patrick Hennessey still had two more years in jail. "The innocence of youth," Charlene said lightly. "Liam doesn't have his face tattooed."

"Before prison, then," he remarked with an accepting shrug.

"You were friends with them too?"

"Nope. I had a job on the boat. Fishing. Finn fell into a rough crowd in high school."

"And now Liam has moved back to Salem for good." Had to be the plan if he wanted to buy the bar from James and Cindy with Patty's 401(k).

"Got out of prison, did his time." Gil scratched his chin. "I heard Patrick died in jail. In New York."

"Oh." Charlene's heart skipped. "How sad."

"Now Liam is all that's left of the trio." Gil tapped the photo. "They called themselves the Lucky Stars. Not so lucky after all."

Shannon joined them, her hands behind her back. "What are you doing? I wanted you to show Charlene the old architecture, not bore her to tears with photos. Oh, heaven, is that Aiden? He had to be five in this picture with Uncle Finn."

"He was really cute," Charlene said. His uncle had his hand on Aiden's little shoulder at an Easter egg hunt. Finn and Aiden were in matching short-sleeved shirts. Finn had a few tattoos on his arms. Was this before or after Liam and Patrick had gone to jail?

"I just can't believe Finn is gone," Shannon said in a thick voice. She swiped her cheeks.

"Ah, Shannon, hon, I'm sorry. Let's go have some tea upstairs." Gil put his hand on Shannon's lower back and led the way to the staircase and the upstairs kitchen.

Charlene had so many questions she couldn't ask. The pair were slowly opening up to her and she didn't want that door slammed shut.

She pulled her gaze from the wall of smiling faces and happy memories captured in time and followed them up the stairs.

The last time she was here, on this landing, Connor had been attacked.

Charlene kept quiet, but rubbed a chill from her arms when they reached the spot on the second floor. "This looks completely different!" she said in surprise.

"Without the green decorations everywhere?" Shannon gave a sniff that was half-cry and half-laugh. "I should hope so. It takes days to get this space set up for Saint Patrick's Day, and days to get it down again. All for one magical dinner party. Is it worth it?" She shrugged.

The question was rhetorical, but Gil patted Shannon's shoulder. "It is, Shannon."

"You only say that because you like being the leprechaun."

"Not true. And this last year wasn't so wonderful. Connor and me . . ." He touched his cheek.

"Cause he was drunk." Shannon squeezed Gil's wrist. "I yelled at him for it."

That was why she'd argued with Connor? Sticking up for Gil? It made sense, in context now.

"Connor was belligerent, demanding real gold. Said to ask you about it and I don't mind saying, that's when I punched him." Gil shook his head.

Shannon blinked and eyed Gil. "You didn't mention that before."

"Because I don't understand. Still don't."

Charlene lowered her gaze and stepped away from the pair. Connor had wanted real gold? Did this have to do with the gold coin at the gravesite?

"Connor shouldn't have come back," Shannon said. "He would still be alive if he'd stayed in California, I just know it."

"Why did he come back?" Gil asked.

"We will never know." Shannon crossed her arms, ending the subject.

Charlene couldn't help but think that the answer was a little too convenient. Connor with his drinking and bad habit of blabbing, made him a dangerous person to have around if one was protecting a family secret.

"This is the kitchen?" Charlene asked, stepping toward an open doorway.

"Yes," Gil said.

"We have a Keurig, so just grab a mug and your pod of choice." Shannon slipped by Charlene and into the kitchen with the ease of someone very familiar with the space. "Tea, cocoa, coffee."

"You both grew up here," she said. "In this club."

"Pretty much." Gil chuckled. "I'll have a decaf. It's just about pub time. I'm going to meet Liam for a pint."

"Liam?" Shannon asked in surprise. Her cheeks reddened. "Liam Kane? Why?"

"Yep. He invited me for a beer. Said he wants to catch up on old times."

Charlene didn't understand the odd vibe between Shannon and Gil at that statement. Had Shannon once cared for Liam, back before the prison tattoos? He'd been very handsome and dashing. So had Patrick and Finn.

"You should join us, Shannon. Maybe we can drag James out from behind the bar to visit too."

Shannon fixed a mug of coffee, decaf for Gil, and handed it to him. "No, thanks. I have work to do." She got down another cup and looked at Charlene. "What would you like?"

"Dark roast is fine with me."

"And I'll have an Earl Grey." Shannon chose those pods from the basket near the machine. "I need a boost so I can finish my report." She handed Charlene a mug with *AOH* on the side and started one for herself. "I still have to plan Finn's service and I just don't have the strength. I'm meeting with Father Callahan at six tonight."

"Is there anything I can do?" Charlene asked, leaning back against the counter. "I'm good at following directions, and I can help with food."

"A stranger is kinder than my own family." Shannon's chin trembled as she glanced at Gil. "If you see James at the damn pub, have him call me, would you? I'd like his support, but he's not returning my calls. Coward."

"You bet," Gil said in a sad voice. He blew on the steaming liquid.

"James and Cindy are gonna sell the pub to Liam," Shannon informed Gil in a stoic manner. "You should know what you're walking into. Another dramatic mess. Liam might want you to bartend or something. I told Cindy you're good with customers."

"A job?" Gil's tone lifted with interest and he looked at Charlene. "I was laid off last week. Fishing industry is slowing down. Shannon's hired me to do the maintenance here, but it's not full-time."

Charlene nodded. She got the sense that Gil would do anything for Shannon.

"They'd be lucky to have you, Gil." Shannon sipped from her mug. "And no matter what, I'll need you to help me with Finn's house. It's been months since he let me inside the place. God only knows what it will be like."

CHAPTER 23

Gil downed his coffee and put a hand on Shannon's shoulder. Charlene couldn't tell if he had taken over the role of big brother or wished for more. What did Shannon want?

"Thanks for everything. I'm going to visit Liam before he hires someone else. You can always count on me, Shannon. Nice seeing you again, Charlene. Take care now." Gil headed toward the stairs.

"Bye, Gil," Shannon said.

"Good luck with the job," Charlene added. The O'Briens and Gallaghers were at odds with each other, but Shannon seemed to have separated herself and Aiden from the pack.

"More coffee?" Shannon asked when Gil was gone.

"No, I still have some." Her mug was half-full.

"Are you running off, then?" Shannon scooted her

chair closer to the table. "Listen, I'm sorry about the other day."

"No! I am," Charlene said quickly. "I open my mouth to help and—"

Shannon raised her palm. "You were right about Aiden, Charlene. I didn't want to hear it." She stared into her mug of Earl Grey. "I wanted so much more for him, you understand? I wanted him to be educated like his father."

Charlene patted Shannon's wrist. She wore a fine gold bracelet with charms.

"I loved Trey Best." Shannon's hands shook a little as she reached for her tea. "He was a jokester who made everyone laugh, and people flocked to him. Mostly women. I tried not to notice, but it wears at you after a while. Always wondering, you know?"

"I'm sorry."

"Don't be. He loved his son very much and was a good man, for all his faults. He didn't deserve what happened to him."

"My husband was killed by a drunk driver," Charlene shared. "She's in jail now, still breathing, while the love of my life is in Heaven."

Shannon dabbed at the corners of her eyes. "What a tragedy, Charlene. Life isn't always fair, is it?"

"Not even close. What happened to your husband?"

"Trey was on a fishing trip with college friends from Boston. They had a cooler of beer and sandwiches. Nothing hard, just a day of fun planned on the water. They'd gone a dozen times. Well, I guess a couple of the guys had words and Trey got into the middle of it—he always thought he could fix things. Somehow, he fell off the boat. The men circled the area." Her voice grew thick.

"Took turns diving in and searching. Finally, they called the Coast Guard, who arrived at the scene within minutes. Didn't find my husband."

"Oh, Shannon, that is so awful. It must have been devastating for you and Aiden."

"It was. Shock at first and the belief that he'd be found. Alive."

Charlene put a hand over hers.

Shannon sucked in a breath and closed her eyes. "Even though it's been ten years, it's still hard to talk about. The following morning, his body washed up onshore. He had fish bites all over him, and I couldn't bear to look. We had a closed casket for the funeral, and no one wanted to talk about the incident. Guess we were all traumatized."

"Of course you were." Charlene could picture a jovial fisherman in the center of friends. "Trey sounds larger than life."

"That sums him up perfectly. He could be really great, except for the times when he wasn't. And now Aiden, he's smart . . . smarter than me and Trey combined. I wanted him to get out of Salem and save the world." Her eyes glistened even as she laughed at her own words.

"It's a terrible blow to lose both your brother and cousin within days of each other, but you still have James and Cindy—"

Shannon shook her head.

"—and Gil to help you get through this," Charlene continued. "And a friend in me."

A fleeting smile graced her mouth. "I don't have a lot of those, and I'm touched at your offer." She pinched her brows together. "Aiden and I had a heart-to-heart about what *he* wants, so I'm grateful to you for that."

Charlene sipped her dark roast, remembering why she

was here in addition to being a friend to Shannon. "Do you think Finn might have left something for Aiden? It might help with school."

"I've got a meeting next week about his will." Shannon sighed. "My brother was going a little crazy, I hate to say. Hallucinating. Talked about seeing Patrick Hennessy, who's been dead for two years now." Her voice caught. "He even told me that Patrick was haunting him for . . . for what Finn had." Shannon gave a cynical laugh. "What would a ghost do with worldly goods?"

Patrick had died in jail, sentenced for multiple counts of theft. Liam had been to jail and done time for aggravated robbery. Liam had wanted to talk to Finn about something—then Finn had died. They all thought Finn was hiding money. Except for Shannon, who knew Finn best.

What part did Connor play in all of this?

Her ghost could do plenty with worldly goods, like the computer and iPad. Charlene just shrugged. Maybe there was a ghost at the O'Brien house, but the culprit was more than likely human. Aiden had also mentioned that Finn had wasted his wealth.

Who had dropped the gold coin?

"Finn had become progressively worse over time. Between hoarding and his being a recluse, I'm sure the house isn't fit to live in right now." Shannon gave another sad smile. "I want to restore our family home back to its original beauty."

"I love my old mansion. Will you hire Gil to do the work for you?"

"He'll be on the team, but it's too big of a job for one man. I'm sure the bank will grant a home improvement loan if I use the house and property as collateral." She tapped her manicured nails to the table in thought. "Depending on the work involved, I'd like to sell quickly and pay off the loan, then reenroll Aiden in med school. He'd lost his scholarship due to bad grades and didn't want to tell me. Figured that if it was his choice, he wouldn't look like such a loser."

"That's positive news. I hope it all works out for you. Shannon, if you need any help emptying the house, I can volunteer an hour or two most days."

"Thanks, but that won't be necessary. Aiden agreed to pitch in after I explained that with the sale of the house, we'd have enough money for his medical school or anything else he's interested in."

"I hope James will step up to the plate to get Finn's place ready to sell." It was awful that her own brother wouldn't call her in these circumstances.

"Finn cut James out of his will years ago, so he won't do a dang thing. I lent James money too, but it wasn't enough. And now James is selling the pub to Liam to avoid bankruptcy—another mistake." Shannon tossed her hair back off her face. "Cindy is no better, though she likes to think so, always with her hand out." Her cheeks flushed. "You asked about Patty, and if she was a friend? Well, Liam and I dated all through high school. He was cute and we talked about getting married one day. Then he met Patty, Connor's younger sister, my good friend, and cousin. Boom—they got hitched within six months with no word to me."

"You must have been so hurt."

"I was until Liam got involved in . . . a gang, and ended up in prison. I bought myself a bottle of champagne that day, I don't mind telling you. And I've been celebrating ever since."

Charlene laughed. "You got the better deal."

"I like to think so. Looking at those tattoos would give me the hives. Kinda feel sorry for Patty. He's nasty to her and she's afraid to fight back in case she loses her cushy lifestyle. Her job at the bank was a parttime teller position."

She thought of the giant diamond on Patty's hand. The cash for the bar. Patty must be living off Liam's spoils. "Despite all the bad, it seems like you might come out on top." Charlene rinsed her cup in the kitchen sink, not wanting to hold Shannon up any longer.

"I will. Never doubt that." Shannon stood as well. Her charm bracelet chimed prettily. Little stars and horseshoes.

"Shannon, just one last thing that I'm trying to put together . . . do you know if Finn's hoard would include a gold coin collection? I saw one with Connor, and then in Finn's grave."

Shannon laughed and brought her tea mug to the sink. "Let me guess: Cindy told you that Finn's rich? She wishes."

Her phone beeped a message from her purse pocket and Charlene quickly said goodbye, with another offer of help. She reached the car and read the message from her dad, who was wondering where she was.

Driving home, Charlene hoped that Aiden would be the son Shannon wished for, going back to school and saving the world. Finn's corner lot was in a perfect spot, just a few blocks off the main road and close to all the good restaurants and shops.

Restored, it would be worth millions. Shannon and Aiden should have no financial worries after that. They'd come out smelling like roses.

When she pulled up to her house, she admired the new plants and the wagon with pots of flowers. She wouldn't sell this place, not for a million dollars, and loved the life she was living, even without her spouse.

The guests were her family, and Minnie and Avery. Jack was her live-in best friend and Sam was always lurking in the background. If he really wanted to get married, he'd find the right woman fast enough. She had a sneaky feeling that he might enjoy his bachelor lifestyle as much as she did hers.

Silva pounced on her as she entered the door, mewing and rubbing her head against Charlene's legs. Where was everybody? "Hello?"

She poked her head in the kitchen, but the silence told her what she knew. Neither Minnie nor Avery or her parents or guests were in the house.

Before she lost her mind with worry, Jack called for her in her suite. She rushed inside. "Where is everybody?"

Jack fluttered a curtain near his armchair. "See for yourself! Teach you to run off and interview possible criminals during bed-and-breakfast hours," he chided.

"You got my note?"

He floated it to her and stuck it on her shirt.

"Funny." Charlene crumpled the note and peered through the pane glass window at Jason, Scarlett, Caleb, and Layla doing a sack race wearing party hats as her parents watched. She turned slowly to Jack. "What's going on?"

"It's Layla's seventh birthday today and her parents surprised her with this! Isn't it fun?"

"Yes, it is." She opened the door and stepped outside. The revelers were bumping into each other and laughing, falling in their sacks and then getting up again to make it to the finish line, where Avery handed out ice cream cones.

Beneath the large oak tree was a blow-up swimming pool filled with dozens of multicolored balloons. Tied to a thick branch was a rope. You could swing and drop into the balloons without getting hurt. She wanted a turn!

Her mom and dad, along with Sheffer, were seated in lawn chairs and shouted encouragement. She waved to her parents, but Sheffer never looked her way. She would find out what he was hiding . . .

Jack stood behind her, close enough to bring goose bumps. "This is the way a home should be, Charlene, filled with laughter. I hope Avery agrees to move in."

Charlene clasped her hands together, eyes shimmering with unshed happy tears. Minnie had put up a long table for small gifts, a huge cake, lemonade, and paper plates and cups. Beneath the table was a small cooler with soft drinks and beer. Three balloons were tied to a pole on one side, and four on the other. Avery whistled encouragement.

"Me too, Jack. Listen, I'm going to go mingle, but when I get back, we have to talk about what I've learned. Do you mind seeing if you can find out how Patrick Hennessy died? Both Gil and Shannon say it was two years ago in jail. Finn claimed to have been haunted by Patrick."

Jack vanished and reappeared by her laptop. "On it— go have a good time! I'll be here."

Charlene scooted over to her mom and dad, ignoring Sheffer except for a brief nod. "Hey, I'm missing out. I wish I'd known, instead of running around doing errands."

"Don't worry, sweetheart," her dad said. "It was a spontaneous, last-minute thing. When Minnie found out it was Layla's birthday, she ran out and bought all this stuff. Even the cake!"

"She's a gem," the three said at once.

"You missed the scavenger hunt," her mother said, brown eyes sparkling. "Your father and I played."

"Sheffer and Jason made up a list of ten things they needed to find." Her dad tipped beers with his new best buddy, Sheffer.

Charlene glanced at Sheffer. "Thanks for doing that. I'm happy to see you here."

"My work is almost done," he answered mysteriously.

"That'll be a relief for you," she answered. *And me.* What did his work entail?

Her mom turned her head. "They had enough prizes for everyone who entered. Your dad got a pack of cards with witches on the back, and mine was a special Salem notepad. Cute stuff."

"I'm interested in that swing," Charlene said. "Looks like fun."

She marched over, eyeing the rope with calculation and excitement. It had been a great many years since she'd done something like this. At ten, she'd gone camping with her cousins. Her uncle had hung a rope over the lake and everyone would take turns jumping in.

Minnie waved at her and she decided the swing could wait. "Before you say a word," Charlene said in a stern voice, "I just want to tell you how much I adore you." She pulled Minnie into her arms and Avery too.

"We missed you today," Avery said. Her short hair blew up on a breeze revealing the tattoo on the back of her neck.

"I expected you back sooner as well. Hope you weren't out giving Sam a heart attack."

"Minnie, that guy is a brick. His heart is encased in stone. And I was just chatting with a few people." People who might have a motive for murder. Shannon had a plan, no matter what was in Finn's will. Same with Cindy and James.

"Here we go again." Minnie swiped a piece of frosting from the cake.

"Ladies." She steered the conversation to a happy place. "Thank you a zillion times over for hosting this birthday party for Layla. A little birdie told me it was your idea, Minnie, and you ran off to get all the goodies."

Minnie beamed. "Because of my grandkids, I had most of it at home. Why not put it to good use?"

"I love you both. Couldn't do without you."

"And we won't let you try," Avery said, handing Charlene a birthday hat.

"Enough gooey stuff! I'm going to round up the birthday girl and Caleb. Want to do the swing with me?"

Avery clapped her hands. "Awesome! What do you say, Minnie?"

"I say I'm not going to make a fool of myself."

"You don't mind if I do?" Avery asked Minnie.

"Go, girl!" Minnie shooed her toward the balloons. "Have fun."

Charlene walked over to where the Montgomerys were sprawled out on the grass. "Who wants to do the swing with me?"

"I did it three times already," Caleb said proudly.

"And I did it twice, but I fell in the balloons once." Layla took off her pink crown that matched her pink dress and handed it to her mother. "Keep this for me, Mommy, so I don't lose it in the balloons."

"Okay," Charlene asked as they faced the long thick rope. "Who's first?"

Caleb yelled, "Me. Please?" He cradled his hands beneath his chin.

Charlene grinned at his antics. "Off you go, then!"

Avery stood on the other side of the balloon-filled pool. "Go, Caleb, go!"

He hooked his legs around the rope and sailed across perfectly, making a Tarzan shrieking noise. Once he was on the grass he made a bow. "I want to do it again."

"You can! But let Layla go next."

Charlene boosted Layla onto the swing and she clung tightly to the rope with a frightened look on her pretty face. Avery gave her a gentle push, but after two seconds her hands slipped, and she fell into the pile of balloons.

Her mother was there in an instant. "You okay, sweetie?"

Layla rubbed her hip. "Yes. But I think I should wait until I'm eight to do it again." Scarlett chuckled and helped the little girl out.

Avery scrambled up to the branch, jumped on the rope, and flung herself well over to the other side of the grass. "That was so cool!"

"Guess it's my turn." Charlene hoisted herself up, using the branch to put her weight on, wrapped her legs tightly around the rope, and shoved off. Instead of crossing the great divide, the rope broke and she dropped bottom first into the pile of balloons.

When her face peeked out, the kids, including Avery, all jumped in, tossing balloons at each other. Jason and Scarlett helped toss them too. Even Minnie got into the action. The laughter and the fun ended when her mom yelled out, "Cake time, everyone."

They all scrambled out and gathered around the table to sing Layla "Happy Birthday" and watch her blow out the candles. Charlene couldn't remember a birthday she'd enjoyed more.

After the party, she and her parents dressed for a fancy meal and she finally got to experience Turner's Seafood dinner for herself. Unlike Sheffer and his rack of lamb, contrary man, she went with the house special, and it was divine.

Later that evening, after everyone had gone to their rooms, Charlene, at last, got a chance to catch up with Jack.

"Charlene, you were right to be curious. Patrick Hennessy was murdered in jail by other inmates. If a ghost can't leave the place they were killed, like it happened with me, then Patrick wasn't haunting Finn."

"So why would he tell his sister that?" She grabbed the afghan for her lap on the love seat.

Jack shook his head and settled back in his armchair. "Mental illness?"

Charlene supposed that was possible. "Patrick, Liam, and Finn were close childhood friends and named themselves the Lucky Stars. What mischief they'd gotten into turned sour when Patrick and Liam both ended up in jail for theft."

"Finn was left behind, living his life out as they paid with hard time," Jack said. "Could that be enough to turn him into a recluse? Patrick was murdered in jail. Liam came home."

"That sounds like motive for murder—if one had gotten away with something and the others did not, don't you think, Jack?"

CHAPTER 24

Sunday morning, Charlene pushed back her covers and accidentally dislodged Silva from her place behind Charlene's knees.

"Yowl!" Silva complained with a smack of her tail to the air. Left, right, *snap.*

"Sorry, kitty cat." Charlene scooped Silva up and dropped a kiss to the top of her furry head.

She carried Silva out of the bedroom to the sitting room, where Jack was watching the news.

"Still no word. It's been a week," he said. He tapped his chin and studied her with her arms full of pouting feline. "Why is Silva so grouchy?"

"I knocked her from her comfy spot on the bed." She rounded the love seat and sat down. "Jack. I'm going to confront Sheffer today, and I'd like backup. You."

"Confront him?"

"Yes. He knows something about Liam and Patrick, and Connor. My brain is insisting he's involved somehow and I think it must do with the time Liam and Patrick did in jail, in New York. I'd like to find out if Connor went to jail in New York too. Saying he was in California could be a cover story."

Jack leaned back and crossed his ankle to his opposite knee. "I can search his room. I know you don't like that, but it would give us immediate information."

It felt wrong to spy on a guest, but what if she was harboring a murderer? He'd told her that his activity was legal, but in this household, she needed proof.

She stood, unsettled.

"I can go right now. He'll never know I was there." In an instant, Jack's body that he manifested for Charlene was gone and all that was left was a cold pocket of air.

"Jack?" Darn it. She'd wanted to discuss it first.

He returned in another flash, a scowl on his face. "Sheffer's not there, Charlene. His bed wasn't slept in."

Her guests didn't have to check in or out. Her bed-and-breakfast was their home while they rented rooms.

Why rent a suite and not sleep there? It wasn't the first time either. "If he's a womanizer, why come to Salem to sleep around? He can do that in New York a lot easier, I'm sure."

"I wish I could follow him and tell you." Jack paced in a flurry of energy.

His essence was tied to the property and he couldn't leave, which meant any old-fashioned following had to be done by her.

"It seems suspicious, doesn't it?"

"Oh yes," Jack agreed. "Where was he the day Connor was attacked?"

"Sheffer is too tall to be the person who attacked Connor, but I would bet the bed-and-breakfast that he's involved somehow."

"You'd put up our home? You must be pretty sure." Jack's image wavered before the television. "What now?"

"It's Sunday. He'd paid ahead for a week, which is up tomorrow. I suppose I could print out a bill and slip it under his doorway. I'd like to see inside the room."

"I can do that for you, be your eyes. What are you looking for?"

"Proof that will tie him to both Connor and Finn's murders."

He nodded and disappeared.

Silva meowed from her spot on the love seat. Jack was here and gone—something they'd learned to accept.

Charlene went to her room and pulled on jeans, a sweater, and comfortable half-boots for tromping around Salem. Her skin had that itchy feeling of something about to happen.

Back in Chicago, she would have ignored the sensation, but since moving here she'd become more open to her other senses. What was taking Jack so long?

She went to the kitchen and helped Minnie put together breakfast for their guests. Her parents hadn't come down yet, but it had been a fun evening of card games that lasted until almost midnight.

Jack appeared at her side while she was stacking toast. Crumbs fluttered to the counter from his whoosh of energy, but Minnie didn't notice. "Sheffer's computer was closed so I couldn't snoop, but he had a printout on Liam Kane and Patrick Hennessy. He also had one on Finn O'Brien."

She knew it! Charlene bit her lip before she asked

aloud where he'd found the papers. "Minnie, excuse me just a second."

She held her hand to her stomach and stepped toward her suite.

"Oh! Take your time. It's seven-thirty and nobody is down yet."

Charlene nodded and went into her living room, shutting the door and locking it behind her.

"Jack!" she whispered.

He appeared next to her laptop.

"Where did you find those papers?"

"Under the printer he'd brought with him. Which was also odd."

"Like they were hidden?"

"Definitely."

She sat at her desk and powered on the laptop. "Can you research Finn, to see if he had any warrants, or if he'd done jail time? Gil mentioned yesterday that Finn had fallen into a rough crowd for a while. Is there a statute of limitations for felons or criminal records?"

"I'll look. And then what? Finn was scared straight?"

"You said it last night. Scared into being a recluse." Charlene's skin tingled. "What if instead of hiding from the world, he was hiding from *someone*?"

Minnie dropped a dish in the kitchen. Charlene couldn't stay to investigate, but needed to help her housekeeper with their guests.

She got up and pointed to the chair. "See what you can find out with your cyber skills. Something happened to Finn and we need to find out what it was. Shannon isn't talking. She steered away from the subject of her brother, actually. She wants to fix up the house and sell it."

"From everything you've said, she is protective of those she loves. Aiden. And Finn."

"Morning, Minnie," a male voice called.

"I see you've got a coffee?" Minnie said cheerily. "Breakfast will be done in fifteen minutes."

"Sheffer's here!" Charlene said. She exchanged a look with Jack, then darted out of her suite through the kitchen to the staircase.

Sheffer had his coat slung over his arm and a cup of coffee from the dining room in hand, one foot on the lower step.

"Let me help you!" Charlene insisted.

"I'm just going to my room." He had dark shadows under his eyes. Growth along his chiseled jaw. He had the look of a man who'd been up all night.

There was no hint of perfume or love kisses on his throat, no sign of passion. Charlene ran down a list of possible explanations: gambler, art thief, stripper, counterfeiter . . . killer?

"I'm right behind you," she said. "I'd like to speak with you for just a second."

His brow arched in annoyance. "I'd rather not."

Charlene motioned for him to continue up the stairs. "It's important."

Jack shimmered at the top of the landing, his arms crossed as he studied Sheffer.

"This better be." Sheffer stopped at the center of the staircase. "I can be outta here in fifteen minutes."

"Suit yourself," she murmured, not allowing him to bully her.

"What kind of hostess are you?" His tone was layered with sarcasm, but she detected a whiff of concern.

Good. No jokes. The time for schmoozing was over. "An observant one. Would you like an audience?"

Sheffer didn't hurry his pace as he continued up the stairs.

She followed Sheffer to his room. Nobody else on the floor was awake. She stood so they were an inch apart before his bedroom door.

"Where were you last night?"

"Don't have to tell you." The vein in his neck pulsed. "I'm free to come and go. Unless you came looking for me, Charlene?" He winked.

Her stomach churned and she retreated a step.

"He's hiding something," Jack insisted.

"Let's talk in your room," Charlene said. "We don't want to wake the others. I have my cell phone and the police on speed dial."

"Police?" Sheffer unlocked the door to his suite and tossed the trench coat to the bed.

She followed him inside and Jack slammed the door. Sheffer didn't notice as he was perusing the desk and bed. A predator sensing another animal in his lair?

"I wasn't in here without your knowledge."

"I know that." He pulled his smartphone from his pants pocket. "I have security wherever I go."

"What kind of man would need that?"

He gave her a half-smile and leaned his hip to the desk. "Sam warned me you were curious."

She wouldn't get sidetracked on how he knew Sam. From New York. Where Liam had done time.

"What do you do for a living? How do you know Liam and Patrick? Did you meet them in jail? They were both incarcerated in New York."

He drew himself up, affronted. "I have never been to prison."

Jack hovered between them, his fists clenched. The air around her ghost was electric with spectral energy.

Sheffer remained unaware of the danger he was in.

"Answer the question, please."

"Which one?" Sheffer was flip in his attitude.

She gave a shake of her head toward Jack, who was looking through Sheffer's trench coat pockets.

Charlene kept Sheffer's focus on her, with Jack at his back.

Jack pulled an object from the inside pocket and it was all Charlene could do to stifle a scream. Was that a gun?

Not a gun, but a Taser.

Jack put it back as Sheffer glanced behind him to the bed when his coat slipped to the floor.

He couldn't see Jack, who was responsible.

Sheffer scowled and put the coat back on the bed. The Taser dropped to the thick area rug with a *thunk*.

"Why do you have that?" Charlene demanded, her thumb over the dial button for the Salem police as she showed him her phone.

"A Taser?" He shrugged. "It's part of the job."

"What job requires a portable printer, staying out all night, and a weapon? Oh, and binoculars."

He tossed his head back and laughed. "You are relentless. And way out of line. Do you treat all your guests like this?"

If he thought to bully her, he was on the wrong track. "Why were you spying at Connor's funeral? What do you know about Finn's death? I saw you there and then you were gone. Give me one good reason not to call the police."

"Fine." Sheffer held his hands out at his sides. "I'm a PI."

"What?" Jack spluttered.

"What?" Charlene asked. Yet it fit. A private investigator had their own rules as they searched for clues to solve crimes. "I understand everything but the printer."

"Sometimes I need documentation that is easier for me to get on my own rather than head down to the local office supply shop. It avoids too many questions. I'm not saying more than that."

She couldn't tell him that she knew he had printouts on Liam, Patrick, and Finn. "Are you investigating Liam?" she asked. "He just got out of jail."

"I know." Sheffer nodded. "That's why I'm here."

"I don't understand."

"A criminal once released will usually return to the nest—in this case, Salem." He watched her like a hawk eyed a rabbit.

Charlene debated what to give in order to get more information. "I saw pictures at the AOH club of Liam and Patrick. And Finn."

"You did?" Sheffer's voice rose. "Can you show me?"

"Maybe." She feared if she cooperated too much with Sheffer, he would shut her out, as Sam did. "Is it important?"

"Maybe." His tone copied hers exactly. Jack snorted.

"Who told you about the pictures?" Sheffer asked. "Shannon?"

"No. Gil."

"Little short dude that plays the leprechaun every year. Interesting character. I wonder if he's involved with the gang, but I haven't found proof."

"Gang?" Charlene glanced at Jack.

"Oh . . . do I know something you don't, Ms. Morris?" Sheffer crossed the room to the desk and switched the chair around to sit.

"A lot, I'm sure. What gang?" Her mind drew up an image of the Lucky Stars.

"The Lucky Stars gang," he confirmed.

Charlene swallowed, her throat dry. "Liam has a tattoo . . . three stars," she said.

"So did Patrick." Sheffer tapped the same place she'd seen the tattoo on Liam. "Inner forearm."

She wanted to connect Connor and the reason he'd been attacked. "Was Connor the third member of the gang?" It made sense to her. She could ask Patty if Connor had that tattoo as well.

Sheffer rubbed his hand through his hair, mussing it in a sexy way. "I have my hunch, but I need proof."

"You sound just like Sam." The two had known each other in New York. Why hadn't Sam told her that? Didn't he trust her?

He shook his head, eyes glittering with suppressed humor. "Sam and I are on the same side of the law, sort of, only I have more wiggle room."

She nodded but stayed on topic. "Did you help put Liam in jail? I read that it was aggravated robbery, among other things."

"I did." Sheffer's voice was proud. "I was hired by the company the gang stole from. I tracked down Liam, then Patrick. Gave evidence to send them away for fourteen years. One of the gang got away, and the other two wouldn't give him up."

"That's loyal."

"My guess is that the person who didn't go to jail stayed out of the spotlight."

"What was stolen?"

"A cargo truck of gold coins worth millions."

Gold coins! Things fell into place. "Connor was talking about gold. He left Salem and then came back. He drank too much and blabbed. Is that why he was killed? Did Liam do it?"

"Slow down, Charlene." Sheffer expelled a breath and leaned his forearms on the back of the chair. "You have a quick mind."

"I saw a gold coin in Connor's grave. When Finn was killed."

"Sam told me about that."

"Why would he tell *you*?"

"Don't be jealous, Charlene. I'm a licensed professional with ties to the case. I'm working for the armor truck company to see about finding—"

"The third man?"

"Nope. The gold."

Jack whirled around the room in alarm.

"You see, Charlene, the stash of gold coins was never found."

CHAPTER 25

Charlene dropped her phone into her pocket as she stared at Sheffer. "The gold was never found? You think that Liam might lead you to it, here in Salem after all this time. Did he have the coins?"

"Not that the cops found." Sheffer got up and twirled the chair back to the desk. "You're pretty good. Sam should hire you."

"I own a bed-and-breakfast."

"You run the classiest B and B in all of Salem, I know." He tilted his head as if to study her. "They say that curiosity killed the cat, but not so with you. You're smart in addition to curious."

"Thanks for your faith in me, and I sure hope you're right. I don't know the connection between Connor and Finn or why they were killed."

"You don't stop." He gave her an admiring look. She

quickly stepped back and opened the door. Jack simmered behind her in anger and she wanted to defuse the situation before he did something crazy, like lift Sheffer off his feet in a flurry of ghostly air.

"Why did Sam suggest you come here? You could have had any hotel in town if you've been hired by a big company."

"I miss home-cooked meals. Hazard of the job. I also prefer bed-and-breakfasts because they're cozier and allow me more privacy." He widened the door and she stepped into the hall. "Usually."

She found herself smiling, albeit reluctantly. "Will you tell Sam about this?"

Sheffer chuckled. "Sam is very protective of you, so I'll leave that in your court. Mum's the word on my end. I need some sleep." He shut the door so hard it bounced in its frame.

She faced Jack and opened her mouth to speak until she noticed her guests emerging into the hall, dressed for Sunday breakfast.

"Are you all right?" one of them asked.

"What was that noise?"

"I'm fine—don't worry! Sheffer just accidentally shut the door too hard. Now, who is hungry?" Charlene raised her hand like a flamenco dancer and led the way down the stairs to the dining room.

Jack didn't join them.

After breakfast and helping Minnie with the dishes, she made sure that her guests were out the door in plenty of time to join their tours for the day. She let Minnie know that she'd be busy for the next few hours and hurried to her suite with a bottle of water in hand.

Jack waited by her laptop. "No Connor Gallagher in prison, so I did some digging on Patrick Hennessy—he was in a different jail than Liam."

"They were known partners in crime, so maybe the police wanted them separated?"

He shrugged. "I hacked into the visitors' log. Patrick's jailhouse wasn't as strict as where Liam was incarcerated."

"Why the visitor log?"

"To see if Connor ever visited and whether or not Finn or Shannon did. I know you like Shannon, but her protectiveness might mean she would cover for her twin if he too was involved."

Charlene hated that Jack was right.

She sat down and he scrolled the log for her.

"Nothing from Connor. Or Finn." He hesitated. "Not Shannon. But there is a woman, Letitia Moor, who visited quite often in the two years before Patrick died."

"Letitia?" She shook her head, not recognizing the name. In truth, she'd half-expected it to be Shannon, or Cindy.

Jack scrolled to a different date. "Here the log reads Letitia Moor, with Hennessy in parenthesis."

"What does that mean?" She glanced at Jack. "Are they married?"

"I don't believe so in the strict sense of the word. Some of the visits are marked *CV*. Conjugal visit."

"Ew!"

"But if at some point they did marry or have a common-law relationship, Patrick might have confided in Letitia. Husbands tell their wives or girlfriends secrets all the time. If he told her about the stash of gold it would give her a reason to stick around."

"That is certainly possible. Jared and I didn't keep secrets from each other."

"You probably didn't rob an armored truck either," Jack teased.

"True." She typed *Letitia Moor* and *Patrick Hennessy* into the search bar, searching for death or marriage records. A news article popped up from the Boston paper.

"Bingo," Jack said over her shoulder. "Patrick Hennessy, deceased, survived by Letitia Moor. Type in *Letitia Moor*."

Charlene's fingers sped over the keyboard. She scored multiple hits and read, "Letitia Moor did a few years in a Boston jail for petty theft. She got out on parole just last month." Hair on her nape rose to attention.

Jack crossed his arms. "That's convenient, with Boston right down the street from us."

She found a mug shot of Letitia Moor. The woman had a square face and body, with hard eyes. Bleached hair. Forty or sixty, it was hard to tell. Covered in tats.

"Letitia is a tough woman. She doesn't look like the type to walk away from a possible fortune, still hidden."

"Exactly. Especially if that was what her common-law husband did time for." Jack tapped his chin, staring at the computer screen.

"She would know about Liam and the third member of the gang."

"And want her share, or she might blab."

Charlene shook herself from her reverie, thinking she needed to warn Shannon. "We have to find Letitia before she goes after Shannon."

"Why Shannon?"

"She's closest to Finn. Jack, Shannon dismissed Finn's rantings that he was being haunted by Patrick as part of his being crazy. Don't forget that the night Connor was attacked, the person called Connor *Finn*. In their youth they resembled each other, and in the dark . . . ?"

"Mistaken identity." Jack nodded. The temperature room dropped a few degrees as he got excited.

"Shannon said that Connor and Finn could have been twins, before Finn became a recluse. What did Sheffer say? Finn hid from the world, staying well out of the spotlight."

"And?" Jack encouraged her train of thought.

"What if Letitia killed Connor somehow, thinking it was Finn?"

Jack agreed. "Are you going to tell Sam?"

Her heart hurt when she thought of Sam. "Right now, Sam is the last person I want to talk to. He knew Sheffer was a PI and deliberately kept me in the dark about it."

"He was protecting you." Jack shrugged as if this might be a gray area. It wasn't to Charlene.

"Sam suggested my bed-and-breakfast and then didn't tell me the truth. He knew I suspected this guest of mine was connected to this case. He had plenty of opportunities to come clean."

"You can't just go after Letitia yourself."

"I know." She exhaled. "I could be wrong, which would also upset Sam." She got to her feet. "I'm going to take Sheffer, and his brains, and his Taser."

Jack chuckled. "Now, that I like. Where are you going to start?"

"The AOH and the gallery of pictures . . . there is one of Finn with Aiden that I'd like to study."

CHAPTER 26

Charlene called Shannon to ask if she could visit the AOH, but the phone went to voicemail. Shannon was probably at church, where she would be safely surrounded by other people. Charlene couldn't wait to see the picture and the tattoo on Finn's inner arm. Confirming his alliance with his buddies, Liam and Patrick, would tell her where to search for Letitia, though she had a good idea where to start.

Her guests were out for the day, so now she pondered her next move. One, get rid of her parents for a few hours. Two, find a way to convince Sheffer to break into the AOH. Surely as a PI, he'd done worse. Jack was spying upstairs and would let her know when Sheffer woke up. She needed to act.

She peeked out the front window at her parents, who

were relaxing outdoors on the Adirondack chairs after their big breakfast. Looked like her dad was napping and her mom was busy with a crossword puzzle.

Minnie's routine was to bake and while the food was in the oven, to vacuum and dust. She was only working a half-day today.

Charlene perched on one of the stools, an ear out for Jack and Sheffer. "What time are your grandkids coming over?"

Minnie checked the timer on the bread. "Three or four. They're not so anxious anymore to see Papa and me. Teenagers just want to be with their friends or on their phones. Not sure what this Snapchat is all about, but they're glued to their screens."

"Closest I have to understanding that is Avery." Talking about it no longer made her feel sad. This was her journey and time to embrace it, not wish for things that might have been. "At least you get to see them every Sunday for dinner. You're a lucky woman to have family so near."

"I am. I was so excited when my youngest girl married a professor from BU. I knew that'd keep them close for a while. Jake, as you know, went to college at Penn State, met a girl, and decided not to come home. Twelve years it's been." She wiped her hands on her apron. "They come to visit a few times a year, and I can always take a quick visit to them, but it's not the same."

"I suppose that's how Mom and Dad feel. I was their everything."

"You still are." She nodded toward the front porch. "Nice day out there. You should take them on a day trip."

"Wish I could, but there's something I need to do." Charlene grinned. "It involves Sheffer. Could you help me out? I need him out of bed. He pulled an all-nighter and is in la-la land as we speak."

"What are you scheming?"

"Your vacuum. While you bake, I'll bring it upstairs and run it right outside his door."

Minnie chuckled. "You really don't like him much, do you?"

"I don't . . . however, he's one of the good guys, which I will explain later."

Minnie's eyes locked on hers. "You be careful. Don't be foolish."

"I will—that's why I'm taking Sheffer along."

The timer beeped. Minnie removed the bread and popped in a casserole, then grabbed the vacuum. "I'll get him awake while you arrange an outing for your parents." She hustled toward the staircase, where Jack waited. He saw Minnie with her vacuum and laughed.

Charlene dreamed up a stellar idea. Her mother had said she'd wanted to see the vineyard, and her friend Brandy owed her a favor, or two.

She dialed and Brandy answered on the second ring. "Hey, stranger. What's up?"

"My parents are in town."

"You need a magic potion or something? You know I could go to jail doing something like that."

"No," Charlene said with a half-smile. "Matter-of-fact, we are having a wonderful visit. Best ever."

"Not sure if that's a good thing or not. A sudden change of heart could mean early dementia," the practicing witch said with a snicker.

"You can see for yourself. I need a favor! Would you be able to give them a tour of the winery, with lunch included?"

"Sure." Brandy sighed. "What are you up to?"

"Nothing yet. I'll send them in a cab, since I need my SUV."

"Don't be silly. I'll have Serenity pick them up."

"All the better. My folks will think they're getting the star treatment. She's doing good, right?"

"Serenity couldn't be better."

"Thanks, Brandy. I owe you one."

"No, you don't. We'll call this even."

The call ended as the vacuum roared to life upstairs in the hall. Her parents came inside to the foyer and Charlene told them the plan for the day.

They were delighted, of course. They'd met Brandy and her mother, Evelyn, and Charlene knew her mom was quite bewitched by them. Brandy would make sure they enjoyed themselves, and perhaps give them a tarot reading.

"Brandy's daughter, Serenity, will pick you up in an hour. I have things to do this afternoon but should be done by four. Can't miss happy hour, can I?"

"You run your errands, Charlene," her dad said. "We'll bring home some wine to share."

"If we don't drink it first," her mom said, raising a brow to her husband of fifty years. Not one snarky word from her mom about not spending time with Charlene. "Annabeth says that wine is one of God's best gifts."

Annabeth was a miracle worker, Charlene decided on the spot. She heard loud shouting. Jack floated up and down the stairs, laughing hard.

Her parents had just reached the top steps to get ready for Brandy's when Sheffer barreled down past them, anger on his face. Her dad paused but she waved for them to go on to their room.

"What do you not understand about *do not disturb*?" His eyes were steely as he moved into her space.

A rush of cold air split them apart: Jack to the rescue, his humor tampered down.

"I need you, Sheffer. And those are words I never expected to say."

The PI froze and slowly unthawed as he deciphered her meaning. "You have new information? What happened while I slept?"

She wanted an answer first. "Where do you go at night?"

"Recon. Liam likes his dive bars." He scowled, his eyes still bloodshot.

"What about Aiden?"

"He's all right. I checked out his story. He dropped out of college due to bad grades from partying and didn't want to tell his mama."

She looked him over in his sloppy sleep pants and a long-sleeved T. "Go get dressed. Not your good clothes. I think we might get dirty."

He opened his mouth, then closed it tight. "I'll be down in ten."

Jack followed her to her suite. "You have your pepper spray? A full charge on your cell phone?"

"I do! Don't worry. We need proof that Finn is the third member of the gang, and then we'll call Sam. I think I know where Letitia might be."

Jack walked her and Sheffer to the porch and waited until she drove to the end of the driveway. He waved until she was out of sight and she knew he'd be waiting for her return.

"What's the plan?" Sheffer asked.

"I want to check an old photo of Finn at the AOH, and

Shannon didn't pick up when I called. I'm quite sure that he had a tattoo on the inside of his arm. If it is stars, that would physically tie him with Liam and Patrick and the Lucky Stars gang."

"All right . . . What do you need me for?"

"I don't have a key and nobody's there. I'd like you to break in for me."

Sheffer spluttered and scratched his jaw. "And what if I said no?"

"I'd have to do it myself, then drive over to Finn's house and break in there. You'd miss out on all the fun." She glanced at him. "If something bad happened to me, Sam would be furious with you."

He stared at her, then started to laugh.

"Does that mean yes?"

"You are one crazy lady. I sure don't want your giant detective coming after me with a loaded gun. So, yes. I'll help."

"You won't regret it, I promise."

When they arrived at the AOH the parking lot was empty.

"We should go around to the back entrance, which will lead to the main floor. I was on the outer stairs second floor when Connor was attacked. Someone raced past me."

"Did you see his face?"

Charlene kept her thoughts on the attacker being a woman to herself until she was sure. "Of course not, or the case would be wrapped up by now."

Sheffer rolled his eyes and hurried around the back and out of sight from the street. She watched as he put on gloves, tried the door handle—locked—then he jimmied it open in a matter of seconds. He waited for an alarm.

Nothing. He pushed the door and turned to her with a satisfied grin. "Easy when you know how."

As she brushed past him, she asked, "You earn your living by jacking cars?"

He snorted. "Nope. Had a rich daddy, so got a college degree."

She kept her smart retort to herself.

Charlene took him down the hall to the wall of portraits. Sheffer recognized the main characters. "All childhood friends, I see. Liam. Patrick." Sheffer slowly perused each photo. "Here is our man Finn. He does look like Connor when they were young." He tried to take the picture off the wall, but it was stuck. He shrugged and removed a pocket magnifier from his pants. He held it up to Finn's arm and then stepped back. "You're right. Stars on his inner arm. He's the third member they protected. Why would they do that?"

It was obvious to Charlene that Finn had hidden the gold somewhere for his mates.

Sheffer took a few pictures with his iPhone, grabbed her arm, and led her back to the door. "What's next?"

"Finn's house." They hurried away from the AOH to her SUV and got in.

"What do you hope to find?"

"Same as you," Charlene said. "The gold."

He gave her a half-smile. "Glad you didn't attempt this on your own."

"You give some legality to our breaking and entering. I don't want Sam hauling me off to the police station and questioning me again."

"He did *what?* That's a story I wanna hear." Sheffer leaned against the interior passenger door.

"Later. Once we find the gold and capture the person who murdered two people. Before a third dies." She drove out of the parking lot.

He shot her a look. "My interest is in returning the gold to the company who hired me. Sam can take care of the rest."

She liked that—everybody safe and happy. "There's something I don't understand. If the killer believes that Finn has the gold hidden somewhere, why not keep him alive to find it?"

"Murder never makes sense, except to the people who committed the crime."

Charlene decided to take a chance. "Sheffer, do you know Letitia Moor?"

"Nope. Never heard of her. Why?"

"She was a common-law wife to Patrick Hennessy."

"Oh? Huh." Sheffer tapped his thumb to the passenger-door handle. "You know, I *do* recall that name. She was a criminal too. I could never tie her to the robbery."

"She just got out on parole last month."

"No way." Sheffer thought, then said again, "No *way*." He typed something into his cell phone.

"What are you doing?"

"Searching her name." A noise sounded on his device. "Score!"

"What?"

"Letitia was picked up again right after parole for robbing a Walmart. Probably still in jail. It's a lifestyle. Can't believe I didn't follow that trail. Don't matter, though. I'm betting on James and Cindy. They're in deep money problems with the bar."

Letitia in jail? Darn it. Charlene turned toward Finn's house. She didn't think James or Cindy. But Liam? Mistaken identity would still work. Liam hadn't seen Finn in fourteen years. Liam had wanted to talk to Finn, probably about the heist. Which would explain Connor's death, but not Finn's. "Liam put in an offer for the pub. Cash." He smoked. He was the right size.

"That right?" Sheffer pursed his lips. "I'd love him to go back to the slammer. What do you think of Aiden and Shannon? They were pretty mad about Connor busting into the party."

"Even if Shannon needed money, I don't think she'd kill her twin for it. Shannon loved Finn."

"I agree with you. I think she loved him enough to protect his secret all these years. Makes you wonder about human nature, doesn't it? He becomes a recluse and doesn't spend a dime on himself or to help out his sister or any family members. That could make a lot of people mad."

Charlene nodded. "I hope Shannon returns my call soon. I'm worried for her."

"She'll be fine so long as she pleads complete ignorance. We need to get in and out of Finn's without alerting the police—gold in hand." Sheffer's eyes twinkled and she was reminded of the night Sheffer had baited Sam at the table. A competition.

Was Sheffer the real deal or was he playing his own game? If the criminal was Liam, he wouldn't be hiding out at Finn's, which eased her mind about breaking in to find the gold. The house should be empty. She'd been wrong about Letitia, which made her glad she hadn't told Sam her theory.

"There's a lot of gray area for people like me," Sheffer continued. "A private investigator wouldn't be worth his salt if he couldn't discover personal items, hidden safes, dark secrets, or cheating spouses. The police leave us alone for the most part, since we find their criminals for them."

She chuckled at his audacity. "Interesting perspective. I'd love to hear Sam's version."

"Hey, don't bring him into this. You and I are going to bring back the gold, baby!"

That just might keep her out of trouble with Sam. Results.

She rounded the corner and glimpsed the huge monstrosity partially hidden by a wall of evergreens. A large black fence split the property and bracketed the brick and stone house.

Whatever yard work Aiden had done in the front was unclear. Brown and straggly bushes, some half-rooted, surrounded the porch. Overgrown trees had shed piles of dirty leaves to blanket the bumpy driveway full of potholes. Weeds had grown around the house as high as four feet, only slightly hiding the peeling trim on mildewed window frames.

Shannon had a lot of work to do to get this disgrace habitable, never mind attractive to buyers. Tearing it down would be far more logical—unless somewhere inside the walls was a hidden fortune.

CHAPTER 27

Charlene parked the Pilot behind a large oak where it would be less noticeable to road traffic and people passing by.

Sheffer jumped out of the car without waiting for her. It was impossible to reach the back of the house because of the ten-foot fence and overgrown trees. There was a door to the right and he ran to it, jimmying his second lock of the day.

Putting her pepper spray in the side pocket of her handbag, Charlene exited the car and looked around the unkempt yard. She didn't see or hear anyone, though there were certainly places to hide. She hurried inside the dilapidated mansion as Sheffer held the door ajar.

"We need to be quick." Sheffer glanced toward the street. "This is a hot spot as far as our officers of the law are concerned."

"All right," she said, hunching her shoulders.

Instead of tiptoeing as her instincts urged her to do, she rushed ahead of him. Where would a miser hide gold? The side door led to the mudroom, and beyond that was the kitchen. The interior was dim and gloomy. Much worse than she'd thought.

Charlene covered her nose to prevent gagging as she and Sheffer picked their way through the disgusting filth on the floor. It was like stepping through a minefield, afraid every second her foot would disturb a rat.

Her body grew cold with fear. Not of who might be lurking behind, but what critters she might find during their search.

"Sheffer?"

"Yep?"

"I'm glad that you're with me right now."

"Me too. But Charlene, why are we whispering?"

She giggled, then slapped a hand over her mouth. Stepping in farther, her nose twitched. A familiar tang. "Do you smell a cigarette?" She shifted in the dim interior. Someone had been here recently. Maybe still was. Charlene imagined Liam somewhere hiding and hugged her purse, with the pepper spray, to her chest.

"Yeah." Sheffer shuffled ahead of her, past the kitchen that was overrun with pots and pans. Empty boxes.

The only person she knew who smoked was Liam. They were in a hallway, but leading to what she didn't know. It was hard to get her bearings due to the dark interior. Window curtains and blinds had been pulled shut. She dragged her fingers along the wall as her eyes adjusted.

"I think I found something," Sheffer said, opening a

door to their right. "This must lead to the basement. Good place for gold, right?"

Suddenly someone jumped out at them from their left. Cackling. The person pushed Sheffer down the wooden stairs, then ran out of sight. She could hear his body as it thumped on each step.

Charlene stifled a scream. What if he were dead? Holding onto the doorjamb, she peered down to see if he was alive. "Sheffer." Then louder. "Sheffer! Answer me."

From behind, a cold hand rested on her shoulder . . . so cold it reminded her of Jack, but it wasn't. Could Finn have been haunted by Patrick's ghost after all?

Petrified, she stood still, heart hammering loudly in her chest.

"Do you want to join him?"

Her mind grappled with this new info—not Liam, but a woman's warm cigarette-scented breath heated Charlene's neck, sounding like a horrible stepmother from a wretched Disney movie. Female. Human.

She jerked away. *Okay*. This was no ghost and Charlene's life was in danger. No one knew where they were.

"Who are you?" Charlene spoke in a loud and firm voice. She tried to turn to see.

Without answering, the woman spun Charlene by the arm and slammed the door separating her and Sheffer. She locked it. Sheffer couldn't help her now.

Charlene scanned the crowded hall for an escape. It probably led to bedrooms or a sitting room, since they'd already passed the kitchen. In silhouette, she could see that the woman was her height, stocky. A fedora covered short hair. The man at the funeral. Connor's attacker. Finn's killer. Letitia Moor—obviously out on bail, contrary to Sheffer's intel.

Anger surfaced. "I know who you are." Charlene dipped her hand into the side pocket of her purse and grabbed her pepper spray. Her self-defense classes had armed her for this situation and she was ready.

The woman chortled in surprised amusement and kicked it from Charlene's hand. Her fingers stung and her weapon was gone.

"Get away!" Charlene fumbled for her cell phone now, her confidence rattled.

"I'm death. Comin' to you real soon." The woman reached into her back pocket and brought out a—sling-shot? It would sling pebbles or stones . . . to the temple. Who would think a stone to be deadly? Who would look for one as a weapon? Small rocks had been all around the graveside in the dirt. Would there have been a rock in the AOH? It was too late now to search for one.

Charlene hurried backward. The woman followed and chopped down with her hand on Charlene's wrist. She dropped her phone and cringed when she heard the screen crack. "Ouch—stop! Why are *you* here?"

"Same reason as you. To get my share of the gold."

The woman lunged for Charlene and slammed a fist into her belly. Charlene gasped for breath, seeing stars. She had to defend herself or she would be done for. The woman punched again, but Charlene grabbed her fist and shoved it behind her back, yanking it upward as she pushed the woman against the wall.

Leaning in, Charlene said, "I know your name. Letitia."

The evil woman snagged her leg around Charlene's, making her stagger backward. She pushed Charlene to the floor and held her down with a foot to her throat. Charlene had to improvise. Quick.

Bracing herself, she bit the woman's ankle showing

through her pants above her black boots. Hard. Pushing herself forward, Charlene snagged the woman's wrist and gave it a sharp twist. Still on her knees, Charlene tried to crawl away, but the woman was bigger than her and meaner too. Letitia had the advantage of prison yard brawls.

"You're not going anywhere." Letitia plonked her weight on Charlene's back and tied a scarf around her throat. "You know my name? Well, so what." She tightened the knot. "I'm Patrick Hennessy's wife. How'd ya find out about the gold? Where is it?"

Charlene gasped. "Why did you kill Finn? He'd tell you." She choked. "Can't breathe. Lemme help you!"

The grip loosened. "You know where it is?"

"Finn. Lucky Stars gang," Charlene managed to spit out. "Armored truck robbery."

"Where's the gold?" Letitia sat back a tiny bit.

Charlene sucked in a big lungful of air and wriggled her body. Letitia tightened the noose and cut off her windpipe. Charlene gathered her strength and knocked Letitia's head back. She heard the crack of Letitia's nose. The fedora landed to her side. Letitia let go of the scarf and fell backward with a yowl, skittering away from Charlene.

Charlene struggled to her feet as Letitia, nose bleeding, pulled a folding knife from her back pocket. The woman was an arsenal. She probably had to be, to survive prison.

Letitia flicked it open and waved it at her. "You want this—" She moved menacingly toward her with a nasty grin. "Tell me where the gold is, and I might not kill you." Her crazed eyes told Charlene that her threat was real.

"How long have you been hiding here, scaring Finn, pretending to be your dead husband?"

Sanity flickered in the woman's hard gaze. "This is my house now. Finn owes it to me." She wiped spittle from her chin. "You know why it's mine?"

Charlene was standing now, her back to the rear door leading to the yard. "Squatter's rights?" She had her hands behind her and fiddled with the lock.

"Don't be *stupid*. Finn was cunning like a fox. He didn't get tossed behind bars like Liam and Patrick, did he? No, no." Letitia shook her head. "He had the gold from the robbery. Paid Patrick monthly to keep him from spillin' the beans. Guess he did the same for Liam, through Patty. Cold bitch, that one."

That explained Patty's money and why she wouldn't divorce Liam and give up her cushy life. Telling her friends it was a 401(k) would stop rumors. "And then Patrick died."

"Finn cut me off. Two years I been plannin' this to the last detail. Men's clothes. A fedora like Patrick used to wear. Did push-ups and bodybuilding for this moment. I can kill a bird from a hundred yards with a rock and my slingshot—girls inside were right scared o' me."

Charlene was also frightened. She twisted the knob behind her back, but the lock didn't budge.

"Finn shoulda paid me." Letitia snickered. "You shouldn't be here. Now I gotta kill you too."

"Wait!" Charlene stalled desperately, her fingers examining the smooth metal around the knob. "I don't understand—why Connor?"

Letitia scraped a dirty hand through her short hair. "Thought Connor was Finn that night. Realized my mistake when I retrieved my lucky stone and got close

enough to see his features. It was you there on the staircase, wadn't it?" Her eyes narrowed. "Shoulda knocked
you over the side."

"I didn't see you. You can let me go." The click of the
doorknob signaled the lock had sprung when she'd pressed
a button. Her pulse raced. "Why did you kill Finn?"

"Didn't need him, not with his sister alive." Her laugh
was ugly and evil.

Charlene had the door open and rushed through it, tee-
tering at the top stair. A long staircase twelve steps deep
descended before her. Where could she go to hide? The
backyard was a series of overgrown trees and holes dug
in the ground. By Letitia? A toolshed was to her right.

She fled down the stairs, Letitia on her heels. After
three steps, Charlene tripped and grabbed the railing to
regain her footing.

An enraged Letitia banged into her, using an elbow to
push her off. Charlene tightened her grip on the rail and
shoved a leg out. With a wail, Letitia dropped, rolling
down the staircase, much as what had just happened to
Sheffer.

Charlene didn't waste a second as she sprinted down
the remaining steps, leaping over Letitia's body. The
ground and safety was only a few steps away when a fist
grabbed at her ankle. She flung herself forward, landing
on the ground headfirst. Charlene's chin smacked and she
tasted blood from her split lip. She crawled to the harsh
gravel to the side of the staircase.

A shovel leaned against the shed a few steps away.
Charlene got to her feet and armed herself with the thick-
handled tool, then turned to Letitia, who hadn't moved.
She flipped the woman over to see the folding knife em-
bedded in her chest.

Charlene's stomach clenched. After all of that, Letitia had accidentally killed herself.

Just then Sheffer burst through the door and Shannon followed, pulling duct tape from her mouth.

"I found her bound in the cellar," Sheffer said. "She knows about Finn and the gold. Protecting him, like I thought."

"He's my brother," Shannon said weakly, holding the rail as she took the stairs down and collapsed on the bottom step, her gaze flicking over Letitia. "What happened?"

Charlene put her hand to her throat. "She fell on her knife."

Sheffer bent down and pointed to the blood pooling around the knife handle. "We better call in the cops."

"Sam too. My phone is inside somewhere." Charlene sank next to Shannon, who wore her church clothes of a blue dress and short heels. "I know where the gold is." Precious metal needed to be stored in a dry, dark area. Not the dirt. It was hidden in plain sight.

Shannon's blue eyes widened.

Sheffer made the call, pacing on the grass and avoiding the holes.

"Not in the ground." Charlene gestured to the toolshed where she'd found the shovel. It wouldn't be inside the shed, but below it, probably in a vault of some kind. "It's sitting under that thick slab of concrete. Dad and I used to go to a lot of museums and archeological digs. I remember hearing that gold has to be kept in a dry area in the dark."

Sheffer tugged on a heavy lock that sealed the shed tight, then broke it open with a rock. He peered in. "Empty." He kicked the slab and grinned. "Hope you're right, Charlene. I better get a raise after this."

Shannon stared down at Letitia without a word. Shannon had known all along, Charlene realized. She had been complicit in the heist not only by her silence. Aiden must have discovered the truth while visiting his uncle. What a mess.

"Shannon," Charlene said softly. "You helped Finn launder the money through your accounting business, didn't you?"

Sheffer sucked in a breath while Shannon cried. She didn't confess, but the tears were enough for Charlene.

They heard the police sirens and Sheffer leaned against the back railing, pulling some papers from his back pocket. "I found these letters from Letitia to Finn in the basement. Got a feeling Detective Holden will want these."

"What do they say?" she asked.

"Letitia wanted Patrick's share of the gold. Finn didn't agree that she was entitled, so she followed through on her threat to kill him, betting that Shannon would know the location of the stolen coins. Obviously, Letitia had been unsuccessful looking on her own." He nodded at the holes in the dirt.

Shannon bowed her head and swiped her cheeks. "That horrid woman said she'd hurt Aiden."

So, she'd given up the secret she'd held for years. If Charlene and Sheffer hadn't arrived when they did, Letitia might have gotten away with the coins, and Shannon would most likely be dead.

Charlene turned toward the sound of metal screeching as the gate separating the front yard from the back was torn down, and Sam raced around the lawn. He stopped to stare at her, breathing hard. Sam joined Sheffer near the toolshed and gave him a manly punch on the arm.

"Thanks for watching out for her. She's quite the handful, isn't she?"

"You can say that again." Sheffer rubbed the spot Sam had punched. "We could use someone like her. She'd be an asset to our investigation team in the city."

Sam grimaced, crossed the dirt to where she stood by the stairs, and put a finger under her chin. He looked back at his friend. His tone was light, but Charlene knew he wasn't kidding around as he said, "Don't make me hurt you, man. She's not going anywhere. Charlene is my lucky charm."

CHAPTER 28

Charlene drove back to the bed-and-breakfast a few miles over the speed limit, hyped on adrenaline and fear that her parents (her mother) would be upset if she missed happy hour after not spending the day with them at the winery.

Sheffer had gone to the police station with Sam, who'd promised her that he'd drop by later after they finished booking Letitia. The woman wasn't dead after all—the muscle she'd built from working out to be bulky like Patrick had saved her heart. This time she was going to jail for good, and the guards would be warned about her affinity for slingshots.

Had Sam meant it, saying that she was his lucky charm? She'd seen a hint of jealousy at Sheffer's suggestion that she help him with the private investigations.

Grinning wide, Charlene parked in the driveway of her

home. At half-past three, the sun broke from behind a cloud, hinting at a glorious sunset later this evening. She might suggest jackets and hot cocoa with peppermint schnapps on the widow's walk.

Right now, it felt good to be home.

Jack met her on the front porch, his image vibrant and strong. "How did it go? What are those marks around your neck? Your lip is split." A rush of air as he moved closer to her made her shiver.

In her joy of catching the killer, she'd completely forgotten the beating she'd taken. She hurried up the porch steps. "I'll tell you when we get to the room. Are my parents here? I don't want them to see me bruised up."

"They're in the living room with Avery, in very jovial spirits thanks to the winery visit."

She hesitated, then skipped down the steps to go around the back and through her private entrance.

"Good thinking," Jack said. "Meet you there." He disappeared.

She went up the back stairs to her porch and into her sitting room as stealthy as she and Sheffer had snuck into Finn's and the AOH.

Jack waited with an alarmed expression, pacing before the love seat. "What happened?" He studied her with doctorly concern.

"We were right, Jack. It was Letitia. Sheffer thought she was in jail, but she wasn't. Finn had been paying Patrick off to stay quiet about the robbery, through Letitia, his common-law wife. When Patrick died, Finn got cheap and quit paying. Letitia wanted 'her' share."

Charlene dashed into her bedroom and headed to the bathroom mirror. Jack hovered at the threshold.

He wasn't invited into her bedroom. It was off-limits,

but the open doorway didn't count. Silva, curled up on the bed, blinked her golden eyes at Charlene and stared at her as if to see for herself that her owner was all right.

Charlene gasped when she saw the dark purple finger-prints around her throat. A tiny amount of blood caked her skin from Letitia's fingernails digging into her flesh.

"Shower, and a turtleneck."

"You really could have been hurt, Charlene. I hate that I can't be with you. I want to protect you."

"I know, Jack. You help me here and you and I tracked down a killer." She held his gaze from across the room. "I couldn't do this without your assistance."

Jack blew a raspberry. "Sam." His smile showed he was mostly teasing her. "He needs us."

"Sheffer offered me a job practically, but Sam nixed it." She kept the lucky charm comment to herself.

A knock sounded on her suite door. "Charlene?" her mom called. "Are you home?"

"I'll be right there, Mom!"

"No rush. Avery and I put the lasagna bites in the oven already."

She grinned at Jack and whispered, "We need to send Annabeth a thank-you card."

A half-hour later, dressed in a turtleneck with long sleeves to cover more bruises from her battle with Letitia, Charlene accepted a generous pour of wine and a seat before the fire in the living room.

"I feel like I'm the guest," she said, sitting back after a delicious sip. The house smelled like garlic from the savory appetizers.

Avery brought her a dish and a napkin. "You deserve to be spoiled. You do so much for everyone."

"Avery was just telling us how you're helping her with

college and getting her driver's license. Charlene, we want to pitch in too," her dad said. "Avery is like family now."

Charlene's throat thickened with emotion and she cleared it, setting the small dish to her side. "I agree. She is." She reached for Avery and squeezed her fingers. "I'm glad you see it too."

Avery smiled shyly. "I got an email earlier from one of the colleges I applied to with a full scholarship. I was on the waiting list, remember?"

That had been hard, watching her sweet girl not get everything she wanted. "Yes?"

"I got in! Full tuition to Boston Academy. I just need to commute. Other than being homeless since Jenna wants to move in with her new boyfriend instead of me, everything's great." Avery's smile widened to a grin. "I'm being positive, like Charlene."

Charlene laughed, her heart soaring at Avery's hard work paying off. "Would you consider the bed-and-breakfast your forever home? You can have one of the rooms on the top floor free of charge."

Avery's jaw dropped and she sank to her knees by Charlene's chair. "Really? I don't have to find an apartment?"

"I would love it if you would consider this your *home*, Avery. I love you."

"I love you too!" Avery wiped happy tears from her cheeks. "I can't wait to tell Janet. I know she's been worried about where I'll end up, but now—well, this is perfect."

Brenda exchanged a look with Michael, then said, "I couldn't be happier for you both. What a great solution. Michael?"